SCENE OF THE CRIME

"When you were in the barn, did you see a jack?"

"Yes, so?" I flailed my arms in the air. "I saw it, Chief Kennedy and half the police force saw it!"

"It was broken."

"And your point is?"

"It looked like it had been done intentionally."

I narrowed my eyes at him. "What makes you think so?"

"The pin holding the axle support in place had been sheared off."

My breath caught in my throat. A few minutes ago, while the possibility of murder had hung in the air, the probability of it had suddenly come slashing down like the sharply honed blade of a French guillotine. "So you do think it was murder? You think someone snuck up on Chick and broke the jack? With him under the car?"

Paul bobbed his head and I shivered. That was a cold and brutal move . . .

Books by J.R. Ripley

DIE, DIE BIRDIE

TOWHEE GET YOUR GUN

THE WOODPECKER ALWAYS PECKS TWICE

TO KILL A HUMMINGBIRD

CHICKADEE CHCKADEE BANG BANG

Published by Kensington Publishing Corporation

Chickadee Chickadee Bang Bang

J.R. Ripley

LYRICAL UNDERGROUND
Kensington Publishing Corp.
www.kensingtonbooks.com

LYRICAL UNDERGROUND BOOKS are published by

Kensington Publishing Corp.
119 West 40th Street
New York, NY 10018

All Kensington titles, imprints, and distributed lines are available at special quantity discounts for bulk purchases for sales promotion, premiums, fund-raising, educational, or institutional use.

Special book excerpts or customized printings can also be created to fit specific needs. For details, write or phone the office of the Kensington Sales Manager: Kensington Publishing Corp., 119 West 40th Street, New York, NY 10018. Attn. Sales Department. Phone: 1-800-221-2647.

Lyrical Underground and Lyrical Underground logo Reg. US Pat. & TM Off.

First Electronic Edition: September 2017
eISBN-13: 978-1-5161-0312-6
eISBN-10: 1-5161-0312-2

First Print Edition: September 2017
ISBN-13: 978-1-5161-0313-3
ISBN-10: 1-5161-0313-0

Printed in the United States of America

*Thank you to John Scognamiglio and the whole
Kensington crew for the incredible job you do; to
Priya Doraswamy at Lotus Lane Literary for
representing me so well; and my family, friends
and fans. Together, you make what I do possible
and worth the doing. And if you like a story,
posting a positive rating or review somewhere is
a great way to help the authors you enjoy.*

1

"It says here," read Kim, "that the black-capped chickadee is slightly larger and a tad brighter than the Carolina chickadee." She had her nose in a well-worn copy of one of my birding field guides.

"What good does that do us?" whispered Otelia, hovering nearby like a baby jay. "We have nothing to compare it to." She cinched her light sweater tighter. A small but cool breeze had kicked up.

Sally Potts snapped her chewing gum and the little bird jumped to a farther branch. It was late September and leaves were beginning to fall from the trees, but there were still plenty of yellow-orange leaves on the maple to obscure our bird.

"Shh." I pressed a finger to my lips. The bird in question was the chickadee singing in the tree overhead, but I wasn't sure yet which species it belong to. "Go ahead and read some more, Kim," I suggested softly.

"Umm."

I watched for a moment as Kim's eyes scanned the page, then lifted my binoculars and trained them once more on the small chickadee.

Chickadee-dee-dee! The bird extended its neck and shook itself briskly after singing its signature song—a sure sign that we were spooking it.

John Moytoy, a Ruby Lake librarian, lowered his binoculars and rubbed the bridge of his nose where his eyeglasses hit. "The Cherokee called it *tsikilili* because of the sound it makes." John was well versed in the Cherokee heritage, being of Cherokee descent himself. He had jet-black hair and was cherubic in body and spirit. He'd been letting his hair grow out and it was now long enough that he sported a ponytail.

"Thanks, John," I said. "Like many other animals, numerous birds are commonly named for the sounds they produce, such as cuckoos and bobolinks."

"And whip-poor-wills, right?" That was Tiffany LaChance. Tiff worked as waitress at Ruby's Diner. She was a buxom blonde who was very easy on the eyes. Hers were green. She was a few years older than me but had already been married and had a child. She had been wedded to Robert LaChance, but I didn't hold it against her because they were divorced now. Robert and I have had our differences. Tiffany and her eleven-year-old son lived in a condo by the lake.

"Good example," I whispered. Tiff wasn't one of my regulars, so it was especially nice to see her join us.

Kim cleared her throat. "It also says that the black-capped chickadee has a larger area of white behind their, um, aur-auriculars." Kim paused and shot me a questioning look. She's a long-legged, blue-eyed blonde who can eat any amount of food and get away with it, as evidenced by the tight jeans hugging her hips. Life really wasn't fair.

"That's right," I said. "Go on." Kim and I were both in our midthirties. The blue eyes were practically all we had in common physically. On a good day, I was a tad heavier than her—a tad being measured in five-pound increments—but I also had an inch on her height-wise. While Kim often goaded me to dye my hair blond like hers, I was sticking with the chestnut brown I'd been born with.

Kim took a sip from her water bottle, then read a little more. "The Carolina chickadee's auriculars are more grayish." She closed the book and looked up into the maple.

"What the heck is an auricular?" Karl scratched the side of his head and pushed his thick, black-rimmed eyeglasses back up his nose for the hundredth time since our in-town bird walk had begun. He owned an ancient pair of binoculars that he'd had since his younger days. The weight of them strapped around his neck threatened to bring him to his knees.

"The area around the ears." I replied. "That's the name for the feathers that cover their ears." The four-inch gray, white, and black bird hopped to yet a higher branch. The black-capped chickadee and the Carolina chickadee share a territory and their markings are quite similar, making them difficult to differentiate. The fact that they sometimes interbreed makes it nearly impossible to distinguish such birds with the naked eye.

"Like a covert?" Floyd asked.

"Exactly." I smiled. "In fact, they are also called coverts because they protect the ears." Floyd had once told me that in his younger days he had been a duck hunter, so I wasn't surprised to see that he was familiar with the coverts that hunters often utilized in the field. I was glad he'd given up shooting ducks. Not only for the sake of the ducks. Floyd's eyesight wasn't the best. He occasionally mistook branches and even rocks for birds.

"So what do we think? Black-capped or Carolina?"

"I vote black-capped," answered Kim. She stuck her water bottle back in its holder attached to her belt.

"I vote Carolina," countered Sally Potts. Sally's a slender woman with red hair and sharp green eyes.

"I vote lunch," came Steve Dykstra's reply. Steve was also new to our group. He'd come into the store once or twice for birdseed with Olivia Newsome. He had been mentioning lunch ever since the group had met up after breakfast.

"I'm thinking Carolina myself," I said, studying the little bird closely and ignoring the digressions that always seemed to pop up on these walks.

"Look at that beauty." Karl whistled. "White with teal accents."

"Where?" I turned and followed the line of his binoculars. "I don't see anything."

There was too much traffic. My little group and I were on a birding walk in the city and had stopped at the Town of Ruby Lake's spacious town square to observe the large variety of birds that could normally be found there.

People who weren't into birding didn't realize how many interesting species lived in an urban setting. Though *urban* was being generous when describing our modest town nestled among the Carolina foothills.

I moved my binoculars back and forth. Could Karl have possibly seen a blue-winged teal? The ducks were rare to this part of western North Carolina, but it wouldn't be impossible to see one—especially with the lake being so near.

And with the fall, we would get our share of migrators.

"Right there!" Karl said loudly. "Heading east. You can see its rear end!"

"I can't see anything," complained Otelia, a fiftyish brunette with a beehive hairdo. She owns a local chocolate shop that I'm drawn to like a bee to nectar.

"Me either." That was Kim.

I refocused my binoculars on an elm across the road.

Karl lowered his glasses. "It's gone now. Turned the corner. What do you think, Floyd?" asked Karl. "Was that a fifty-seven Chevy or maybe a Pontiac?"

I lowered my glasses and gaped at Karl. "What?"

"That was no Star Chief," Floyd said, lowering his own glasses and wiping the eye pieces with the corner of his shirt—something I'd warned him a hundred times would only scratch them. "Didn't you see those taillights? Definitely a fifty-seven Chevy Bel Air. Man, what a beauty."

"You guys were looking at a car?" I shook my finger at Floyd and Karl. "We're supposed to be bird-watching."

"Yeah, but not just any car, Amy," explained Karl. "That was a fifty-seven Bel Air."

The corners of my lips turned down. "So I heard. Can we get back to bird-watching now, do you suppose?" I added a smile to my request.

Karl nodded sheepishly.

Floyd nudged his buddy Karl and said in a stage whisper, "That car's not from around here. I'll bet it's in town for the car show."

The car show in question was part of an upcoming annual event in town. Among the myriad of special events the Town of Ruby Lake helps organize, each fall we host the Ruby Lake Fall Festival. It's held annually the first weekend after the fall equinox. The Fall Festival includes a number of popular events, such as the classic car and tractor show and a baking competition. The local residents enjoyed it, the tourists came for it from miles around, and the merchants loved what it did for their bottom lines.

I was hoping it might do the same for mine, though I wasn't sure I could count on an uptick in my bird-store traffic from fans of classic automobiles and farm equipment, or even baking. But you never know, and I was participating like most every other business owner in town. Kim had suggested we bake up a couple dozen mock four-

and-twenty-blackbird pies. But considering we ran a shop catering to birders, it seemed a bit tasteless to me. No pun intended.

We did intend to have an outdoor presence along with dozens of other street vendors, and we'd be selling my mom's surprise hit, Barbara's Bird Bars, along with other food and bird-watching and -feeding products.

To my surprise, the Birds & Brews trailer that I had found myself a reluctant partner in, due to the machinations of my mother and the business owner next-door, could just prove to be a winner. We were planning on setting up the trailer, which had been built to look like a giant red birdhouse, along one of the streets surrounding the town square.

That former camping trailer still gave me the heebie-jeebies, considering that it had once belonged to a friend of mine who'd met an untimely end. Buying it had not been my idea. That idea had been my mother's and Paul Anderson's doing. Now I was stuck with it and doing my best to make the most of the situation—and bury the unpleasant associated memories.

Paul Anderson, my neighbor and now business partner, had taken care of the business permits and Cousin Riley had remodeled the interior of the trailer, which had once served as my friend's home away from home, into a proper mobile storefront for Birds & Bees and Paul's business, Brewer's Biergarten. We'd even sprung for a fancy solar-lighted sign reading BIRDS & BREWS, which Cousin Riley had affixed to the roof.

"I'm pooped," said Steve. In his early fifties, Steve was one of the youngest of our group. He was tan and fit, with coppery hair swept back dramatically atop his head. His eyes were painted bunting blue. Having come dressed in white slacks and a raspberry-red sweater, however, he might have been having a negative impact on our bird sightings.

Birds are visual creatures and communicate a lot with color. Red and white are danger signals to birds, as they are to other animals. The flash of a bird's white tail feathers or a scared deer's white tail warn of trouble. The best way to see birds or any other wildlife in a natural setting was to blend in. That meant wearing neutral colors.

Steve and Otelia were dating. He worked as a mechanic at Nesmith's, the gas station on the edge of town. The next closest stations were out along the highway. I didn't know him well, having only a nodding acquaintance from seeing him around the gas station where he pumped gas, in addition to the time or two he'd been in the store with Otelia.

"I'm starved." Otelia looked meaningfully across the town square, her eyes smack on Jessamine's Kitchen, our planned lunch stop.

I looked at my watch. It was a little early, but I could see that my flock's attention was beginning to stray. "Fine. Let's eat. Besides, if we dine now, we can beat the lunch crowd." Normally, I liked to start my bird walks early in the morning. That was the best time to spot birds as they busied themselves in search of breakfast, but in an effort to appease the group, we'd picked a midmorning start with lunch afterward. I had reconnoitered the proposed walk the day prior and was confident we'd see plenty of birds.

We had. Despite the time of day and Steve's clothing choices. Proper clothing was something I might have to bring up with the group before our next walk.

Using my mobile phone, I snapped a quick photo of the chickadee in the tree for later inspection.

We cut across the town square with Steve and Otelia leading the way. Tiffany waved to Aaron Maddley, who was working out of his stall at the farmer's market. Their relationship seemed to be developing into something beyond casual dating. Good for them.

Aaron, dressed in blue jeans and a gray T-shirt, was selling farm fresh arugula, lettuce, radishes, and other fall vegetables under his tent. Besides being good at working the earth, Aaron was good with his hands. He provided me with handmade bluebird houses and other nesting boxes for the store.

"Go on without me," Tiffany said with a big smile on her face. "I'll catch up in a minute."

I smiled back. "Okay. Say hi to Aaron for me." My relationship with Aaron was still a bit strained. He was having a hard time letting go of the accusations I'd once wrongly levelled at him. When we'd first met, there may have been something between us.

Now that something was a lingering animosity on his part. Still, I was happy for him and Tiffany. I was even happier for me and Derek Harlan, the handsome and steady man I'd been getting closer to since returning to Ruby Lake to open Birds & Bees and be nearer to Mom and the rest of my family.

I couldn't get much nearer to Mom. We shared an apartment above Birds & Bees.

My flock and I waited for traffic to clear, then moved as a group across the street to Jessamine's Kitchen, a homey Southern-style restaurant that had only recently opened. I had called Jessamine Jeffries yesterday to let her know our group would be coming in.

A high school girl I knew greeted us at the entrance. "Hello, Ms. Simms. You're early." She had a laminated menu in her right hand.

"Hi, Lulu. It won't be a problem, will it?" Lulu Nowell was a chipper young blonde who worked to pick up some spending money on weekends and occasionally after school, and on weekdays when her strict mother and father would let her.

"None at all. Jess has your table all ready."

"Great."

The layout of Jessamine's Kitchen was simple and the décor was as cozy as the food. The furnishings included Shaker-style tables and chairs. Blue and white checkered tablecloths covered the tables. In the evening, the waitstaff placed beeswax candles on the tabletops in small cut-glass bowls shaped like tulips. The floor was old pine, reclaimed from a local barn that had been torn down. The local lumber yard sells tons of the stuff.

There was a black cast-iron woodstove near the center of the room, though I hadn't seen it lit yet. With winter around the corner, I was sure it wouldn't be long.

I followed Lulu. Several tables in front of the window overlooking the town square had been pushed together. Two vases near each end of the joined table held fresh bouquets of sunny yellow coreopsis.

I took a seat at the far side. Floyd and Karl opted for spots against the window, looking inward. A flamboyantly dressed man and woman, who appeared to be in their late fifties or early sixties, sat at the small round table nearest us. Their plates were piled high with fried chicken and hush puppies. My mouth watered just looking at them.

"That sun is bright," Karl said. "Hurts my eyes." He made a show of removing his eyeglasses and vigorously rubbing his eyes with his fists.

Floyd agreed. "It is kind of bright." I had a feeling both were more interested in having a good vantage from which to view Jessamine than they were in protecting their eyes from the sun's rays.

Steve held out a chair facing the window for Otelia. Sally sat at the opposite end of the table. Kim squeezed in beside her, and John Moytoy sat beside me.

A lanky waiter, approaching forty by my guess, came to the table and took our drink orders. Karl and Floyd ordered beers and the rest of us settled on a shared endless pitcher of iced mint tea.

As the waiter set down our drinks, Tiffany came hurrying in. "Sorry I'm late!" Floyd scooted over and she took a seat beside him.

"Have some tea." I filled Tiffany's glass.

She pulled off her sunglasses and unbuttoned her green sweater. "Aaron was telling me all about the work he's been doing on his truck." She jiggled her brow. "The man about talked my ear off."

"Is he having a problem with it?" bellowed Steve from across the table. Steve wasn't much for whispering, a trait I was trying to instill in him if he was going to go bird-watching with us. Birds have a way of disappearing if you go thrashing about and talking at the top of your lungs. "Maybe I can help!"

"Thanks, Steve, but there's nothing at all wrong with it," called Tiffany from the other end of the table. "He's getting it ready for the car show." She picked up her napkin and unfolded it. "Polishing thingies, tuning the engine, replacing parts." She laid the white cloth napkin in her lap. "You name it, he's doing it."

"Don't tell me Aaron is all caught up in the car show this year, too," I groaned.

Tiff smiled my way. "Oh, yeah. Big-time. I can't believe it. Just my luck, I go from being married to a car dealer to dating a car nut!" She laughed as she said it.

"Hey," Steve said, "I resemble that remark." He grinned. "I've been parading my car every year in the car show. It's fun." He picked up his iced tea. "Besides, we raise a lot of money for charity."

The stranger at the next table barked out a laugh. He leaned over and touched my arm. "I can't help hearing you all talking about the car show," he said loudly. "That's what me and Belle come for, isn't it, doll?" He winked at his wife, who beamed in return. "That and to see a man about a car."

His *doll* nodded. "Like the man says, I'm Belle," the woman said with a quick smile. Her unnaturally orange hair was tucked neatly atop her narrow head. She wore a yellow knit sweater and jeans. "This handsome devil with me is my husband, Emmett."

The handsome devil in question laughed uproariously. "Emmett Lancaster," he said, thrusting out a hand. We shook.

"Pleased to meet you both," I replied. His fingers were icy cold, probably from the soda his hand had recently been wrapped around. His cheeks were puffy and pink and he had a cleft chin. His eyes were pulled close to his bulbous nose, under which grew the beginnings of a sparse moustache. He wore a baggy tweed jacket. Its mottled white and brown pattern reminded me of a wood thrush's belly.

"Are you local?" I asked. The pair didn't look familiar and I was certain I'd remember if I had seen the two of them before.

"Nope." Emmett tugged at the linen napkin tucked into his collar. "We drove up from Trenton. That's out east. We love cars and car shows. Don't we, Belle?" He reached under the table and patted his wife's knee.

"That's right," agreed Belle. "We go to as many as we can."

"Have you got a classic car yourselves?" asked Floyd.

Emmett puffed out his chest. "Do I have a car?" He laughed loudly. "Hear that, Belle? He wants to know if we have a car?" He laughed once more. "I've got a car, all right." He laced his fingers over his belly. "And before we leave your little town, I expect to have another."

Steve coughed and reached for his iced tea. John and I looked at one another and suppressed our grins.

"You hoping to buy a car from one of the folks showing at the festival?" asked Karl.

Emmett shook his head. "Nope. Not that I won't keep my eyes open for the right car at the right price." He shook his head. "No. I've arranged to meet a man named Hernando, who's offering a car on one of the classic car websites."

"Em's been drooling over that car for weeks," added Belle.

"Hernando?" Karl pulled at his chin. "Can't say as I know the man." He looked around at our group and we all shook our heads in the negative.

Emmett chuckled. "Yeah, like Belle says, I guess I have been overanxious about this deal. We've been dickering back and forth over the internet for weeks. We finally agreed on the price. Now all I have to do is make sure the car checks out and is everything Hernando promises she is." He leaned toward me. "And it better check out. I sent the man a ten-thousand-dollar deposit."

Floyd whistled softly. "That's a lot of money for a car you haven't seen."

"Tell me about it," said Emmett's wife. "But that's my husband." She grabbed her coffee cup. "He's always been the impulsive type. We got married after courting for only two weeks!" She brought her cup to her lips and smiled at her husband as she drank.

"What model car are you buying?" demanded Karl.

Emmett smiled enigmatically. "Oh, no," he said with a wagging finger. "I can't tell you that. You might just try to outbid me!"

I didn't think there was much chance of that. "What car are you driving now?"

"We have a 1939 Oldsmobile Business Coupe," the man named Emmett said proudly. "I bought her when I was eighteen years old with my very own money. It took me five years and two layers of skin off of these two hands"—he thrust out his hands palms up, and the sleeves of his jacket rode back to reveal a pair of slender, hairy arms—"to restore her."

"I'm not familiar with the model," Steve said, clearly intrigued.

"Me either," admitted Karl.

"Let me tell you," began Emmett.

"Now look what you've done," Belle said with a chuckle, "you've done set him off." She waggled her fork at her husband. "Once you get Emmett cranked up on the subject of his Business Coupe, you'll like as never get him off it!"

"Now, now. The man asked," replied her husband. "It would be rude of me not to answer." He swirled his cola, sipped through his paper straw, then twisted his chair at angle to our table. "Let me tell you, the Business Coupe was, and still is, a real beauty. She was a favorite of traveling salesmen because of her large trunk and reasonable price."

"Yes," added Belle. "The car has no back seat, but the trunk is big enough to hold an elephant. And seeing how we don't travel light and Em is a traveling salesman, the Olds is perfect for us." She removed a tube of red lipstick from a skinny black leather purse on the edge of the table and ran it across her lips.

"What line are you in?" inquired Steve.

Emmett shrugged his sloped shoulders. His ginger hair was thinning at the front. "Like Belle says, I'm a salesman. You name it, I've sold it." I noticed a cellophane-wrapped cigar protruding from his pale blue breast pocket.

Steve worked his lower jaw back and forth. "Would you consider selling the Olds?"

Emmett barked. "Not for all the corn in Iowa! But if you'd like to see her, come around to the motel. Me and the wife will take you for a ride."

"I just might take you up on that," Steve replied.

"Great. You show me yours and I'll show you mine," Emmett belted out with a lascivious grin.

"Good luck with that," Otelia said. "Steve here won't even let me see his precious car lately. Says he's keeping it clean until the parade."

Steve's face turned red as a scarlet tanager. "I spent twenty hours detailing her, Otelia. I've got to keep her spic-and-span."

She pulled at his sleeve. "I'm just teasing, Steve."

Emmett Lancaster turned to his wife. "Ready, doll?"

She tucked her lipstick tube back in her purse and nodded. Emmett rose, helped her with her chair. He withdrew a fat black wallet from the inside pocket of his sports coat and tossed a few bills on the table. "See ya' at the show, folks." He waved a meaty palm in farewell.

The smell of fried chicken and gardenias lingered in the hole they'd left.

Steve watched them maneuver out the door, then dug into his sandwich.

"Sounds like that fella has a real classic," Sally Potts said.

Steve looked put out. "I suppose."

"I've always admired your car, Steve," Floyd said, pulling at his mustache. "My pa had a '42 De Soto. I wish I had it now."

"Well, mine's not for sale," Steve said. "I've owned her for twenty years and put twenty years of my life into restoring her."

"She's a fine car, all right," Karl said with a touch of envy. "But me and Floyd have a car of our own that we plan on showing this year. Don't we, Floyd?"

Floyd jerked to attention. "We do?"

"Of course, we do." Karl shook his head. Both men had gray hair, though Karl's was by far the thicker of the two. "My pal here is a little senile."

Karl rubbed his hands together. His gray eyes seemed to say that they held a secret. "Just wait and see what we've got. Boy, she is something. I tell you."

Karl Vogel and Floyd Withers were retired. Both lived out at Rolling Acres, a senior living center. Karl was the former Town of Ruby Lake chief of police. Floyd was a retired banker who had lost his wife in the past year.

"Dan's planning on showing his Firebird, so I feel your pain, Tiffany," Kim said from across the table.

"Really?" Tiffany actually looked interested. "What year is it?"

"It's a 1980 Firebird Trans Am. He bought it from Robert a few years back as a project car. He gave me a ride in it once. Mostly we take my car or his truck because the Trans Am's parts are spread around his garage."

Tiffany laughed. "If he bought it from my ex, I'm sure *project* is the right word for it."

"What color is it?" asked Steve. "Red?"

"Black," answered Kim. "With pinstriping."

"A muscle car, eh?" Steve nodded appreciatively. "Well, all I can say is good luck if you think any of you are going to win a ribbon this year." I sensed some good-natured ribbing in Steve's voice.

John turned to me. "Wasn't this supposed to be a luncheon in which we talked about the birds we had seen this morning?" He riffled through the notebook he'd been carrying with him on our two-hour walk. John was a fastidious note-taker. He'd even added tiny pencil sketches of several of the birds—a sparrow, a mockingbird, and the chickadee.

"That was the idea." I shot Karl and Floyd each a *behave yourself* look.

"Uh-oh," Karl said, nudging Floyd with his elbow. "Looks like you're in trouble."

"Me?" gasped Floyd. "What did I do?"

The former police chief ignored Floyd's agitation. "You have to admit, Amy, that '57 Chevy was something."

I looked down my nose and across the table. "I barely saw it. *I* was watching the birds."

"Like you always say, Amy," Karl said, "a good birder keeps his or her eyes open for anything, anywhere." He picked up his beer and drank it half down, then smacked his lips with satisfaction. I wasn't sure that satisfaction was with his beer or from having thrown my own words back in my face.

Two, or in this case three, could play that game. "I'll have you know," I said, folding my arms across my chest and clamping a hand down on each upper arm, "Derek and Paul are also planning to enter a car in the competition this year."

"They are?" Steve and Karl replied as one.

"Yes, they are."

"What kind of vehicle have they got?" demanded Steve.

"Now, now, Steve," Otelia interrupted. "Like John said, we're here to talk about birds, not cars." She patted his knee. "All this shop talk can wait." She giggled.

Unfortunately, I couldn't resist a little good-natured trash talk myself. "It's a 1961 Chevrolet Impala SS convertible."

Steve whistled through his teeth and brought his hands to his cheeks, making him look like a chipmunk with indigestion.

"That's some car, ain't it?" Karl remarked.

"Can we see it?" asked Floyd. "Please?"

"Sorry, Floyd. Derek and Paul have sworn me to secrecy." The two men had been huddled out in the detached garage at Paul's unfinished house practically every night for the past month. Plus weekends. I barely saw Derek, at least when his hands weren't covered in grease and grime and he wasn't smelling like an auto repair shop. "To tell you the truth, I haven't seen it lately myself."

"A '61 Chevy Impala convertible," Steve said, his voice just above a whisper. "That's some car, all right."

"An Impala *SS*." I couldn't resist correcting him.

Steve nodded. "Yeah. SS." He looked at Karl. "We've got some competition this year."

Karl twisted his lip. "We ain't worried, are we, Floyd?" He turned to Floyd, but Floyd's eyes and attention had been drawn elsewhere.

2

"Good afternoon." Jessamine's sultry voice brought our friendly bickering to a standstill. "How is everyone today?" She made a point of making eye contact with each of us in turn.

"Hello, Jessamine," Karl and Floyd said in unison.

A retired accountant from Greensboro now following her passion for cooking, Jessamine was a zaftig woman of sixty-some years with shoulder-length brown locks and brown eyes. A divorced and unattached woman, she was receiving the attention of many of the older and even some of the younger men in town. She seemed to be having a certain effect on Floyd and Karl—more than birds or cars, that was for sure.

"Hi, Jessamine." I leaned sideways as she lightly kissed my cheek.

"How was your bird-watching?"

"Bird-watching?" I quipped. "If you'd have heard our conversation you'd realize we'd actually been on a *car-watching* expedition this morning."

That earned me a laugh from the group and a flush on Karl and Floyd's faces.

"I'm new to town, but running a restaurant I hear what's on the town's mind." Jessamine picked up the tea pitcher and refilled each of our glasses in turn as she spoke. "And what's on it these days is the Ruby Lake Fall Festival and the classic car and tractor show."

"I noticed you have one of their posters in your window," I said, turning my head toward the entrance.

"I have two. One on each side of the front door. Mrs. Sudsbury is quite a force." Jessamine ran her hands along her hips. She wore a simple black dress with an antique silver necklace and matching bracelet.

I grinned. "Sudsy is a force to be reckoned with, that's for sure." She had anointed herself director of the festival during its infancy and no one had ever dared refute her.

"Sudsy?" Jessamine asked.

I cleared my throat. "I wouldn't go calling her that to her face," I warned. "Elizabeth 'Sudsy' Sudsbury once got annoyed when I dared to call her Betty."

Kim snorted. "I remember that! Hilarious. You should have seen the look on her face. If looks could kill!"

The waiter returned and stood by quietly as his boss continued the conversation.

"I won't," promised Jessamine in response to my advice. "As a newcomer, I want to stay on everyone's good side."

"I'm sure you won't have any problems at all," I said. "I have a feeling you know how to handle yourself."

"Do like the rest of us," said Floyd. "Give her what she wants."

"May as well," Karl said. "What she wants, she gets." Karl motioned to the nearby waiter for another beer for himself and Floyd. "The woman was always getting on my case. Telling me how to do my job." His fingers went to the cigar he always kept on him though he rarely lit up. "You never saw me trying to run her fancy jewelry store."

"Are all you men parading your automobiles this year? And," our hostess added, "not to be sexist, any of you ladies?"

All the guys starting talking at once.

Jessamine's earthy laughter and accompanying smile brought them to a halt. "You know," she said, leaning over the table, displaying a glimpse of cleavage, "I'm hearing a lot of talk about Mr. Chick Sherman. One of my patrons, I don't remember who, said Mr. Sherman is going to have the car to beat all cars. A special car. A car he designed and built all by himself." She wriggled her brow provocatively.

"That crackpot?" scoffed Steve. "He says that every year." Steve shook his head in disdain. "And every year he has nothing."

Jessamine shrugged lightly. "He says this year is different."

Steve, Karl, and Floyd looked at one another.

"He's always had old cars," Karl said. "He never shows those."

"Apparently, this is a prototype," Jessamine replied.

"You mean he actually managed to finish it?" Floyd tilted his head toward Jessamine.

"He says he did."

"Nah, I don't believe it," repeated Steve. "The man's a nut."

"That's not a very nice thing to say," John interjected. "I've seen Mr. Sherman at the library quite a lot. He's always checking out all sorts of books about engines and the like. Maybe he really does have something."

"Maybe," Steve agreed albeit reluctantly. "I'll believe it when I see it."

With that, Jessamine nodded to us all and left us to enjoy our lunch. Thankfully, with John's help, I was able to get the subject back to birds for the remainder of the meal. Afterwards, I collected everyone's money and everybody went their separate ways while I waved down our waiter to pay the bill. I left a generous tip on the table.

Outside at the curb, waiting for Kim to bring her car around, I saw Floyd and Karl talking to Steve next to the mail drop box at the corner. A moment later, Steve waved and departed. He turned the corner, so I couldn't see whether he was driving the antique De Soto he'd been bragging on and on about.

"Come on," I overheard Karl say. The two men were on the deaf side and tended to speak loudly to one another. "Let's get down to LaChance Motors. I saw a couple of good options there."

Floyd was shaking his head. "I don't know why you told everybody we got a car to enter in the car show, Karl."

"Because I'm tired of guys like Steve getting all the ribbons." He clapped Floyd on the back. "Let's get ourselves a ribbon, Floyd. We can do it!"

"You're crazy, Karl. You know that?"

Kim pulled up and tooted her horn. The paint job on her blue Honda was fading and the wheels were scratched from too many encounters with curbs. She, for one, wouldn't be winning any ribbons at car shows anytime soon. "Get in!"

I held up a finger indicating that she should give me a minute. "Do you boys need a ride?" I called to Karl and Floyd.

Floyd and Karl turned, halfway in the middle of the street. They looked at one another. I heard Floyd say, "It's a long walk to the car lot from here and the bus doesn't go that way, Karl."

"How did you get to town this morning?" I asked.

"The shuttle from the senior center drove us out, but we said we'd catch the bus back."

"It sounds to me like you could use a ride, Karl."

"Fine." Karl nodded. "Don't mind if we do."

The two men hustled over and climbed in the back. Kim hit the button to unlock the rear doors. "Going home to Rolling Acres?" she asked.

I sat in front beside Kim. As always, her car smelled like a perfume lab. I glanced at Karl and Floyd in the rearview mirror as Kim started out into traffic. "I believe these two gentlemen are on their way to LaChance Motors."

Karl and Floyd expressed surprise.

"Sorry, I couldn't help overhearing." I swiveled my head around as Kim zipped down the road—it was better than watching her drive. "You don't actually have a car, do you?"

"No," Karl muttered sheepishly after a moment. "We're going to get one though!"

Floyd gazed at his friend. "It better be cheap."

Karl waved off the remark. "Trust me, Floyd. You don't want cheap, you want classic." He fanned his hands.

"Classic?" Floyd frowned. "That sounds expensive."

I chuckled. "Frankly, I think it could be a good hobby for the two of you." Then a problem popped suddenly to mind. "But I'm not sure how Rolling Acres is going to like you keeping a project car on the premises, let alone working on it there."

Visions of the elegant yet stern Millicent Bryant, who oversaw the day-to-day operations of the facility, came to mind. She barely tolerated my bird feeders and was constantly complaining about the sunflower-seed shells littering the grass. What would she think of two of its residents making like grease monkeys in the parking lot?

Karl replied, "You let me worry about that. First, we need a car."

"Who is this Chick Sherman?" I asked as we headed toward the edge of town, where the space between houses grew larger and the fields began to spread.

"You don't know him?" remarked Floyd.

I said that I didn't. Ruby Lake is a small town but not so small that we all know one another.

Thank goodness.

"He came down from Asheville a good twenty years ago."

"That's right," agreed Karl. "Asheville. And I'll bet the town was happy to see him go."

"Why do you say that? Is he trouble?"

"No," Karl said, "not trouble exactly."

"Unless he burns your garage down!" Floyd said with a snort.

"Excuse me?" said Kim. "Why would he burn somebody's garage down?"

"Accident," replied Floyd. "He was working on something in his garage, the way I heard it. There was an explosion. *Ker-pow!*" Floyd threw his hands in the air. "The next thing you know, his garage is on fire and so's the one next door."

"Lovely," quipped Kim, swerving to avoid a squirrel that couldn't make up its mind whether or not to cross the road.

"Nah, nothing like that." Karl squinted as he squeezed between the front seats and looked at the dashboard. "Say, Kim," he said, "not that it's any of my business anymore—I am retired—but did you know you're going nearly twenty miles over the speed limit?" He pointed to the needle of the speedometer.

"Oops."

I felt Kim ease up on the gas and mouthed a silent thank-you to Karl. "What's the scoop on this Sherman character?" I asked.

Karl leaned back. "You might call him a tinkerer," answered Karl from behind me. Floyd sat behind Kim.

"A tinkerer?"

"Always inventing stuff," filled in Floyd. "One time he built a hot air balloon that he said could double as a boat."

My eyebrows went up. "What happened to it? Did it work?"

"Sank like a stone," deadpanned Karl. "The dang fool almost drowned. Me and my men had to rescue his butt." His eyes drifted to the past. "The balloon and basket are still at the bottom of Ruby Lake."

"For years he's been telling everybody that he's building a special car." This from Floyd.

Karl snorted. "He claims it can go two hundred miles an hour on land, three hundred in the air, and do forty knots per hour on the water."

"Can it?" I asked, though I was dubious.

Floyd shrugged. "Nobody's ever seen it."

"That's because it doesn't exist," Karl said firmly.

"What does this tinkerer do to earn a living?" Kim asked, turning her head to talk to Karl.

"Eyes on the road!" I yelled as we drifted over the line.

Kim scooted back into our lane. "Sorry."

"He doesn't do much of anything. Not for as long as I've known him." Karl coughed. "He runs an unofficial junkyard."

"Unofficial?"

"He hasn't got a business license to operate," Karl explained. "But no one's ever seen the harm in it."

"His wife tells fortunes," added Floyd. "They sell used goods out of their house, too."

"She says she's a gypsy." Karl rolled his eyes and stuffed his cigar in his mouth.

"Don't you dare light that thing," Kim warned.

Karl frowned at her reflection in the mirror. "But who ever heard of a gypsy from Kentucky?"

"You know that little white house near the lumber yard?" Floyd tapped the side window. "It's coming up ahead."

I nodded and glanced to my left. The long, low sign mounted between two sturdy six-by-six posts read: MOUNTAIN LUMBER. The signage separated the road from the gravel and dirt parking lot. Trucks and pickups filled the spots nearest the unremarkable brown structure. Two men in flannel shirts loaded long, wide boards into the back of a slat-sided truck.

A minute later we passed the small white house Floyd had mentioned. It looked like an old sharecropper's house. "Do the Shermans live there?"

"Nope," Karl answered. "They've got a shack farther out. Just down that dirt track. Trudy, Chick's wife, keeps this place for the tourists."

Kim slowed as we passed. There was a crystal ball painted on the unwashed plate glass window and a green globe on a white pedestal in the rather bleak-looking yard. The sign on the door was written in red: FORTUNES TOUTED, MISFORTUNES ROUTED. A phone number was displayed in small black numerals below.

Those were strong claims.

Little did I know then how my fortunes and those of my friends were going to change.

3

Kim pulled in to the used car lot of LaChance Motors. Second-hand cars were all he sold. He also ran a repair shop.

The big boss himself, Robert LaChance, stood on the wooden deck attached to the double-wide trailer from which he ran his business operations. Several white outdoor molded-resin seats were scattered about—the kind you get at the big box stores.

The car salesman's hands gripped the railing. A gold ring with a ridiculously large diamond, real or not I couldn't tell, flashed almost as brightly as his unnaturally white teeth as we came to a halt. Robert seemed to be tan no matter the season and was fond of pinstripe suits. His wavy dark hair was beginning to gray at the temples. Tiffany told me he bought his suits at O'Neill's Men's Clothing here in Ruby Lake. I wasn't sure where he bought his tan.

When Robert wasn't driving one of the many heaps he was selling, he was driving an old red Ferrari that he seemed to love more than anything. If he'd loved his ex, Tiffany, half as much, maybe they'd still be married. Not that she wasn't better off without him.

Besides, he'd taken up with his secretary, a redhead named Monica somebody. And she had some body.

Robert LaChance beamed and started down the deck stairs toward us, waving off the two salesmen in sport coats and brown slacks seated on their own white plastic chairs under a red and white striped awning protruding from the service area.

I'd heard Robert kept fit playing tennis out at the country club three days a week. I'd also heard that he worked out quite often with his redheaded secretary, who was a good ten years younger than him. Monica favored tight sweaters that pushed out in all the right directions and short skirts that did nothing to protect her legs from the viewing public.

Karl and Floyd climbed out. "Thanks for the ride, ladies." Karl slapped the trunk.

"Shall we wait for you?" I asked. "You don't mind, do you?" I said, turning to Kim.

"Not at all."

"That might not be a bad idea." Floyd zipped up his light jacket. The breeze was picking up. I hoped it didn't rain. I was looking forward to some quality time in my garden later. The flowerbeds needed reworking.

"That won't be necessary," countered Karl. He thumped the roof of Kim's car. "We'll be driving ourselves home." He waved us off.

"Hold on there a minute." Robert stepped in front of Kim's Honda. Kim and I eyed him curiously.

Confident that we weren't driving off, Robert removed himself from the front bumper and came around to the driver's side. Kim rolled down her window.

"Good afternoon, ladies." When he smiled, his teeth seemed bigger than his whole head. He smelled of drugstore cologne. "I can give you a good price for this thing if you're looking to upgrade." His hand stroked the A pillar. "Seven-fifty toward any car on the lot." He waved said hand in a broad gesture.

"No, thanks." Kim went to roll up the window. "And my car is not a *thing*."

Robert's hand held the window in place. "I'll make it a thousand and throw in a sixty-day warranty on any vehicle you buy. What do you say?"

I leaned toward him from the passenger side. "We say goodbye." I tapped Kim on the shoulder. "Let's go."

"Karl and Floyd are the ones looking for a car," Kim explained.

"Really?" Robert looked across the car lot and I saw dollar signs flash in his eyes.

"Something *old*," added Kim.

"Old, you say?" Robert rubbed his hands together as he smiled. "I always get a few cars in special around the time of the classic car and tractor show. It never fails that we don't get one or two interested buyers around this time. Discerning buyers, I might add." He smiled devilishly at Karl and Floyd. "I've sold two in the last ten days."

"I'll bet," I said. "Tell me, Robert, is your girlfriend entering the Miss Fall Festival pageant?"

The corner of his mouth turned down. "You know that's only open to women under twenty-one."

"You didn't answer my question." I batted my eyelashes innocently.

"Say," interrupted Kim, extending her neck and clutching the steering wheel as she lifted up from her seat, "how much is that cute little BMW convertible?"

"The blue one?"

Kim nodded. Before LaChance could answer, I did. "More than you can afford. Come on, Kim. Let's get out of here before you do something you'll regret."

Kim moaned but cranked the engine. "Are you sure Floyd and Karl are going to be okay?"

I looked across the lot. The two salesmen were double-teaming the guys. "Karl and Floyd are old enough to take care of themselves. Besides, I don't think they want us interfering. Let's go."

Robert backed away from the car as Kim turned around and headed for the road. I lowered the visor and looked in the mirror. Karl and Floyd were pawing and drooling over a seafoam-green behemoth with chrome wheels and fat whitewall tires.

As LaChance Motors faded into the distance, I noticed a trio of turkey vultures sitting on the roof of Robert's trailer office. Whether that was an omen or a marketing plan, I wasn't sure.

As we approached the small, untidy white cottage along the roadside that housed the fortune-teller's business, I turned to Kim. "What do you say we get your fortune told?"

Kim's brow wrinkled up. I felt her foot lift from the gas pedal as she looked my way. "I thought you didn't believe in such things?"

"I don't," I replied. "That's why I said we'd get *your* fortune told."

"Why the sudden interest in fortune-telling?"

"Who knows? It might be fun. Aunt Betty loves all this psychic mumbo jumbo. Maybe she's on to something. Look how well she's turned out."

Kim eyed me skeptically. "Your aunt has been married three times."

"Yeah, but she's perpetually happy."

"I suppose." Kim pulled off the highway and stopped in front of the house. "It looks closed."

True enough, the windows were dark. "Let's check." I climbed out.

A young couple sat on the corner of the intersection of the dirt road and the highway, on the same side of the road as us. The young man had scraggly black hair to his shoulders and was as skinny as a proverbial beanpole. The girl was just as skinny with pale pink skin and light brown locks clipped atop her head. When she turned to glance our way, I noticed that the hair on that side had been dyed blue and green.

The young couple had rigged up three wooden broom handles and a yellow bedsheet for a makeshift covering over their goods. They appeared to be hawking their possessions. Everything from kitchen utensils, to posters, to used clothing lay spread around them. A pair of bicycles, one red, one yellow, lay side by side with a black backpack atop the red one.

The pair eyed me as I approached the fortune-teller's door. I tried the worn brass knob. It jiggled loosely in my hand but would not turn. I peeked in the window. Midnight-blue curtains covered the walls. A small wooden table with the obligatory crystal ball and two chairs occupied the center of the room.

I returned to Kim's car and climbed in. "The place is locked and I couldn't see anyone inside." I slammed the door closed.

"What? No spirits of your dead ancestors floating about in the ether?" Kim asked with a smile.

"Thankfully, no." I ran my hands down my legs. "It's getting chilly out there."

A car came quickly out from the dirt road, paused at the highway, then lurched toward town. "Hey," I said, "that must be the car that Karl and Floyd were so keen on this morning."

Kim glanced over her shoulder. "The color is right. Teal and white."

"What did they call it? A Bel Air?"

"I think so." Kim laughed. "I know just about as much about cars as I do birds."

"Which isn't much at all," I teased.

Kim shrugged. "I'm learning." She turned the key in the ignition. "Ready to go home?"

"Why don't we drive down the road a bit? Karl said the Shermans live out that way. Maybe we can get a look at this special car half the town says Chick Sherman is working on."

"The guys also said that Mr. Sherman won't let anybody see it. It's supposed to be top secret."

"Yes," I said, with the beginnings of a smile, "but maybe he'll show it to us if we play our cards right."

"You mean the feminine wiles card?"

"I say cards, you say wiles," I answered with a shoulder shrug. "Imagine the look on Paul and Derek's faces when they learn that we've seen Chick Sherman's car before they have. Maybe I'll get a picture on my cell phone."

Kim was smiling now, too, as she carefully made a three-point turn to avoid running over the two young sellers and started down the dirt track. "Dan's going to be green with envy."

"That's the spirit!" I laughed as the Honda bounced up and down along the dirt track through the woods.

"How do you think I'd look with blue hair?" Kim asked, glancing at her reflection in the rearview mirror as we passed a couple of narrow, tree-shrouded lanes with mailboxes. Kim slowed as we did. None of the post boxes belonged to the Shermans.

"Like a blueberry with legs," I quipped.

Kim stuck her tongue out at me.

"Real mature." I pointed. "Watch the road, blueberry girl."

Before long a ramshackle thirty-foot-tall windmill came into view in a small clearing surrounded by pine forest. Its green-jay-colored sails rotated anemically. A battered mailbox in the shape of a black cow sat atop a post at the corner. The name SHERMAN had been hand-painted on the cow's side in white letters. A smaller sign on a stick pounded into the earth had a white arrow painted on it. It pointed to the right, and so we went.

Kim turned into the sandy drive indicated. Several junkers, two pickups, and an unidentifiable sedan sat around the yard the way others might arrange large boulders for yard décor. We'd bounced along for about a quarter of a mile and the Honda was covered with dust.

I rolled down my window and took a look around.

It wasn't quite the shack that Karl's words had me envisioning. We were looking at a Folk Victorian–style house with white clapboard siding, jigsaw bargeboards, and elaborately carved spindles.

The shutters were bluebird blue. There was a small second story with a chimney running along the side.

A brown squirrel danced on the sagging porch. The shingled roof was sagging, too. In fact, the whole house looked rather tired or as if it had grown just too hard to stand straight any longer. A flat carport extended from the house to a rather large unpainted clapboard barn whose pine had faded to a silvery gray.

There was junk everywhere. Old rusted buckets, statuary, some with limbs and heads missing, a push mower, parts of old farm equipment, and a gas pump with the image of a green brontosaurus on its belly that looked like it might have come from the Ruby Diner, which had originally been a gas station before being converted to the eatery it was now.

The wind picked up, sending a gust of chill air through the clearing and in the car window. An eerie sound like the groaning of demons accompanied it. The little hairs on my arms bristled.

The front door to the farmhouse stood open. Painted on the front window were the words THRIFT GOODS & ANTIQUES.

I pushed open the passenger-side door and climbed out before I could change my mind. "Shall we?"

"If you insist." Kim cut the engine and buttoned up her sweater.

She followed me up the short flight of steps to the main door. The dancing squirrel hopped to the rail, then leapt to the ground and disappeared in some untrimmed hedges.

"Hello?" I stomped across the porch, making sure we'd be heard and weren't catching anyone unaware. "Is anybody here?"

A cedar birdhouse that didn't look like it had had a tenant since the Eisenhower administration hung over the front door. There definitely wasn't anybody at home there.

I stepped across the threshold.

Kim grabbed my sleeve. "Are you sure we should be doing this?"

I pointed to the sign on the door, a cracked and split orange and white plastic job that read OPEN.

The inside was more cluttered than the outside. Antique furniture, mirrors, toys, car parts, two spinet pianos, a hand-crank sewing machine, whatever the heart desired. You name it, it was there.

"Wow," whispered Kim.

"Yeah, wow," I whispered back. I reached over and picked up a brass table lamp from a coffee table that looked ready to collapse. A faded price tag had been tied to its base with a piece of blue string. "Two dollars." The living room, now a jumbled sales floor, smelled of sage and patchouli.

"It's a steal," quipped Kim. She wound her way through a stack of old newspapers and magazines. "Hey, look at this."

"What is it?" I sneezed from all the dust and dander that had found its way into everything including my nasal passages. I rubbed my nose and worked my way across the room. A threadbare lilac rug covered the hardwood floor visible along the edges of the room—at least those edges not covered with bric-a-brac. The only light came from the afternoon sun cutting at a slant through the living room window.

"Come see."

I found Kim slowly thumbing through a stack of bird prints. "How about that," I said, my voice low. "These are lovely. These look like original Audubon bird prints." I sidled up next to Kim and watched as she flipped through the stiff prints. Some were pen and ink. Others were watercolor. "Or very good copies."

In fact, the whole corner seemed to be devoted to birds and other wildlife, boasting everything from a stuffed owl and a stag's head on a mounting board, to various animal artwork, including framed oil paintings and engraving plates.

There was a row of books bound in red Morocco leather. I scanned the titles, seven volumes in all. "This is an old copy of John Audubon's *Birds of America*. The Royal Octavo edition." The edition contained five hundred beautiful lithographic prints. The small white sticker on the last volume indicated that the price was one hundred dollars for the complete set, which seemed more than reasonable.

I stopped at a delicate-looking card-backed illustration featuring three pairs of birds, a male and female specimen of each. A hanging gourd-shaped nest hung from an upper branch. The pair of chestnut-backed chickadees sat to the left and the bushtits on the right. The black-capped chickadees sat near the bottom on another willow-oak branch. The marvelous nest would be the work of the bushtits, who were known for creating these architectural jewels using nothing more than moss, spider webs, and grasses.

"This reminds me of the chickadee we saw this morning."

"Yeah, I guess so." Kim was busy examining a tray of pinned moths.

"I wonder how much it costs?"

Kim bent and looked behind the artwork. "Ten dollars is written in pencil on the back." She squinted. "I think."

"That's a bargain. At these prices, Trudy Sherman is probably more successful as a fortune-teller than she is an antiques dealer." I stared at the illustration appreciatively. I held it at arm's length, trying to see it in better light. "This would look lovely behind the cash register, don't you think?" I turned to Kim, but a big shadow moving in the front door caught my attention and I froze.

"Are you okay?" Kim looked at me funny.

"We have company." I set the sketch carefully back on the tray that held it and all the others. "Hi." I smiled brightly though my heart was pounding in my chest. "Mr. Sherman?"

Kim moved behind me, knocking over a stack of big-band-era LPs mixed in with some original Broadway recordings that under normal circumstances would have caught my attention. "Oops!" She rushed to pick them up and restack them.

"Just leave it," said the man. "We'll clean it up later." His tenor voice was firm.

Kim gulped, nodded, and set the half-dozen LPs in her hands back down inside the upended crate that had held the vinyl records. She wiped her dirty hands on her sweater. "Hi." She glanced at the disarray. "Sorry about that."

The man stepped farther into the room. "Who are you ladies?"

I stepped forward, pulling Kim with me. "I'm Amy Simms. This is Kim Christy. We're from town. We heard you and your wife had some interesting items and wanted to see for ourselves." I waited for his reply but one wasn't forthcoming.

"You are Chick Sherman, aren't you? I feel terrible if we've come to the wrong house." I started for the door, wondering if I'd made a mistake. The Sherman house might have been farther down the dirt track. "We're sorry to have intruded. Come on, Kim. We must have the wrong house."

The strange man maintained his position in the doorway. "You're in the right place." The stern, suspicious look on his face faded away, making him suddenly seem far less imposing and dangerous. When he wasn't glaring suspiciously, Chick Sherman looked rather boyish, with wavy ginger hair and vigilant green eyes.

"I'm Chick Sherman." He pulled a white handkerchief from the rear pocket of his baggy jeans and wiped his hands before extending his right one. "Pleased to meet you."

He had full cheeks and looked like he was kept well fed. A faded blue flannel shirt hung loose from his shoulders. Underneath was a yellowed V-neck tee from which sprouted a clump of hair.

Kim and I shook his hand in turn. Dirt and grease had worked their way into every fold and crevice of his clothes, and his hands were calloused.

"Was there something particular you were interested in?" He stuffed his hankie back in his pocket and smiled broadly. His teeth were uneven but white.

What I had come to see was the car he claimed to be secretly working on, but having seen the bird art, my interests had changed. "I was admiring that pen-and-ink sketch of the titmice."

Chick Sherman glanced toward the cluttered corner housing the bird and animal miscellany. "Yeah, the paintings ain't bad if you're into that sort of thing."

"Believe me," Kim said with a smile, "Amy is really into birds. In fact, sometimes I think she's bird crazy."

I tilted my eye at her. "Thank you, Kim." I turned back to Mr. Sherman. "I would like to buy that first print there. Ten dollars?"

Chick Sherman shrugged. "If that's what's written on the back." He sniffled. "My wife handles all that."

"It's a deal," I said. I headed toward him. "My purse is in the car. I'll go get it."

Mr. Sherman stepped aside to let me pass.

Kim followed me outside. I opened the passenger side, dug around in my wallet and extracted a ten-dollar bill. When I turned around, Chick Sherman was standing there waiting mere inches from me. He held out the illustration. "Is this the one?"

"Yes, thank you." I took the piece and carefully laid it on the back seat. It looked even lovelier in the sunlight with its subtle coloring and touches of pastel. I would get it framed at the craft store in town. "You know," I said, "I might be interested in buying the entire lot of prints. How much would you charge me if I took them all?" I'd counted more than a dozen similar sketches.

Chick shook his head. "I don't have a clue. You'll have to come back later when Trudy's home. I'm sure she'll work something out if you take the lot of them."

"You have a lot of interesting things," Kim chirped.

"What's in the barn?" I asked as casually as I could. The structure had a cupola toward the rear with a rooster weathervane circling atop it. The big wooden doors were shut. A dark tarp had been placed over the loft door. "Do you keep horses?" *Like three hundred and fifty of them with a five-speed transmission?*

"Nothing special." He lifted his left leg and knocked the heel of one boot against the other.

I nodded.

"That's not what I heard," blurted Kim.

"Pardon?" The secretive inventor lowered his brow.

I *accidentally* stepped on her foot.

"Ouch!"

A black and tan hound of some sort, with a short, dense coat, trotted from around the corner of the house, its drooling tongue hanging halfway to its doggie knees. The hound woofed at us and wagged its tail. I rubbed the dog's muzzle.

"What's up, girl? You hungry?" Mr. Sherman thumped the dog's ribs. "Feeding time, ladies."

That was our cue to leave. And it was a good thing. If we stayed any longer, Kim would have spilled every last bean in the can.

"Thanks again!" I called as Kim took her seat behind the wheel. I opened my door once more and started to climb in beside her.

Kim shoved the key in the ignition. "What's going on? What did you shut me up for?" She pouted. "And you didn't have to stomp on my foot to do it." She rubbed her foot through her shoe. "I thought you wanted to get a look at this mystery car he's supposed to be building."

"Sorry. I do," I replied quietly, my fingers on the door handle. Man and dog turned the corner where a rain spout ended at a squat wooden rain barrel.

I slowly slid out of Kim's car.

"What are you doing?"

"I just want a quick look." I had my mobile phone in my hand. "One picture is all we need."

"I don't know . . ." Kim looked nervous. "What if he sees you?"

"He won't. Start the engine," I motioned with my hands. "He might wonder what we're up to if he doesn't hear the car leaving."

Kim sighed as if I'd just asked her to carry the weight of the world, but complied.

I raced on tiptoe across the yard. A gust of wind came out of nowhere followed once again by a long, low, and lonely wail. I thanked my lucky stars it was still daylight. This place and that sound would have given me a heart attack after dark.

A crooked horseshoe had been mounted over the double doors, heels up. That was supposed to denote good luck. I'd also heard that the devil won't enter a room with a horseshoe over the door. There was no such prohibition against bird-store owners.

Glancing over my shoulder for some sign of Chick Sherman or his dog, I reached the barn door. There was a latch with a cross bar. I lifted the wood beam that held the barn doors in place.

A sharp voice stopped me. "I wouldn't do that!" Chick Sherman stood at the side of the house, one hand on the rain barrel. His hound dog sat at his side.

"Sorry." I lowered my hand. I smiled. "Just curious, I guess."

Chick came toward me and the dog followed. "Do you see any cats around here?"

I squeezed my brows together as I pondered the odd question and looked around the cluttered yard. "Nooo." I drew the word out.

Chick was within arm's length of me when he stopped. "That's because curiosity killed the cat."

He was smiling when he repeated the proverb, but I headed full tilt for Kim's car and didn't take a breath until we were a mile down the road.

4

"That went well." Kim laughed.

"Very funny." Despite the chill in the air, a layer of perspiration had sprung up on my forehead. I wiped it away with the back of my hand.

Kim slowed as we passed the young couple hosting the garageless garage sale at the side of the highway.

"They'll be lucky if Chief Kennedy doesn't come along and force them to shut down." I waved to them through the window as we passed.

"Should we warn them?"

I thought about it. "No, I suppose not. Warning them might just make them nervous and the police may never bother them at all. No point upsetting them over nothing."

"I'll ask Dan not to give them a hard time. Though there's little he can do if Jerry tells him otherwise."

As we reentered town, I said, "Speaking of Jerry Kennedy, isn't his vow-renewal ceremony coming up soon?"

"Yep. They're holding it the last day of the festival. Don't tell me you forgot?" Kim stopped as the light ahead turned from yellow to red. I had noticed, since she began dating a police officer, that Kim was better about stopping before the traffic signals turned red rather than her usual habit of racing through them.

"No, I haven't forgotten."

"You're still coming, aren't you?"

I pulled a face. "Yes. If I don't, my mother will kill me." Mom was a stickler for civility. Jerry Kennedy and I had a history and it wasn't a good one. We had dated. Once. Just long enough to know that we never wanted to try a repeat performance. Things had only gotten worse since I'd returned to Ruby Lake.

Jerry claimed I was constantly interfering in his police work. I claimed he kept pilfering the bird food I sold by the pound in bins at the front of the store.

"Great." Kim pulled to a stop outside Harlan and Harlan, Attorneys-at-Law. Derek and his dad, Ben, share a small office space just off the town square.

"What are we stopping here for? The office is closed. Derek's out with Paul, working on their car, remember?"

Kim climbed out. "Didn't I tell you?"

I grabbed my purse and followed Kim. "Tell me what?"

"My dress is ready."

"Oh, right. That I did forget." Her date, Dan, was one of the groomsmen, and Kim had ordered a special dress for the occasion. She had begged me to come and I had begged and begged her not to make me. Kim outbegged me and I was going. My pleading with Derek to accompany me had fallen on deaf ears. He said he was still smarting from his own wedding.

Kim stopped outside the display window of Dream Gowns, a recently launched boutique catering to brides and belles. She pulled on the handle and held the door open for me. "Is there a problem?" she asked when I didn't budge.

"You know there is." The store in itself was fine. It was one of the store's partners I had the problem with. She used to be the partner, as in wife, of the man I was now dating. The fact that she had opened her shop right next door to her ex-husband's law office was hardly a coincidence, though she insisted it was. Derek appeared to believe her. Men can be so oblivious.

Derek and his ex had a wonderful young daughter named Maeve, whom I'd met on several occasions. She was a quiet girl with a sweet disposition, much like her father. Thank goodness.

Derek also happened to be living in the apartment above Harlan and Harlan.

His ex-wife's name was Amy, too. That made me Amy Two.

"Don't worry. I talked to Liz."

"Liz?"

Kim nodded. "Liz Ertigun. She's one of Amy's partners. She

mentioned that Derek's ex was down in Charlotte for the weekend doing some shopping."

That was a relief. I blew up my cheeks, let out a breath, and marched inside. It was warmer inside the boutique than it was outdoors, so I loosened my jacket.

An elegantly dressed woman in a slimming plum-colored dress walked toward us. I'd met her once before, briefly, on the one and only other time I'd been to the store. She squinted her meticulously made-up eyes at me. "Don't I know you?"

"N-no," I stuttered. "I don't think so." There was no point reminding the woman that I'd once spilled a potful of soil all over her new carpets—and a brand-new designer wedding gown. I held out my hand. "Amy Simms."

"A pleasure." The woman's hand was as cool as her disposition. She had alabaster skin, platinum hair that fell perfectly to her bony shoulders, and blue eyes that gave me more chills than a late-night horror flick.

"Amy's with me," Kim said, pushing past me to receive a dispassionate kiss on the cheek from Ms. Ertigun.

"Good afternoon, Ms. Christy. Your dress is back from alterations. I'm sure you'll be very pleased." Liz Ertigun eyed me curiously a moment before turning. She moved to the nearest rack. "I don't understand . . . it was right here."

She flipped through several dresses in quick succession. "Someone must have moved it. Follow me, please. I'll ask Amy. She'll know. She is with a customer, but I'm sure she won't mind the interruption."

I stopped dead in my tracks and shot my best friend a look that should have stopped her dead in hers, too. Unfortunately, her back was to me. My deadly looks are ineffective against thick craniums.

The aloof Ms. Ertigun twisted her head around as she walked. "Would either of you like some tea?"

"No, thanks," Kim replied.

I could have used a hot cup myself, but that would have meant sticking around longer than necessary. Maybe we'd stop off for a cup at the Coffee and Tea House on the square afterward.

The salon had been painted off-white. Fashionable, pricey gowns hung from long, chrome clothes rods along the walls. Low glass-topped tables placed strategically about held a small assortment of accessories, including veils, belts, and crystal-covered shoes. Perfectly spaced chandeliers provided ambience.

As I remembered, there were two rows of pale pink satin-curtained dressing rooms toward the rear with a riser and three full-length mirrors between them along the far wall.

As we wandered toward the consultation area and changing rooms, I saw Amy-the-ex seated on a raspberry-colored, armless leather sofa with a quilted back. Her legs were crossed. She wore an elegant deep brown dress that, if she were standing, would have fallen somewhere between her knees and ankles but was riding high now.

"What's *she* doing here?" I muttered. "You told me she was out of town."

"Oops," Kim replied without breaking her stride.

I noted Amy-the-ex was still blond like she'd been the last time our paths had crossed. The first time I'd met her, she'd been a redhead. What nature intended for her to be, I had no idea.

The last time I'd seen her, she'd asked me to stay away from Derek.

Fat chance.

Across from her, on a matching sofa, sat Jerry Kennedy and his wife, Sandra. Sandra's eyes were on the dress displayed on the glass table between the Kennedys and their host. Jerry's eyes, though I couldn't swear on it, seemed to be on Amy-the-ex's long legs.

Jerry managed to remove his eyes from Amy Harlan's legs as we approached. "What are *you* doing here, Simms?"

"Hello, Jerry. I'm here because Kim's here to pick up her dress and she's my ride."

"Hello, Kim. Hello, Amy." Jerry's wife wriggled her fingers at us. "Dan tells me you're his date, Kim."

"That's right."

"I'm glad you could come, too, Amy."

"Hi, Sandra. Thanks."

Jerry made a face at his wife. "One more mouth to feed," he grumbled. "You must've invited half the town by now." He was out of uniform, dressed casually in a pair of denim jeans, cowboy boots, and a gray sweatshirt. Beside him, a windbreaker with a Town of Ruby Lake Police Department patch on the front sat in a rumpled heap.

Sandra chuckled. "Don't mind Jerry. He's only teasing."

"That's a beautiful dress." I waved in the direction of the table. "Is it yours?"

"Yes." She smiled brightly. "Do you really like it?"

"I adore it." Sandra Kennedy had chosen a fit-and-flare dress with a lace top. It was the delicate shade of a pink cockatiel.

"Me too." Kim said, stepping in and running the silky fabric through her fingers.

"Thank you. I'm so glad." Sharon was a trim woman, the same age as me. Except that she was married and had a child already. Her hair was light brown and bounced as she talked. Long lashes accented her wide brown eyes. She and Jerry had married early, fresh out of high school. Sharon worked for a local insurance company part-time.

Amy-the-ex turned her attention to me. "Was there something you wanted?" Though she smiled sweetly, no doubt for the benefit of Jerry and his wife, I sensed an undercurrent of hostility. Amy-the-ex made no secret of her desire to get her husband back.

Liz answered for me. "Ms. Christy is here to pick up her dress for the Kennedy affair."

"Of course. I placed it in the storeroom. I had it pressed. Can you get it, Liz?"

Liz nodded and started down the hall that divided the dressing rooms on each side.

The sound of a curtain being pulled caused us all to turn our heads. A charming young woman in a below-the-knee yellow gown appeared from the dressing room. "What do you think, Mom?" She was beaming.

"You look beautiful," Sandra replied, rising to meet her daughter. She turned to her husband. "Doesn't she look beautiful, Jerry?"

Jerry stood, beaming. "That she does. Just like her mother!" He winked at Cassie.

"You really do look beautiful, Cassandra," I said. "Is this your dress for your folks' ceremony?"

"Oh, no," answered Cassie, her hands ruffling the skirt. "This is for the festival."

Sandra smiled. "Cassie is entering the Miss Fall Festival pageant." She ran her fingers through her daughter's long locks. The Miss Fall Festival pageant was one of the highlights of the weekend. The winner received a five-hundred-dollar scholarship and a bejeweled silver crown.

"That's wonderful!" Kim cried. "Did you know I was Fall Festival Queen?" Kim's crown from all those centuries ago sat in a place of honor on her mantel at home.

Cassie's eyes grew wide. "You were? Do you have any advice for me?"

Kim brought her index finger to her cheek and tapped it while she thought. "Just be yourself. That's what the judges are looking for. Poise, thoughtfulness, honesty. And a big smile."

Cassie grinned ear to ear.

Kim laughed. "Yeah, like that."

Kim laid a hand on Cassie's shoulder and said mock conspiratorially, "Don't tell anybody I said this, but you don't have to know a thing about classic cars or tractors." She winked at us all. "I didn't."

"Trust me," I quipped. "She still doesn't."

Kim turned to me. "For the record, you don't know so much about cars and engines and mufflers and stuff either."

"True. But at least I know the difference between a bird clutch and a car clutch."

"Very funny," replied Kim. She wiggled her brow. "And, personally, I prefer a buttery leather clutch and matching heels."

Cassie couldn't stop giggling. "Were you ever Miss Fall Festival Queen, Ms. Simms?" she asked.

Jerry snorted.

I shot him the evil eye before answering. "No, I'm afraid not. Good luck."

Liz Ertigun appeared from the back with a dress bag on a hanger. "Here we are." She lifted the bottom of the bag, revealing Kim's long silver dress. "What do you think?"

"It's perfect," said Kim. "But I'll try it on to be sure."

Kim took the dress from Ms. Ertigun and disappeared into a dressing room. Cassie and her mother went back into Cassie's dressing room, leaving me alone with Jerry, Amy-the-ex, and Liz Ertigun.

I shifted my feet uncomfortably. I cleared my throat. Nothing I did made the time go any faster or any easier. "How's it going in there?" I called to Kim.

"A minute longer," Kim replied. "Could you give me a hand, Liz?"

"Of course." Liz quietly slipped into Kim's dressing room.

I frowned, thinking of all the places I would rather be than alone with Amy-the-ex and Jerry. "So"—I cleared my throat a couple more times as if trying to disgorge an alien—"I met Chick Sherman today. He's an interesting fellow," I said mostly to Jerry.

"Chick?" Jerry's brow quirked up. "Interesting? Talk about your odd bird."

"I hear he's an inventor."

"He's a crackpot." Jerry fell back onto the sofa and folded his arms across his chest. "So's his wife."

"I hate to disagree," interjected Amy-the-ex, unfolding her legs and running a finely manicured hand down the outside of her right thigh, "but I've had several readings with Trudy. She's wonderful. So perceptive."

Amy-the-ex leaned forward, giving off a light scent of floral perfume. "You wouldn't believe some of the things she's told me."

"Such as?" I asked.

Amy-the-ex slowly turned her attention to me. "Madame Trudy told me the future." She tilted her head appraisingly. "And it's looking quite rosy." The beginnings of a smile crossed her face. "For some of us," she said rather smugly.

I detected a note of challenge.

"Bah!" Jerry shook his head. "Nobody can predict the future. If they could, my job would be a whole lot easier."

"I agree." I picked up a lacy veil from a display table, held it against my head, and looked at myself in the mirror. "Jessamine Jeffries told me that Chick told her that he was going to have his prototype car ready for the festival this year."

This brought another snort from Jerry. "The man's sixty-some-odd years old, and even if he lives another sixty, he'll never have that car, so-called car, of his ready."

Jerry stood as his wife and daughter reappeared, Cassie wearing a second dress, a simple dark blue A-line with a tapered waist. "Well, well, don't you look like a princess!"

"You really do," I was quick to agree.

"Like a true Miss Fall Festival Queen." Amy-the-ex rose, took Cassie by the hand, and led her to the dais so she could see herself in all three mirrors at once.

But Jerry wasn't done railing about Chick Sherman yet. "I'll tell you this about Chick Sherman. The man's never held a job, never done a day's worth of honest work, never paid any taxes near as I can tell, and I expect will sooner drop dead than he will finish that car of his."

5

Kim dropped me off outside Birds & Bees. I carefully took my pen-and-ink sketch off the back seat. Kim's dress hung on the hook on her side of the car under a protective cover of plastic. "Aren't you coming in?"

Kim shook her head. "Nope, I'm having dinner with Dan. What are you up to tonight?"

"A quiet night alone."

Kim grinned. "A Broadway musical marathon?"

"You got it. I see a lot of reading, bird-watching, and TV in my immediate future."

"Is that what the mysterious Madame Trudy would predict?"

"No, but what with Derek and Paul going full steam to get their car ready for the end of the week, I have a hunch that will be the extent of my social life."

I leaned my head in the door. "How did you get Dan to agree to dinner? I thought he was bent on getting his car prepped too?"

"I told him that if he didn't take me out to eat someplace nice, I was going to show up at his boss's vow renewal in a burlap sack and a straw hat."

I nodded appreciatively. "I might have to try that on Derek sometime."

Kim waved and drove off. I glanced next door. The outdoor patio of Brewer's Biergarten was crowded. There was no sign of its proprietor, Paul Anderson, but then I hadn't expected there to be. Like I had told Kim, he and Derek were probably still out at Paul's house working in the garage.

The house Paul Anderson had purchased when moving to town was still being rehabbed. In the meantime, he rented an apartment from me. It was on the second floor, the same floor as Esther Pilaster's apartment. Esther had come with the house. Her lease would be up in a matter of months.

There would be no more playing cat-and-mouse with Esther the Pester, as I sometimes referred to call her, over the cat I was sure she kept—against the rules. It was nothing personal against felines, it was simply that I was allergic. And the cigarettes I was convinced she was smoking—again very much against house rules.

Esther was now working for me part-time. My mom had offered her the job—without consulting me. At first, I'd complained but, truth be told, Esther could sell. Partly, I feared, because customers were afraid to tell her no. She'd been angling for me to give her the title of assistant manager. I'd been avoiding the subject.

I'm not saying I was afraid to deny her the title. I simply didn't feel like arguing with her about it.

I was looking forward to my mother and I having the big house to ourselves one day. Maybe by the time Esther's lease was up, Paul's house would be finished and he'd be out, too. I was thinking of remodeling the second floor to give my Mom and me some extra room. I had lofty dreams of adding a spiral staircase that would connect the second and third floors, creating one spacious apartment for the two of us.

I hadn't figured out yet where I was going to get the money to satisfy that dream. A consultation with Madame Trudy regarding winning lottery numbers might be in order.

The tiny silver bells attached to the inside of the door jingled as I walked into Birds & Bees. There wasn't a soul around, customer or otherwise. "Hello?" I walked between the aisles and down to the kitchenette in the far corner. "Anybody?"

"Why would they leave the store unwatched?" I muttered. I couldn't vouch for Esther, but it certainly wasn't like my mother to be so careless and irresponsible.

I returned to the front, set my new artwork on the countertop and my purse underneath, next to the cashbox. "Yoo-hoo?" I walked to the stairs in the center of the first floor. I kept it roped off with a sign that read: PRIVATE RESIDENCE. The rope was in place. "Mom? Esther?"

I cocked my ear. I thought I heard voices coming from the storeroom in back. But when I got there, it too was empty.

Nothing but boxes of surplus merchandise and cleaning supplies. Then I noticed that the back door was ajar.

I peeked through the crack and saw nothing but a streak of red. Convinced that no harm was awaiting me, I pulled the door open.

"Hello, dear." My mother smiled. "Isn't it magnificent?" She waved her hand at the magnificence in question.

"She's a Chrysler 300B," Karl declaimed as proud as a papa. He had an unlit cigar in his mouth.

I squinted at the behemoth occupying a quarter acre of my back lot. The car was red with tan leather interior. "What does the B stand for?"

Karl looked taken aback. "I don't know." He pulled open the driver's-side door. Floyd sat behind the wheel and Esther sat at the other end of the bench seat. Two more people and an ostrich could have fit between them. "Hey, Floyd," Karl yelled inside. "What does the B stand for?" The dash was two-tone, red and tan.

Floyd blinked and cupped his hand to his ear. "What does a bee sound like?"

"No, no." Karl shook his head. "The B. The B on the Chrysler 300. What does it stand for?"

"I don't know," Floyd confessed. "I figured you did." He looked past his friend to me. "Hi, Amy!"

"Hi, Floyd."

"You seemed really impressed when Mr. LaChance said it was a 300B," Floyd added. "It's got to be better than a 300A, right?"

"Hey, yeah." Karl hitched up his trousers. He patted the car's tall roof. "Looking good, eh?"

"She's a piece of work, all right." There was a certain beauty to the retro contours of the body if one was into such things, but I noticed patches of rust along the door panels and fenders. The frame's bent appearance also had me wondering if the old car hadn't been involved in an accident or two. "Did you buy this car or are you taking it out for a test drive?"

"It's a 1956 model!" Esther shouted from her side of the oversize coupe. Esther's a small, narrow-shouldered, elflike septuagenarian with a hawkish nose, sagging eyelids, and silvery hair. Gray-blue eyes hide under wispy white eyebrows. The woman has absolutely no filter.

"Karl and Floyd bought it," chimed in Mom. She stroked the

long, sloping hood. "And I think it's wonderful. It reminds me of when I was a girl." She looked out into the distance. "And of when your father was alive."

I felt an ache in my heart. I leaned over and gave Mom a kiss on the cheek.

She appeared surprised as she rubbed her cheek. "What was that for?"

"For being you." I waved to Karl and Floyd. "Good luck with the car, guys. You've got a lot to do if you want to have it ready in less than a week."

"A little elbow grease, a coat of wax." Karl rubbed his hands together. "She'll be good as new."

"We don't expect to win any prizes," Floyd put in. "But it will be nice to take part in the parade."

The classic car and tractor parade took place the night of the two-day festival, Saturday, as a prelude to the crowning of that year's Miss Fall Festival Queen. "If you say so."

I was a little dubious myself. And I hoped that Robert LaChance hadn't taken advantage of the two men and overcharged them for the automobile. As retirees, and not wealthy ones, their funds were limited. "Are you sure there's still time to enter? The parade's only days away," I cautioned, not wanting the guys to get their hopes up.

"Don't worry," replied Floyd. "Karl's got some pull."

"It doesn't hurt to be the former chief of police," Karl said with a wink. "Not even a Sudsbury's gonna say no to me. I know where all the bodies are buried."

"Gotcha," I said. "Good luck!" I waved to Floyd as I patted Karl on the forearm and started for the rear door.

"Where are you going, Amy?" Mom said. "Karl and Floyd were about to take us all for a ride!"

"Thanks. Another time, guys. After all, somebody has to mind the store. We don't close for another couple of hours."

Mom's face fell. "Oh, no." She clapped her hands to her cheeks. "Esther and I forgot all about the store."

"Oh, yes," I replied, wagging my finger at her. "You did."

Kim came by as I was fixing dinner for one in my third-floor apartment above Birds & Bees.

"What's up?" I asked with surprise on finding her at my door. I had a cheese-covered wooden spoon in my left hand. "I thought you were going out with Dan tonight."

"I am." Kim came in and shut the door behind her. "I hope."

"Come on. I was just making some mac and cheese."

She tossed her coat at the sofa. It fell to the floor and remained there as she followed me to the kitchen. I suppose it's the thought that counts. She stuck her finger in the pot and took a taste. "Not bad."

"You want some?" I stirred. "There's enough for two. And I'll probably eat it all if you don't save me from myself."

Kim took a spoon from the drawer and helped herself to a mouthful. "No, thanks. Dan's supposed to come by later and pick me up here. If that's okay? He's taking me to the Lake House." The Lake House was a romantic, upscale restaurant located at the nearby marina. There was a million-dollar view of the lake from its windows and outdoor seating area. Though the nights were chilling down, tonight promised to be a great night to sit out of doors and dine by candle- and starlight.

Suddenly, I was envious.

"Of course." I grabbed a bottle of red wine from the fridge and pulled the cork. "Join me?"

"That I will." Kim grabbed two glasses from the cabinet and filled them while I retrieved a plate for my dinner. "Where's your mom?"

"Having dinner with her sister. What's up?"

"Dan had to go out on a call the minute he got to my house."

"Oh?"

"Yeah. You remember that guy we met today?" Kim set down her glass and grabbed an open bag of barbecue-flavored potato chips from the top of the fridge and set it down between us.

"Which one?" I reached for a chip.

"Chick Sherman."

I chuckled. "How could I forget?"

"Yeah. He was an oddball, all right."

"Let's just say he's eccentric, shall we?" I raised my glass and sipped. "What about him?" Red wine and barbecue flavor wasn't the best combination, but I hadn't had a bite since lunch.

"He was involved in a wreck."

"A car wreck? Where?"

"Yes. Out near his place, I guess."

"Was anybody hurt?"

Kim was looking at her mobile phone. "I don't know. But you can ask Dan yourself. He just pulled up outside. That reminds me," she said, as she shoved her phone back in her purse, "I texted you twice. You didn't answer."

"I must have left my phone downstairs." I explained. "Is Dan driving his project car? The Trans Am?"

"No, the pickup. He's keeping the Trans Am clean for the parade. Heaven forbid the floor mats get dirty before then," Kim called as she started for the door. "I'd better go down and let him in."

There was a sharp knock on the apartment door as she reached it. "Who could that be?" she said. She pulled the door open. "Hi, Dan. I was just coming down to let you in."

"The front door was unlocked and there was a light on, so I let myself in." He wiped his feet on the mat outside the door, then stepped inside. "Hello, Amy!" He waved at me.

"Hi, Dan."

Dan gave Amy a peck on the cheek. "You really should lock your door after business hours, Amy. Ruby Lake is a pretty safe town, but still . . ."

"Yes, Kim," I said, from the stove. "You really should lock the door at night."

Kim blushed. "Sorry about that."

Dan unzipped his jacket.

"Can I pour you a glass of wine, Dan?" I called, even as I reached for a third glass.

"Well . . ." Dan looked inquiringly at Kim.

"We have time, Dan. Come on in." Kim led him to the kitchen, where I handed him his wine. "I was just telling Amy about the accident you were called out on." Kim pushed the bag of chips toward him.

Dan took a sip and swirled the wine around in his glass. "This is good." He ran his tongue over his lower lip and dropped himself onto a barstool at the counter. Dan was young and stocky, with brown eyes. He was half Hawaiian on his father's side. "Yeah. It was the darnedest thing."

"How do you mean?" I turned the burner down to low and covered the mac and cheese with a lid. I had some frozen peas waiting in a dish in the microwave. One good blast and I'd meet my green veggie requirement for the day.

"Sherman swears somebody tried to run him off the road."

"Oh my gosh!" gasped Kim. "That's terrible!" She pulled out the stool beside him and sat with her elbows on the counter.

Dan shrugged as he grabbed a handful of chips. "But there was nobody else near when we got there. And there was no sign of any other vehicles." Dan stopped and drank thoughtfully. "When I got there, the chief was already on the scene with Officer Pratt. Chick was mad as a hornet."

"Officer Pratt?"

"Albert Pratt. He's a new guy the chief hired. He just moved up from New Orleans."

"I've met him," Kim said. "His ancestors came over as slaves. Can you imagine?"

My brows went up. "Jerry actually hired somebody new? I'm surprised, number one, that the town had the funds to spend and, number two, that Jerry was willing to spend some of them on a new hire." I'd heard him squawk about wanting bigger, badder, better high-tech gear, but never more officers.

"It was Jerry's idea," Dan explained. "He asked the town council for the money. The chief said—" Dan clammed up.

I eyed him warily. "He said what?"

"Well . . ." Dan's face reddened and he looked to Kim for assistance. She gave him none.

"What did Jerry say, Dan? I mean, come on," I wheedled, "is he expecting the zombie apocalypse or something?"

"Not exactly." Dan tugged at his collar.

"What is it, Dan?" Kim pushed. "Tell us."

Dan frowned. "The chief says he has a call for more officers because . . ." His eyes rolled over me and Kim once more. We waited rather impatiently. "There's been a lot more crime since you came back to Ruby Lake, Amy." He diverted his eyes to the TV, which wasn't very slick considering the set wasn't on.

Kim laughed.

I was at a momentary loss for words. I thumped down on my stool.

"Who called in the accident?" Kim asked, after an unsettling silence.

"A family of tourists from Virginia. They didn't see it happen, but they were driving by and spotted Chick off the road with his car butted up against a tree and smoke coming from the engine compartment."

"Is he okay?" asked Kim.

"Yeah. I mean, I guess." Dan set his glass down and inhaled. "Speaking of smoke, that smells good." He pointed to my saucepan. "What's cooking?"

"Homemade mac and cheese. Would you two care to join me?" Dan's words were still sinking in. Did Jerry blame me for all the murder and mayhem in our little town? "I cater to bird lovers, not axe murderers!"

"Excuse me?" said Dan, looking at me funny.

"Sorry, that just slipped out." I turned toward the stove. "I think dinner is a good idea. A very good idea." When in doubt, eat. That's my motto.

"Oh, no." Kim stood. "You promised me dinner, Dan."

"This is dinner," I replied.

"At a restaurant." Kim folded her arms.

Dan chuckled. "That I did." He polished off his potato chips and washed them all down with the rest of his wine. He dusted off his hands.

"Wait," I said. "You saw Chick's car? Was it this prototype everybody is talking about?"

A slow smile developed on Dan's face. "Oh, yeah. She's a beauty, all right." He lowered his brow. "Looks more like a vehicle you'd ride to Mars than a car you'd drive to pick up groceries. At least she did. She's a bit mangled now."

"That's a shame," I said. "Yet you say Mr. Sherman was uninjured?"

"I'm not saying he was uninjured. I'm saying he refused treatment. He appeared to be limping, favoring his left leg."

"So he's in the hospital?" I asked.

"Chief Kennedy was ordering him to go with the medics to the hospital, but he flat out refused." Dan rose and stretched. "He wouldn't even let us touch his precious automobile."

Kim pulled her brows together. "You mean he just left it there? That doesn't sound like him at all. I mean, if he's as possessive and secretive about it as everybody says."

"He said he was going to use his tractor and a chain to pull it out himself. The wreck happened right near his place." Dan grabbed the doorknob. "There's a dirt road that connects to the highway. That's where he says he was run off."

I thought about the young couple who had been selling at the roadside earlier in the day. They hadn't had a car, at least not in the vicinity, only the two bicycles.

"And Jerry just left Chick alone there? He didn't make him go to the hospital or even haul off the car?" I asked as I followed them to the door. I would have expected to at least write Chick Sherman up for reckless driving. Jerry wasn't stingy when it came to giving tickets.

"Chief figures Chick lost control of that crazy car of his and hit that tree with nobody's help at all." Dan chuckled. "It wouldn't be the first time."

"He's done it before?" I asked. "Then why wouldn't he just say so?"

"The chief figures he was too embarrassed to admit it."

"I know I would be," Kim confessed.

Dan shrugged. "Besides, you know how it is. Folks around here pretty much leave the Shermans to fend for themselves. And the chief feels the same way. He says the man's more trouble than he's worth." With that, Dan said it was time to get going.

"Give me a second to get my coat, Dan." Kim pulled open the coat closet next to the door and began rummaging around.

I laid a hand on Kim's shoulder and turned her around.

"Oh, thanks." Kim moved toward the sofa and picked her coat up from the floor.

I followed them out to the top of the landing. "And don't forget to lock up when you leave!"

"I won't!" Kim called back.

I didn't believe her for a second, but with a police officer accompanying her, I knew at least one of them would remember to secure the entrance.

Maybe it was OCD of me, but I waited until I heard them leave, then ran downstairs to double-check. I tried the door handle. Locked. I turned on the porch light and turned down the store lights. I went behind the sales counter and pulled out my purse. Everything that should have been there was.

Except my artwork.

I drummed my fingers on the counter and cursed.

Then I frowned as I ran my hand over the empty counter. "What the devil?" I looked on the floor directly beneath me. The floor was empty. I went to the customer side and examined the floor.

Nothing.

"That's strange," I said to no one. I planted my hands on my hips. "I know I set that sketch here." When had I last seen it? I walked slowly up and down the aisles, wondering if a gust of wind caused by the opening and closing of the front door might have sent it fluttering.

But I found nothing.

Mom or Esther must have moved it, put it away somewhere.

I climbed the stairs, leaving the chain at the bottom unattached. I didn't want Mom bumping into it when she returned. I stomped to the third floor, thinking about my missing sketch.

A gray-haired head attached to a pink and blue housecoat appeared on the second-floor landing and glared up at me. "What's all the hubbub?" demanded Esther. Her hands were in her pockets. Her robe was pulled tight around her waist. Her feet were bare.

"Hubbub?"

"Sounds like a staircase stampede."

"Sorry," I said. "Kim and Officer Sutton just stopped by and I went down to look for my cell phone. Have you seen it?"

"Nope."

"How about an Audubon illustration of chickadees and bushtits?"

"No, thanks."

"I meant have you seen one. I left it on the counter when I got back to the store this afternoon. I bought it from Chick Sherman. I believe it may be an Audubon original. I thought I'd hang it in the store."

I frowned. "Come to think of it, I don't remember seeing it at all after that." I stared into space. "That's odd."

"Yeah, well, when you find it just tell me how much you want for it."

"I don't want to sell it. I bought it because it's pretty—a work of art. It will be part of the ambience."

Esther snorted. "Put a price on it and it can be part of the profits!"

I could see that a discussion with Esther over the merits of art over commerce would lead us nowhere. "Care for some mac and cheese?"

Esther looked at me like I'd just asked her to take a trip with me to Mars—in Chick Sherman's spacemobile. "No, thanks. It's Tuesday night. I always have meatloaf, take a bath, and watch my shows."

"Okay." I turned to go, then stopped. "How was your ride in Floyd and Karl's car?" They'd all been gone a very long time and I'd locked up the store myself.

Esther nodded appreciatively. "You really missed out. That's some hot rod."

"Hopefully, I'll get my chance soon."

She grinned. "That Floyd is something too."

"Care to elaborate?" I wriggled my brow.

"There's nothing to elaborate." She waved her hand at me. "I'm just saying."

"And I'm just listening." I took a step closer.

"I've got a bath getting cold." Esther tugged at the belt of her tatty robe. "Try to keep it down up there."

I promised I would. "Are you sure you wouldn't care for some mac and cheese? I made it myself."

"Nope. Gotta go."

"Perhaps your cat would like some?"

Esther eyeballed me. "Are you mad?"

"Mad?" I drew back. "No, I'm not mad. Why should I be?"

"I don't mean mad angry." She tapped her skull hard. "I mean mad as in addlebrained. Daffy as a duck."

"Sylvester as a cat?"

Esther snorted. "Batty, that's what you are. You ought to call your store Birds and Bees and Bats!"

And so the dance continued. My ruse to get Esther to admit keeping a cat in her apartment had once again failed miserably.

"Good night, Esther. Enjoy your bath. I'm going out for a few minutes and then I think I'll take a bath myself. Save me some hot water."

The old tank was slow to refill. Being located in the basement, it also had a long path to take before reaching the third floor bathroom. Hot was barely the word for it at the best of times.

"Where are you going at this hour?" Esther wanted to know. Anything after eight p.m. was the middle of the night in Esther's world.

"I must have dropped my cell phone out at the Shermans' house this afternoon." After Kim's comment about texting me, I realized I had not seen my phone since then.

"You're going out to the Sherman house at this hour? They may not like being disturbed by some stranger."

"I won't go in. I won't even knock on the door. I just want to pick up my phone. I probably dropped it right outside the barn."

That was the last place I could remember having had it. I'd pulled it out to take a picture of Chick's mysterymobile when the man himself had surprised me. I must have dropped it there. It was the only answer I could come up with for my phone's whereabouts.

"Why not call them or wait until tomorrow?"

"That's a good idea."

"Of course it is." With that said, Esther retired to her own apartment.

I couldn't help smiling as I listened to the sound of Esther slamming her apartment door behind her. Truth be told, I'd developed a bit of a soft spot for the Pester. And she had literally saved my life once.

I returned to my unit and looked up the Shermans in the local directory that I kept in the drawer of one of the living room side tables. There was a phone number, but when I dialed it a recording came on telling me that I had reached Madame Trudy and that I should leave my name and number. Madame Trudy promised to call back to arrange a reading.

If I wanted my cell phone, I'd have to go get it. I wasn't sure how well it would hold up to the night's elements. The weather forecast had stated there was a 30 percent chance of rain.

My luck, it would all fall over the Shermans' homestead and I'd be forced to buy a new phone. That was one expense I didn't need. The store was barely breaking even as it was.

The draw of the Fall Festival would, hopefully, put a few extra bucks in my till as much as it did those of my fellow merchants and those of the regional growers. It promised to be a big week.

But not in the way I expected.

6

To the soundtrack of Angela Lansbury enthusiastically belting out "Everything's Coming Up Roses" from her Broadway revival of *Gypsy*, I headed out into the darkness. Only three speakers remained working in the old van, so it wasn't exactly high fidelity but it was good enough for me. Traffic was thick through town but dwindled as I reached the outskirts. It didn't take me long to return to Madame Trudy's studio, which sat dark and quiet at the edge of the road.

I slowed, knowing that the dirt track to the Sherman house was nearby. The van's headlights swept over the trees, largely white oaks. With fall upon us here in the Carolinas, the leaves were beautiful to look at when the sun was shining, all brilliant reds, yellows, and oranges. Now they were nothing more than gray-black smudges. A little light can work wonders.

There was no sign of Chick Sherman's prototype car by the side of the road. He must have succeeded in towing it home, as Dan said he was planning to do. The only indications of a recent accident were some deep gouges along the shoulder of the road, no doubt the tracks of his vehicle as it ran or was run off the road and smacked into one of those massive oaks, and some larger tracks that would have been the tractor he'd used to pull it out.

A car moving fast from the opposite direction hurtled past me, its brilliant headlights washing over my windshield and nearly blinding me. I threw up my arm to protect my eyes and pushed my van to the right as far as I dared.

The van rattled and shook as my tires rode the uneven gravel before I got it back on the smooth pavement. Once again the road was quiet but for me, and all was dark. There wasn't a streetlamp for miles.

A minute later, I found the dirt track and swung to the left, bouncing over the uneven ground that Kim had crossed earlier in the day. A creaking old pickup truck with a camper shell came toward me and I moved as far as I dared to the right to let it pass. The moon hung between two towering dark oaks as if suspended between their branches. Black clouds filled half the sky.

A frisson of uneasiness crept over me, but my not wanting to have to shell out another couple hundred bucks on a new mobile phone was stronger. As much as I appreciated Angela Lansbury as Mama Rose, it was hard to get past the fact that she was also Jessica Fletcher and constantly falling over dead bodies. I was beginning to get a little spooked.

I turned off the CD player.

The road seemed to follow the moon. I rolled down my window as I bounced into the clearing and listened. The buzzes and clicks of nocturnal insects and the humming of the Kia's motor were all I could detect. From where I sat at the edge of the yard, I could see that there was a light on in the front room of the Sherman house, though the porch light was off.

I glanced at the house nervously, wondering if I had made a mistake in coming. Esther was right, the Shermans might not take too kindly to me showing up on their doorstep, unannounced, at this relatively late hour.

I considered turning around and going home, coming back tomorrow, but a flash of white light in the clouds hanging over the mountains to the south of me, and the fact that I had already come all this way, kept me from deciding to go home empty-handed. If rain burst from those storm clouds, my phone would be a paperweight. A very expensive paperweight.

I'd do just as I told Esther I would. I'd look for my phone outside the big barn. Of course, the smart thing would have been to bring a flashlight.

I sighed in frustration. "I am such a birdbrain." No offense to birds. They're some of the smartest creatures around, especially when you factored in their relative brain to body size. I'd read books about it and watched documentaries in which birds, in particular those of the corvid family, like crows, performed the most cunning feats, including making and using tools.

A crow worth half his salt probably would have remembered to bring a flashlight to go scrounging around outside a rural barn in the dark.

Of course, I had a flashlight on my cell phone. A fat lot of good that did me. The phone was what I'd come here to look for.

I didn't dare use the van's headlights, though they would have been perfect for the job. They also would have alerted anyone and everyone within a mile of my presence.

I killed the engine there at the edge of the clearing and buttoned up my jacket. Unless someone looked real hard, they might not even notice my Kia. I left the keys in the ignition and opened the van's door as quietly as possible.

"Please don't let the dog be loose," I whispered as I stepped down to the ground, half expecting a canine to clamp her sharp fangs down on my calf for a late-night snack.

But none did. The dog must have been inside the house or put away in a kennel. Maybe the hound was on a doggie date. If so, she was luckier than me.

I thanked my lucky stars as I gently pushed the door closed. I paused for a moment and watched the house. There had been no signs of movement or life of any kind. No smoke came from the chimney, but it really wasn't cold enough to warrant a fire this time of year, so that meant nothing.

Ditto the barn. After his accident, Chick Sherman had probably hauled his automobile into the barn and retired for the day. That's what I would have done.

I moved awkwardly over the uneven ground, bound and determined to find the phone quickly and quietly. Then I would leave before anyone was any the wiser.

As I angled from the van to the barn, I noticed a faint, flickering yellow glow between a gap in some distant trees. I also realized there was a light coming from the crack between the two barn doors.

I crept up. Every few steps, I glanced back toward the house for any sign of man, woman, or beast. There was a definite line of light from inside the barn. The crossbar was lying on the ground, but the latch held the doors together.

Unfortunately, there was no sign of my phone. I bent down and groped about in the dark. The moon was half hidden by dense clouds now. The wind blew and a spooky, wavering wail rose with it.

My flesh went all tingly. I wondered if it was Trudy Sherman's doing. I pictured her sitting around a crystal ball in a dark, patchouli-filled room inside the house. She might have been calling up the spirits of the dead.

Maybe even the undead.

I dropped to my knees in the soft dirt and patchy weeds and fumbled around some more. The phone had to be here somewhere. Unless Chick or his wife had found it and taken it indoors. That's what I would have done. I could have saved myself a lot of trouble by checking with them first, but it was too late for that now.

I moved in a growing circle on my hands and knees, thinking there had to be a better way to spend a night. Weeds, rocks, and something squishy that I could only hope hadn't once belonged to a cow were all I found.

I rose and cursed under my breath. The storm appeared to be getting closer. I studied the house. There was still no sign of life. As I paced in front of the barn doors, trying to figure out my next move, I felt something hard underfoot.

I froze and fell to the ground. My fingers searched the earth. "Got you!"

It was my cell phone.

I straightened, brushed it off, and thrust it deep inside my pocket. I started for the Kia, then turned around. I could still get a picture of this car everybody was talking about.

I tiptoed to the barn and peeked through the crack between the doors. A tractor sat in the middle of a dimly lit space. A clutter of tools and various gadgets and gizmos lay against the walls. I slowly pulled open the door on the right and shivered as it creaked.

But nobody appeared. There was no sign of Chick Sherman. I now realized that that barn wasn't simply one large box as it appeared from the outside. It consisted of the large room at the entrance plus two smaller rooms to the right. I stepped toward them. The first room was dark. Something bulky lay under a heavy tarp in the center of the space. By the shape of it, long and wide, my guess was a vehicle of some sort.

I heard a rumble above me. The storm was coming closer.

I moved on to the second room, where the dim light was emanating from. Was Chick Sherman in there working on his mangled car?

A small sound caught my attention, but I couldn't figure out what it was. It might have been the wind shaking the barn or twisting the weather vane. "Hello?" My mouth and throat were dry as paper.

A thunderclap loud enough to wake the dead shook the barn and everything inside it—including me. A gasp escaped my lips and I froze in horror, waiting for a response from whoever was in the next room, but no response came.

The lights flickered and went out.

I ran my tongue over my lips before cautiously rounding the corner. I stuck my head in the second room and blinked. The space was large and shadowy, but by the light of the half-hidden moon coming in through a loft window on the side, I saw a car sitting near the center of the space.

Various devices, gizmos, and gadgetry hung from the ceiling. I had no idea what most of it was and what I could see was dark and dim. The walls were lined with workbenches and drawers and the floor was covered with more equipment. Tall tool boxes on casters, sitting in a group like rectangular soldiers, occupied one corner of the room.

I slipped my phone from my pocket to get a picture of the car. There might have been a light switch or a fuse box around someplace, but I wouldn't have dared turn it on even if I'd known where it was.

Though my eyes were adjusting to the darkness, there wasn't enough light for picture taking. I'd have to count on the flash of my phone to get a decent photograph of Chick's mysterious automobile. I wondered how badly the vehicle had been damaged. I approached the car and my hand touched metal.

I moved around to the side so I could get a shot of the car in profile. Then I'd get one from the front.

And then I'd get the heck out of there.

As I moved around the rear fender to the side, my feet caught on something hard. I tripped and fell forward, my knees banging the ground with jaw jarring force.

My phone slipped from my hand and I heard it hit the ground somewhere to my right. I scrambled to pick it up. All I wanted to do now was leave. "I must have been crazy coming in here just to take a photograph of some stupid car," I sputtered.

As I scrambled to my feet, my fingers touched something hard yet soft. "What on earth?"

I felt loose material. It felt odd yet oddly familiar.

Two overhead shop lights sprang to life in the other room.

It wasn't much illumination, but it was enough.

I looked in horror from the lights above to my hands below.

I was clutching a pair of legs! Human legs!

The lower half of a man's denim-clad torso protruded from the underside of an exotic-looking automobile. Heavy work boots covered the man's feet. If I remembered correctly, those boots belonged to Chick Sherman.

"Mr. Sherman!" The heavy car was resting on his thighs.

I heaved at the side of the car, but it wouldn't budge. I stuck my head under it, but it was too dark to see much. "Mr. Sherman?" I hollered. "Mr. Sherman!"

I felt the bile rising in my stomach and fell backwards on my rear end. I dug my phone from my front pocket and hit the button on the side to bring it to life.

Only it didn't. It didn't do anything.

I pulled it closer to my face. Nothing. I ran my fingers over it. The face was cracked. Chick Sherman must have accidentally run over the phone with his car or tractor earlier in the day. Maybe both. All I knew for certain was that my mobile phone was as dead as Chick Sherman now seemed to be.

"Hold on!" I shouted, knowing that my words were probably wasted. "I'll get help!"

I ran from the room, across the barn and out of doors. A light, cold drizzle hit me as I raced toward the house. Without waiting to knock, I yanked on the front door knob and pulled. Mercifully, the door was unlocked.

I stepped inside. "Hello?" Breathing heavily, I listened acutely. "Is anyone here?" I stepped farther in. "Mrs. Sherman? Trudy?"

I heard the woof-woof of the Shermans' hound dog and a second later the dog appeared. She took one look at me and wagged her tail. "Hi, girl," I said. The hound stood about two feet tall at her shoulders. "Where is everybody? Are you the only one home?"

She came closer and I patted her head. I asked her where the phone was, but she didn't know or didn't care to tell me.

I was on my own and every minute counted. Assuming Chick Sherman wasn't deceased already. I had to at least try to save him.

The room, as I'd discovered earlier, was as much a jumble and maze as the yard itself. "Phone," I muttered, "where's the phone?"

Assuming the Shermans even had a landline. They may have been using only cell phones. Chick's would probably be in his pocket, and I wasn't sure I could even get to it.

My eyes darted about the room. There was a light on toward the back. I remembered glimpsing a bit of a kitchen that way. If there was a phone to be found, that might be the place to find it.

I skirted through the cluttered space and started toward the rear of the house. The sound of a siren pierced the night air. I stopped and hurried to the front door, tripping over a stool and landing on my elbows.

I cried out. The front door hung open. The hound dog stood on the porch barking at the police car that came straight for us, wipers swishing, lights flashing.

I scrambled to my feet.

Behind the squad car, a pickup truck with a whirling blue light screamed to a halt.

7

Jerry hopped out from the passenger side of the squad car. A big black man in a brown uniform extricated himself from behind the wheel and lunged at me.

The dog barked and stepped aside. I realized I still didn't know the dog's name.

I opened my mouth to speak. "Wh—"

The burly officer was on me before I could get out the first consonant. "Hands where I can see them, ma'am!"

I didn't know which I was madder about, being treated like a criminal or being called a ma'am. Nonetheless, I froze and timidly put my hands in the air.

His hands quickly and efficiently searched my clothing. I'd never felt so embarrassed, or fat, in my life.

"That's enough of that, Pratt!" Chief Kennedy flapped his arm at the man.

"Sir?" He had swung my hands behind my back with his left arm. A pair of shiny, stainless steel handcuffs dangled from his right hand. He smelled of cloves and lime and his short black hair wound in tight curls was visible along the edges of his hat.

Jerry stomped up on the porch beside me. "What are you doing here, Simms?" He tipped back his cap with one finger and he didn't look happy.

Pratt looked from his chief to me. The chief nodded and Pratt let go of my wrists.

"Me?" I replied as I rubbed my wrists in a desperate attempt to get the circulation going once again. "What are you doing here? I mean, I'm glad you are." I looked in confusion from Jerry to Pratt to Dan Sutton, who had been driving the pickup truck that had come flying behind them. Dan was now walking toward our little group on the porch. He was in his civilian clothes—his going-on-a-date-with-my-best-friend-Kim clothes, to be precise.

"We got a call about a problem out here. Some sort of an accident," explained Jerry. He planted his hands on his hips. "Was that you who made the call?"

"No. I mean, I wanted to call. I was just looking for the phone when you showed up."

Pratt clipped the handcuffs back on his leather belt.

Dan stood off to the side. He petted the dog and nodded to me. So much for the intimate dinner date that Dan had promised Kim.

"What's this all about?" demanded Chief Kennedy. "I had plans this evening."

"Me too," muttered Dan.

"There was an accident," I said, still rattled by Pratt practically tackling me to the ground and Chick Sherman lying smushed under his car. "I think it's Chick Sherman."

"What about him?" Jerry asked. "The caller said something about the barn?"

The sharp cry of an ambulance cut through the cold night air and drizzle. A moment later the glow of the ambulance was clearly visible down the road. Then the emergency vehicle swung into the yard. Two men and a woman hopped out.

I nodded briskly and pointed. "That's right. He got trapped under a car."

"What?" Jerry jumped to attention. "Show me."

With Jerry leading the way, we moved as a group toward the open barn. "Keep that dog away!" Jerry ordered.

Officer Pratt escorted the hound dog back to the house and shut the front door, then rejoined us. The rain had stopped but the moon had disappeared completely. I couldn't blame it. This was no night to be out.

The lights in the big room glowed yellow, providing a modicum of light. Jerry, Dan, and Pratt all pulled flashlights from their belts and flicked them on. Three beams bounced around the cluttered walls and floor. "Which way?" Chief Kennedy asked, waving his flashlight into the first of the smaller rooms.

"Back here."

With the EMTs bringing up the rear, we reentered the room where I'd found Chick.

"On the ground," I found myself whispering. "Under his car. He must have been trying to repair it after crashing earlier."

Jerry cleared his throat as all three angled their flashlights at the ground. Chick, if that's who it was, was still there and it was clear that he was dead. His body lay lifeless, protruding from the heavy car that sat atop it.

"No way he survived that," noted Jerry. "Somebody find a light switch."

Officers Sutton and Pratt swept the room.

"Found it!" hollered Pratt from my right. He flicked a switch and the smaller room filled with light that reflected off the car, which I now realized was a convertible with a creamy white and green interior.

One of the medics scurried over, bent low and stuck his head under the car for a look, and extended his hand. A moment later, he rose and dusted himself off. "He's gone."

Dan slipped his flashlight back in its holster and was studying a mechanical car jack lying on its side near the rear tire.

Jerry's sigh filled the space. "All right." He pointed to the jack. "It looks like the jack failed." He frowned and clicked his tongue. "By the looks of it, I'd say he built it himself. Just plain foolish. And now it's killed him."

"Looks that way," drawled Officer Pratt, blinking rapidly.

"Let's get him out of there. Check the other side, Al."

Officer Pratt walked around the car. "This thing is a beauty, isn't she?" He ran a thick hand across the rear bumper. The exterior of the automobile was jade green and silver. I had no idea what the make or model was. The vehicle was unlike any I'd ever seen.

As if reading my mind, Officer Sutton spoke. "It's a '56 El Morocco." He peered at the dashboard. "Heavily modified, of course."

He walked around to the front. "That's a bumper from a '37 Dodge truck, I believe." Dan turned to me. "But this isn't the car we saw wrecked earlier today."

"It isn't?" I paced around the car. "I just assumed."

"All right, all right," grumbled Jerry. "Let's get Chick out of there."

"If it *is* Chick," I added.

That earned me an ugly look from Jerry and perplexed looks from Pratt and Sutton.

I shrugged. "Well, we can't be sure. We won't know for certain until you extract him, right?"

Jerry shook his head. "Give it a rest, Simms. Why are you always looking for trouble? This is the Sherman house. This is Chick Sherman's barn. This car on top of him is *his* car.

"It's pretty clear to me that we are going to find one dead Chick Sherman under this car." He stepped toward me. "If you ever keep quiet long enough to let me and my men do our jobs!"

Dan cautioned me with his eyes. "I'll see if I can find another jack, Chief," Dan said. "I don't trust this one." He tapped the Chevy. "This car is so heavy, I don't think even all of us lifting at once could get it off him."

"Simms, why don't you go wait inside the house?" Jerry stated. "Where's Chick's wife, Trudy? Isn't she here?"

"I haven't seen her at all. But the lights were on in the house when I got here."

"What were you doing out here at the Sherman place at this hour, anyway?"

"I dropped my cell phone when Kim and I came by this afternoon. I wanted to retrieve it."

"Where is it now?"

"Here," I dug into my jacket pocket. "It's broken."

"Let me see that." Jerry held out his hand and I dropped it in his open palm. "Broken all right."

"I told you." He stuck the phone in a bag and handed the bag off to Officer Pratt.

"Hey, what are you doing that for?"

"Evidence."

"Fine." It was useless to me anyway.

"What were you doing here in the barn if you dropped your phone outside?" He waved his hand at me dismissively before I could answer. "Never mind. You can tell me later. Right now, I've got an accident scene to tend to."

"Fine." I started out of the room. Being around a dead body was one of the least pleasant things I could think of. Being around Jerry ranked right down there with it.

I glanced at the industrial-looking lights over the tractor. "The lights . . ." I turned back to the others. "Wait!"

"What is it?" Jerry glared at me. Pratt was standing behind the car. Dan was rummaging around near the wall. The EMTs huddled together awaiting their unpleasant task.

"I don't think this *is* an accident scene."

"What are you talking about?" Jerry's right eye twitched, a clear sign I was making him mad.

"It's the lights."

Jerry was clearly reaching the limit of his patience with me. "The lights?"

"Don't you see?" Clearly nobody but me did. Maybe that was because they weren't there when I found Chick's body. "Those lights," I said pointed to the ceiling, "were not on when I arrived."

"So?"

"You're saying Mr. Sherman was accidentally killed when his jack thingie broke and the car he was working on fell on him."

"Have you got a better theory?" Jerry looked bemused.

"No," I said slowly. "But I have a question: Who turned out the lights? You don't believe Chick Sherman was working under his car in the dark, do you?"

Jerry's mouth fell open. Officers Sutton and Pratt stared at him. I watched Jerry's jaw work back and forth. "Maybe he had a work light of some kind under the car and he was using that."

I shrugged a shoulder. "Maybe."

"We'll know soon enough."

"There's no sign of an electrical cord running under the car," Dan said, after kicking his feet in and around the straw in the vicinity of the body.

I saw Jerry look pensively at the overhead lights.

"I have another question, too," I said.

"What's that?" Jerry plucked his cap from his head.

"If it was an accident, why the anonymous phone call?"

8

Jerry questioned me for about an hour. We sat in the kitchen of the Sherman house, a room that looked straight out of the forties. The kitchen table was a small, porcelain-topped rectangle with a cracked, red vinyl chair at each side.

He'd made a pot of coffee in a percolator that neither of us was very familiar with. The coffee tasted like shoe polish, sweetened shoe polish when I added sugar.

There was still no sign of Chick's wife. Princess, his black and tan hound dog, kept us company, though she seemed to fade in and out of consciousness constantly. I knew her name was Princess, or at least assumed so and was going to go on that assumption, because that was the name inscribed on the metal dog dish resting on a black rubber mat between the back kitchen door and the trash can.

I spread my fingers across the warm table. Decades of nicks and scratches crisscrossed the white porcelain. "And you have no idea who called to report the"—I hesitated since the jury was still out—"accident?"

"Not a clue. But we're working on it. Maybe we'll get a lead on him. Dispatch took the call. All we know for sure is that it was male, or at least did a good enough job of imitating one."

"That's about half the population." I added another spoonful of sugar to my shoe polish.

"You didn't see anybody else out here?" asked Jerry.

"Not a soul." I explained that I had passed a few cars on the road. "The house was unlocked but empty when I arrived. And Chick . . ." I let my voice trail off. We both knew the rest of that sentence.

Jerry stood and yawned. "We're done here, Simms. You can go."

I pushed back my chair and rose. There was a knock at the kitchen door. Princess jumped to attention.

Jerry waved and Andrew Greeley pulled open the door and entered. He nodded a greeting to me. "Miss Simms."

"What have you got, Andy?" Jerry placed his cup under the faucet of the kitchen sink and rinsed it.

"Too early to say for certain," Mr. Greeley said, his voice cracking with age. "Massive trauma, gross injuries to the torso and skull." He ran a bony hand through his stringy white hair. Greeley does double duty as the Town of Ruby Lake coroner and owner of the local mortuary.

Greeley was a soft-spoken, kindly gentleman. He was only in his early seventies but looked a couple decades older. Maybe it was an occupational hazard. He'd been born into the family business, Greeley's Mortuary, which had been started by his grandfather in his younger years.

Whenever Andrew Greeley cruised through town, you couldn't miss him. His daily ride was an antique black hearse with frilly white curtains. When he wasn't hauling groceries in it, he was hauling the dearly departed.

Jerry wiped his hands on his jacket. "So you're saying the car did fall on him?"

The elderly gentleman forced a dry laugh. "There's no doubt about that."

Jerry shot me an I-told-you-so look.

I folded my arms across my chest and gave him a look back. "That doesn't mean it was an accident."

Andrew nodded. "No, no, it doesn't." He folded his bony white hands in front of him and winked at the collarless dog. "Hi, girl. Sorry about your master."

Princess wagged her tail, clearly misunderstanding the coroner's words.

"Are you leaving something out?" Jerry asked.

Andrew scratched his neck. He was wearing a tight black suit, white shirt, and slate-gray necktie, like he did almost all the time, funeral or otherwise. I had a feeling the man slept in that suit.

And maybe in a coffin. Hopefully, an open one.

"There is one thing odd." Andrew's blue eyes fell on me. His eyes were the most colorful thing about him.

"And what might that be?"

"There appears to be a sharp trauma to the back of the head."

Jerry pushed his brows together. "So? The man was crushed under his car, for crying out loud, Greeley!"

"Yes, yes, he was." Andrew's voice remained quiet and steady. "But this blow appears to be to the back of the head. And"—he cleared his throat—"as I stated, appears to have been made by a long, sharp object." He reached his right hand behind his own head. "Mr. Sherman was faceup under the car."

I could see Jerry struggling with the information that Greeley was spooning out. He began pacing. "Sherman was in a car wreck earlier," Jerry growled. "Smashed himself into a tree. Couldn't he have hurt his head then?"

"Were there any signs of head trauma at the time? Did Mr. Sherman indicate that he'd struck his head?"

"No," Jerry said reluctantly. "Only his leg maybe."

Greeley shrugged. "Of course, I can't say for certain yet. But, on initial inspection of the vehicle, there also does not appear to have been anything sharp that would explain that particular injury. In fact, that area of the undercarriage is quite flat."

Greeley pulled a pen and pad from his inside coat pocket and scratched down a few words, then returned it to its place. "Those injuries are consistent with the front facial injuries."

Jerry stopped pacing the red and white checkered linoleum and looked from the kitchen to the barn. "Are you trying to tell me somebody *murdered* Chick Sherman?"

Mr. Greeley drew in a slow breath. "It is not my position to tell you anything other than my professional opinion of the cause of death, Chief. You know that." He smiled in my direction. "I leave the events leading to the cause of death up to you to sort out."

Greeley stooped to pet Princess, who rewarded him with a wag of the tail. "Ain't you a sweet old coonhound," he cooed. Princess danced and wagged like a true princess. Greeley's back cracked as he straightened and addressed the chief. "Mr. Sherman's corpse will be taken to county. We should have the full autopsy in a few days."

"I want that report on my desk ASAP!" Jerry replied.

The coroner only smiled, nodded, and left.

I departed in Greeley's wake and followed the glow of his tail-lights back out to the main highway toward town.

I parked behind Birds & Bees and let myself in through the store-room. My body ached. I had a chill that ran clear to my bones and, though I was experiencing a sugar and caffeine high, my brain was oddly numb.

A man I had met just that afternoon was now dead.

I trudged upstairs and was putting the key in the lock when a frigid hand gripped my shoulder. I yelped and spun around. "Paul!" It was my tenant down on the second floor, Paul Anderson. "What are you doing here?" His hair was tousled and damp and his face haggard. He wore a denim jacket, green flannel shirt, and blue jeans.

"You look an absolute wreck." I realized I'd been yelling and lowered my voice. "Is everything all right?"

Paul shot his hands through his hair. "Yeah. I heard you were out to the Sherman place."

I frowned. "How on earth did you know that?"

"Esther told me. She said you drove out to look for your mobile phone." His coffee-colored eyes bobbled wildly.

Of course. Esther. I turned the key in the lock and opened the door. "Come on in."

Paul glanced at his muddy sneakers and kicked them off outside the door, following me in a pair of thick gray wool socks.

"We'll have to keep our voices down." I glanced toward my mother's closed bedroom door. "Mom's sleeping."

Paul nodded.

I switched on the table lamp next to the couch. "Can I get you a glass of hot tea?"

"That would be great." There was a tense weariness to Paul's voice. It wasn't like him. Usually, he was upbeat to the point of annoyance.

I eyed him wonderingly as he slumped down on the brown leather sofa and rested his elbows on his thighs. I grabbed the tea kettle and set it on the flame to boil. My eyes fell on a handwritten note next to the stove. It was from my mother. It read: *Dear Amy, You left your dinner cooking on the stove. Lucky for you, I returned before your*

home and business burned to the ground the way your mac and
cheese did . . . Love, Mom.

   P.S. The saucepan is soaking in the sink. Who knows? In a year or
two the crud at the bottom might loosen up enough for you to scrape
it off!

   I looked in the sink. Sure enough, the now black-bottomed saucepan
sat in a bath of soapy water. I opened the trash bin and discovered a
soggy, gooey lump of blackened mac and cheese atop the heap of
garbage.

   The tea kettle whistled and I quickly pulled it from the flame to
keep from waking Mom. I carried over our two mugs and returned
with the sugar bowl and a carton of low-fat milk that I set atop a birding magazine on the coffee table. "Help yourself," I said.

   Paul added a little sugar and nothing more, though he looked like
he could have used a shot of bourbon.

   "How's the car?" I asked, settling back into the green easy chair
to the side of the sofa.

   Paul jumped, spilling tea in his lap. "Ouch!" He set his mug on
the coffee table.

   "Are you okay?" I set my mug down on the side table and went to
the kitchen for a couple of paper towels. I threw the towels to Paul
and returned to my chair as he dabbed away.

   Paul grabbed his tea, blew across the top of his cup, then sipped.
"Why do you ask about the car?"

   I frowned again. "Because I'm curious? Because you and Derek
have been working on it every chance you get and I haven't seen it in
over a week?"

   Paul nodded in understanding. "Yeah, the car." He forced a smile.
"She's coming along great. Just about ready."

   I lowered my mug from my lips and took a closer look at my tenant. "You were there," I said. "You were at Chick Sherman's house."
I leaned toward him. "You were the anonymous caller!"

   Paul opened his mouth, then shut it again. He toyed with his tea
for a moment, then set it unsteadily on the table, a defeated look on
his face. "How did you know?" He ran his hands along his thighs.

   I pointed to his legs. "That."

   "What?" Paul looked down.

"You've got several bits of wet straw stuck to your jeans." There had been straw in the entrance of the barn.

Paul's eyes widened. "I see." He gingerly plucked one from the side of his pants and held it in front of his nose, twisting it round and round in his fingers.

"You want to tell me what happened out there?"

Paul sighed. "It's a long story."

"So my beauty rest will be curtailed." I stood. "It won't be the first time." I started back to the kitchen. "I need something to eat." Seeing the ruined mac and cheese had reminded me that I hadn't eaten a meal since lunch. "How about you?"

Paul nodded.

"Fine," I said, pulling open the fridge to see what I might scrounge up. "You talk. I'll cook."

"You're right, Amy." Paul turned sideways on the couch to face me as I scrambled up some eggs.

There were some English muffins in the freezer. I pulled them out to thaw in the microwave. "I passed a pickup with a camper shell on my way to the Shermans' house. That was you, wasn't it?"

Paul nodded. "Yeah. I recognized you. I was surprised. You were the last person on earth I would have thought I'd see. It wasn't until I got back here that Esther told me where you'd gone and why."

I pulled the muffins from the microwave and dropped them in the toaster. I lowered the heat to a bare minimum to keep the eggs from drying out. I also refilled the tea kettle and dropped it on a second burner.

I set a couple of plates on the table and Paul joined me.

"I went to Chick's house to pick up our carburetor," Paul said, reaching for the tub of margarine.

"Your carburetor?"

"For the Impala. Chick offered to rebuild it for Derek and me." Paul gave his English muffin a heavy dose of butter. Apparently the man didn't worry about fat or calories.

"Why not take it to one of the garages in town?"

Paul hitched a shoulder. "I guess some of the shops could have handled it, but Chick offered to do it for free. Besides, I figured he owed me."

"And just why did he owe you?"

Paul pushed the second half of his English muffin into his eggs and shoveled egg onto it. "Sherman did some work for me at the brewery. He said he could make some tweaks to the system that would improve our efficiency and give a better brew."

"And?"

"And he mucked it up good." Paul chomped into his eggs and muffin and chewed. "He said he knew what went wrong and promised to get it fixed. But in the meantime, I'm down to half production. Do you have any idea what that's costing my business?"

I didn't really. Birdseed was more my thing. But I could imagine.

"So you went out to Chick Sherman's house to pick up your rebuilt carburetor?" Thank goodness Derek hadn't gone with him. It was bad enough that Paul had gotten himself mixed up in a possible murder.

"I got a message from Chick that the part was ready and that I should come pick it up."

"He called you? What time was this?" My eggs had gone cold and I'd eaten no more than a bite of my English muffin.

"He didn't call. He sent me a text. It was maybe an hour before I got there." Paul fished out his phone and scrolled down.

"Here it is." He aimed the face of the phone toward me. "About eight fifteen. Derek and I were just finishing up for the night, so I offered to go fetch the part. He was hoping to spend a few minutes with his daughter before she went to bed."

While Maeve, Derek's daughter, lived with Amy-the-ex, Derek saw to it that he spent as much time as he could with her. I knew he had intended to pick her up from his ex tonight and that Maeve would be spending the night and the next day with him.

"And when you got to Chick Sherman's house?"

"There was nobody home. I mean"—Paul wiped his mouth with a paper napkin from the holder in the center of the table—"not in the house."

"Were the lights on?"

"Yeah, why?"

"Just curious." I drank my tea. "What did you do next?"

"I went to the workshop."

"The barn?"

"Yeah, same thing." Paul tugged at his jaw. "Anyway, that's when I found him. Lying there . . . under the car."

"Why didn't you call for help right away?"

Paul shook his head helplessly. "I-I panicked. I mean, I could see he was dead. Our carburetor was lying right there on the ground. I called when I got back to town."

"I didn't see anything resembling a carburetor lying beside him."

Paul dropped his gaze. "I took it."

"You took it?!" I groaned loudly, then glanced at my Mom's door. More softly, I said, "You took it? Don't you realize that could be the murder weapon?"

Paul looked absolutely horrified. "What?" He leapt from his chair. It crashed to the ground. "Sorry!" He scooped it up and pushed it into its place under the table. He paced between the kitchen sink and the island. "Murder weapon? Murder weapon? I thought the car fell on him."

"Maybe," I said. I reached for a bottle of Tennessee whiskey that I kept atop the refrigerator for special occasions. Like crazy tenants who might have gotten themselves in a serious jam that could lead to a stiff prison sentence. I twisted off the cap and poured a generous serving into Paul's mug. "Drink this," I said, handing him the cup.

Paul nodded. His hand shook as he drank.

"Where's this carburetor now?"

"In the back of my truck."

I couldn't help shaking my head.

"What? You think I killed Chick?"

"No, of course not. I just think you're doing a great job of framing yourself." I drummed my fingers against the countertop.

"What do you think we should do?" He set the empty cup in the sink, then crossed to the living room, where he flopped down in the green chair I'd vacated earlier.

"We?" I sputtered. Nonetheless, the guy looked so forlorn and helpless . . .

"Fine." I ran my teeth over my lower lip. I hated to bother him, especially at this hour and with him spending some quality time with his daughter . . . but there was really no choice.

I went to the phone in the kitchen and laid my hand on the receiver. "The first thing *we* have to do is call Derek." I picked up the receiver and dialed.

9

"No! Please, Amy, don't!" Paul jumped up, ran to the kitchen and placed his hand over mine.

"Paul!"

"Please, Amy. Help me."

I dropped the phone in its cradle, gently removed his hand from mine, and forced him to look at me. "Okay, Paul. What aren't you telling me?"

Paul ran his hands up his stubbly cheeks and blew out a woeful breath. "We had a big fight in the biergarten."

"We? You and Chick Sherman?"

He nodded. "In front of witnesses—staff and customers."

"About what? Hot rods? What is it with men and their cars?"

Paul chuckled mirthlessly. "I could say the same thing about women and their shoes."

"Touché." I wriggled my fingers in a *talk to me* fashion.

"It was more serious than a friendly disagreement about cars or sports." He swallowed hard, running his stockinged feet against the hardwood. "I said he ruined the equipment and it was killing my business. I told him if he didn't fix everything and fast I was going to kill him."

Paul stared at me as the words came tumbling out, as if daring me to say something. The truth was, I didn't know what to say.

I gawped at him.

"What?" Paul looked at me like I'd offended him. "It's a figure of speech."

I cocked my brow. "Around here those words aren't a figure of speech, they're an admission of guilt!"

"When you were in the barn, did you see a jack?"

"Yes, so?" I flailed my arms in the air. "I saw it, Chief Kennedy and half the police force saw it!"

"It was broken."

"And your point is?"

"It looked like it had been done intentionally."

I narrowed my eyes at him. "What makes you think so?"

"The pin holding the axle support in place had been sheared off."

My breath caught in my throat. A few minutes ago, while the possibility of murder had hung in the air, the probability of it had suddenly come slashing down like the sharply honed blade of a French guillotine. "So you do think it was murder? You think someone snuck up on Chick and broke the jack? With him under the car?"

Paul bobbed his head, and I shivered. That was a cold and brutal move. I'd made up my mind. "I'm calling Derek." I reached once more for the telephone.

"He's with his daughter. You don't want to spoil that, do you? What would his ex-wife think if she found out?"

I poked him in the chest. "That was a low blow."

"I know. Sorry." He hung his head and patted my hand.

"Paul," I said sternly, "we've got to call him. Derek's an attorney. He'll help sort this out." I could feel Paul's hand tense against the back of mine. "We could use a third party to provide some objectivity. And I think you could use another drink." I aimed my eyes at the whiskey bottle.

"Come on, Amy," he wheedled. "You know how Derek is. All by the rules and letter of the law." Paul twisted his hands through his hair. "Please? Can't we at least talk about this?"

He gave me a lost puppy-dog look, the kind men are so good at when they want to get you to do something you know you shouldn't.

"Please?"

I frowned and lowered the receiver. "Fine." I crossed my arms. "We'll talk about it. I'm not saying we shouldn't call Derek and that I won't call him afterward." I grabbed the bottle and Paul's glass from the sink and poured him a refill. I poured myself a small one, too.

"Great!"

Suddenly my mother's door shot open. She had a head full of pink plastic hair curlers and was tying up her terry-cloth bathrobe.

Her face was puffy from sleep. "Amy, what *is* all the commotion?" She suddenly spotted Paul, who had returned once again to the living room and stood looking out the front window. "Oh, hello, Paul."

Mom looked back to me, a hundred questions written on her face. "Is everything okay, dear?"

"Yes, we're fine. Sorry we woke you."

Mom glanced toward Paul once again.

"Yes, I'm very sorry, Barbara."

Mom shook her head. "Well, I'm going back to bed."

"Good night, Mom. I promise we won't disturb you again."

Mom grinned. "I'd appreciate that."

"Don't worry. Paul and I are going out."

From the threshold of her bedroom door, Mom blinked at me twice. "At this hour? Where on earth are you going?"

The corners of my mouth turned down as I said, "I've got to see a man about a carburetor."

Once Mom was gone and I saw the light beneath her door disappear, I whispered, "Show me this carburetor."

Paul nodded. He went to the front door and slipped into his shoes. I locked up behind us and followed him downstairs to his vehicle, which was parked next door in one of the spaces behind Brewer's Biergarten, along with a handful of employee vehicles.

I waited, shivering and wishing I'd brought my jacket, while Paul fished in his pockets for his car keys. "Here it is." He held up his keyring, then crossed to the camper attached to the rear of his truck. "The carburetor is in here."

He pulled open the camper shell door and flicked on a light stuck to the ceiling. I peeked around him. The carburetor lay on the middle of the flat, threadbare brown-green carpet.

"Do you really think this could be what killed him?" he asked.

Paul stepped into the camper and I followed. It was cramped, damp, and smelled like a lifetime of dirty socks. I waved my hand in front of my nose. "Don't you ever air this dump out?"

"What?" The brewer sniffed. "I don't smell anything." He reached for the carburetor.

"Wait." I held him back. "Let's look at it more closely, but don't touch it."

"Why not?"

I shrugged. "There might be blood stains or something."

Paul appeared dubious. "If you say so. But I didn't notice anything. Besides, I've already handled it, remember?"

"Humor me."

Paul turned on a couple more lights and we squatted before the carburetor. After a minute, he said, "It looks good to me."

"The coroner said Chick showed evidence of a sharp blow to the back of the head."

"Maybe whoever killed him hit him from behind with something hard and then shoved him under the car."

"Then dropped it on him to make it look like an accident," I conjectured. "It makes sense."

I turned the carburetor with my finger to get a better look at the other side. "It looks okay to me, too. It's clean as a whistle and dry as a bone."

Paul's knees cracked as he rose. "Chick does good work. Did." His smile turned to a frown. "At least on some machines."

I placed a hand on the table attached to one side of the truck and lifted myself up. "What exactly did he mess up at the brewery?"

Paul sank onto a cushioned bench on one side of the small Formica table. I joined him on the other side. "You know Craig and I got most of the equipment for the biergarten secondhand."

"I didn't, but what about it?" I did know about Craig and wished I didn't. Craig Bigelow was Paul's silent partner, and thank goodness for the silent part. Craig Bigelow—or the gigolo, as I thought of him—had been my boyfriend for nearly six years. What I hadn't known was that he was also the boyfriend of several other women over the course of our stormy relationship.

I thought returning to Ruby Lake would mean never having to see him again. Craig lived in Raleigh. Then he and Paul had bought the empty business next to Birds & Bees and started Brewer's Biergarten. So far, Craig was keeping his distance. I hoped he'd keep it that way.

"Craig bought a lot of our equipment off Chick. He'd salvaged it from a brewery that had gone belly-up." That sounded like Craig. "At first, everything ran okay. But we've been having trouble with some of the PRVs and sample valves."

"PRVs?" A gust of wind picked up and threw the door shut.

"Pressure relief valves on the fermentation tanks," Paul explained, glancing back at the camper door. "To tell the truth, the whole system's been buggy, glitchy." He laced his fingers and squeezed. "Do you have any idea what that does to our production? To our business?" The table bent under his weight. "We're running a brew pub. How can we survive if we can't brew?"

"I understand what you're saying," I began, "but do you understand that everything you're telling me is only going to make you look more guilty? More like you have a reason to want him dead?"

"I didn't kill him!" Paul jerked back. "I needed him alive to fix the equipment." He shook his head. "I'm ruined."

"I'm sure you can get somebody else to make the repairs."

"I suppose. But a lot of what Chick did was custom work, you know? Not all the necessary pipings and connections came with the stuff we bought from him. Chick fabricated the rest in his workshop."

Paul rose and crossed to a small dorm-size refrigerator resting on the floor near the front of the camper shell. He yanked open the door and sighed. The interior was nothing but a black hole. "Nothing."

"Nothing?" I pointed. "Is that mold?" I asked in horror.

Paul slammed the door shut. "I need a drink."

"What you need is to have your head examined. And for more reasons than I can begin to count. Why don't you sell this monstrosity and get yourself a car? It would be a lot easier and more economical to run around town in."

Paul eyed me like I'd asked him to sell his firstborn child. He was stooped over—which was the only way to move around the interior—and looked like an angry hunchback. "Are you going to help me?"

"I don't know what I can do, Paul. I still say we call Derek and then the police. Tell them what you know."

Paul groaned. "Come on, Amy. Poke around a little bit. I know you, you're nosy. Talk to people. Talk to Chief Kennedy. He likes you."

My snort filled the camper shell. "Are you kidding? Half the time I see him, he looks like he's thinking of shooting me just for sport!"

Paul pulled a face. "Give me a day or two. That's all I'm asking. From what you told me, we still don't know for absolute certain that Chick Sherman was murdered or what might have been the weapon that did, if that's what happened."

"Yes, that's all true, but—"

"Please? I promise, if you don't find anything, I'll talk to Derek myself. Please?"

The man was an expert—and, I was beginning to suspect, compulsive—wheedler. "I don't know, Paul . . ."

"You do realize that if I get locked up, even temporarily"—there was a wicked glint in his eye—"somebody's going to have to run the business."

My heart froze in my chest. The man also knew how to ruffle my feathers.

"What's it been since you've seen Craig? A few months?"

I stood abruptly, banging my head against the ceiling. "Ouch!" I bent, rubbed my skull, and headed for the door and threw it open.

Paul followed me out, his hands gripping the sides of the doorway. "Is that a yes?"

I shot him a look. "Forty-eight hours," I found myself saying against my better judgment.

Paul grinned. "You're the best, Amy."

"No," I said. My hand went to my scalp. "I think I just banged my head too hard."

And I was only half joking.

10

Despite my better judgment, I had promised Paul I would poke around a little on his behalf. That's why, instead of enjoying a relaxing morning out on the Birds & Bees front porch, bird-watching and sipping coffee, I was standing at the edge of the road feeling the wind searching out my bones.

I pulled my denim jacket tighter across my chest and stamped my feet as I looked at the white shack. I'd been intending to go to the Sherman homestead, but it appeared that somebody was here at the fortune-teller's.

The sign hadn't changed and I hadn't expected it might have. FORTUNES TOUTED, MISFORTUNES ROUTED. In smaller letters it read: PAST, PRESENT, AND FUTURE —ALL CAN BE EXPLAINED.

"If only that were true," I muttered, pulling on the knob, surprised to find that the door was unlocked and that I was entering an unexpected cloud of patchouli.

Why hadn't she predicted her husband's death? My fingers went cold as I released the knob and stepped inside as the thought occurred to me: Maybe she had.

More than that, maybe Trudy Sherman had had a hand in making certain that it happened. She would not have been the first man or woman to murder his or her spouse. Sadly, not the last either.

"Wouldn't it be ironic if the murder weapon turned out to be a crystal ball?"

"Excuse me?"

I jumped. I didn't realize I'd said that last part aloud or that there was someone else in the room with me. "Oh, hi. Nothing. Just thinking out loud."

I approached a small round table, draped in blue satin, near the back wall. A woman sat stiffly in one of the chairs at an angle to the door. "Mrs. Sherman?"

She nodded. Her slender fingers were wrapped tightly around the handle of a delicate cup. "Yes. I give no readings today." She raised the fragile-looking teacup to her narrow lips and drank. Her long black hair spilled forward and her large brown eyes dug into my soul like fingernails sinking into a loaf of fresh, warm bread. From the redness surrounding them, I sensed she had been crying.

She had an olive complexion and a thin, pointed nose. Pink lipstick highlighted her lips and left an impression on her cup as she set it back down on the tabletop.

"Actually, I didn't come for a reading. I came because, well . . ." My eyes looked slowly around the small room. The only light came from the window. A curtained partition separated the room we were in from the space behind. The curtain ended several inches above the ground and I could see the bottoms of boxes and a dorm-size refrigerator.

Other than the table and two chairs, there was a two-cushioned blue divan with a petite round table beside it, also covered in drapery. Atop the smaller table rested a box of tissues, an incense burner from which gray smoke twisted lazily into the air and disappeared, and a paperback novel with a cowboy on the cover.

Several wall-mounted wooden shelves held small, weird-looking statues whose nameplates identified them as saints, except for one labeled LORD OF DEATH.

Lovely.

"Death brought you."

I gulped. She wasn't wrong. She waved for me to approach the table.

"Sit," she commanded.

I sat.

Mrs. Sherman pulled a lace-edged white handkerchief from the front pocket of her orange and yellow dress patterned in fall leaves. "Would you care for some tea?" She lifted the stainless steel tea kettle and I saw that the tablecloth had been scorched. A faint brown ring traced the spot where the kettle had rested.

I nodded and she rose. Her dress billowed around her as she pushed open the curtain to the back and returned a moment later with a cup that matched her own. She handed me the cup and I turned it over in my hand. Each one was finely decorated with duck-egg-blue roses and gold lace filigree. The rims were pinched. "These are very lovely. Antique?"

Mrs. Sherman managed a smile. "Yes, from an estate sale near Dillsboro some years ago. They are bone china, circa the nineteen fifties, I believe, from Staffordshire, England." There was a husky quality to her voice. I didn't hear Kentucky at all, though that's where Jerry said she hailed from.

I nodded politely as she poured hot tea into my cup. I had heard of Dillsboro, but I had never been. It was a small town west of Ruby Lake and located along the banks of Tuckasegee River. "Thanks."

"You're quite welcome, Ms. Simms. Would you like something for your tea?" Her left hand pushed under the table and she set a mason jar of honey and a bowl of sugar in front of me. "I prefer orange blossom honey, myself."

I poured thick honey into my tea and jiggled my cup to stir it around. I didn't see a spoon and she hadn't offered me one. "How did you know my name?"

"I'm not wrong, am I?"

"No." Had she read my mind? Was she psychic as well as clairvoyant?

"You are the young woman who found my husband's body."

Funny, I wasn't much younger than Chick's widow. If I was right in my estimation, she couldn't be much more than forty years old. Chick had to have had twenty years on her. At least.

I nodded. "Yes, I'm so sorry."

She refilled her glass with a steady hand. "I'm certain his spirit lives on." Her gaze turned toward the window, where a dusty and dinged four-door maroon Camry sat. It must have been Trudy's car. "My husband's essence remains strong. At the farm and in all things that surrounded him and that he had placed his hands on and his heart within."

"Yes," I said, unsure what else I could say.

Suddenly she rose and crossed to one of the dusty shelves. She picked up an eight-inch-tall statue in a red suit and matching top hat. She held it toward me. "This is Baron Samedi, the Lord of Death. Do you know him?"

"Not personally," I replied.

"Death is nothing to be feared, yet not something to be taken lightly. I told my husband that he should not take the afterworld frivolously."

"He didn't believe in the afterlife?"

"He believed in this life. Nothing more." She set the bizarre-looking statue with its skull head and skeleton hands on the table in front of me. "I told him over and over that he should let the Lord of Death be his guide."

I felt a chill in the air, but all the windows were closed.

The seer continued. "The Lord of Death not only guides souls into the spirit world, he protects those who carry him from mischievous ghosts."

I reached out a tentative hand and stroked the skeleton's face. "It's remarkable."

What was Trudy Sherman trying to tell me? That if her husband had had one of these bizarre statues in his back pocket, he'd still be among the living rather than the dead?

Trudy settled herself back in her seat and rubbed her hand slowly over her chin. "The police are at the house now. That's why I came here." She wiped the handkerchief across her forehead. "I did not want to be there while they were on the premises. It's too unsettling."

She turned her gaze on me and I felt like she was seeing every secret I'd ever held. Including the one where I'd snuck out of my house to go on a date with a boy when I was sixteen, for what promised to be my first make-out session.

I squirmed in my seat. "The police are at your place now?"

"They search the house and barn." She offered me more tea, which I refused with a shake of the head. "They asked my permission and I gave it."

"Why? Do they think it wasn't an accident?"

She nodded solemnly. "It seems someone stole Chick's life."

My jaw tensed. I'd been afraid that would prove to be the case. "Do the police have any idea who might have wanted to harm your husband?"

"No," she answered with a sigh. "And neither do I. Chick was not always the most amicable of men and he certainly did not have much use for the townsfolk, but such strong animosity that someone would remove his life force?" She shook her head vehemently. "I cannot conceive of such a thing."

"It's too bad you weren't home. Perhaps you might have seen someone."

Her head moved slowly up and down. "Perhaps." She nailed me with her eyes. "Did you see Chick's spirit, Ms. Simms?"

"His-his spirit?"

"Yes, you were the first one on the scene, besides his killer, of course. Did you see his spirit? Did he speak to you? What color was his aura? Did he reveal anything, anything at all?"

I frowned. "You mean, like who killed him?"

She nodded. When she pressed her fingertips together, her green-painted fingernails looked like flower petals.

I wrung my hands. "Sorry, no. Did the police say how your husband's, ah, life force was taken?"

"A blow to the back of the skull with a sharp object." Trudy's hand went to the back of her own head. "That is all they will reveal to me. Whether it rendered him unconscious and he was then placed under the El Morocco or he was dead already, they say they do not know."

She paused meaningfully. I felt a trickle of sweat run down the back of my neck. "And I've been able to get nothing out of my husband."

My eyes went wide despite myself. Frankly, I'd have been amazed if she had been able to get anything out of him. I swallowed the rest of my tea and stood. "I'd better be going. If there is anything I can do to help, please let me know." I reached into my purse and handed her a Birds & Bees business card. "Here's my contact info."

"Please, do take the statue." She nodded toward the hollow-eyed Lord of Death.

I took it reluctantly. It was cold as an ice cube.

"Twenty dollars, please."

"Excuse me?" I blinked at her outstretched palm.

"The Lord of Death is twenty dollars. Tax included."

I dug into my purse for a twenty. I pushed the Lord of Death into my purse. I saw him staring up at me with those crazy eyes and mad grin and clamped the purse shut as I struggled from my chair. My left leg had fallen asleep.

She rose and followed me as I limped to the door. Unexpectedly, Princess came pushing through the curtain separating the consulting room from the rest of the small house.

"Hi, Princess." I teetered and petted her sides as she rubbed against me. "It's too bad Princess can't tell us who killed your husband."

"Yes," answered Trudy. "But I am afraid a dog's perception is different from our own."

"You never did say where you were when your husband was killed."

She stuck her hands in the deep pockets of her dress. "I was visiting my sister."

"Yes, that's right," I replied. "I remember Chick saying something like that."

She cocked her head. "You talked to my husband? I thought he was dead when you discovered him. That's what Chief Kennedy told me."

"Yes, it was earlier." Apparently she didn't know everything after all. I explained how I'd come out to the house earlier in the day with Kim, dropped my phone, and returned later to retrieve it.

"How fortunate that you did," she answered. "My dear husband may have remained there all night."

"You spent the night with your sister?"

"Yes, I only returned this morning, and there was a police officer sitting on the porch waiting for me when I arrived.

I frowned. "I'm surprised they hadn't called you."

"I do not believe in telephones."

"You don't?"

She nodded. "They are a disruption to the ether. Such devices interrupt the flow of the spirits and the psyche. They aren't natural, you know."

Trudy pointed to the wall where a phone straight out of the sixties was mounted. "We have the phone here with a tape machine in back. Chick installed them both. He was concerned I would receive no clients if I didn't allow it."

I had a feeling that, of the two, Chick, despite his own eccentricities, appeared to be the one in the family with their feet on the ground.

Now that was a scary thought.

"What about your husband? Did he feel the same way?" It was a good thing Paul had made the anonymous call about Chick Sherman's death; I would never have found a telephone at the Sherman house. Unless maybe I'd looked in Chick's pockets, which I wouldn't have dared do even if I could have reached one.

"No, he had his own cell phone. But I never touched the thing." She said it like it was the tool of the devil and, in her mind, it sounded like it pretty much was.

"If you don't mind my asking, do you and Mr. Sherman have any children?"

Trudy shook her head. "None. I lived for my work and Chick lived for his."

I wasn't sure what to make of that statement. "Well, I'll leave you alone, but if you need someone to talk to . . ."

"Thank you, Ms. Simms. I am wondering what I will do with all of Chick's toys."

"Toys?" I pictured a room filled with childhood favorites, from board games and bicycles to toy cars and tractors.

"His projects." Trudy's shoulders rose and fell. With the sun from the open door hitting her, the redness in her eyes was more apparent, and so was her earthy beauty. "Cars and tractors and all the other vehicles he's spent a lifetime accumulating."

I smiled. "Like the car he was readying for the car show."

"Yes. You know, he'd had several gentlemen make inquiries regarding that car. The El Morocco, too."

"Was the El Morocco valuable?"

"He's been offered upwards of six figures for it."

"Six figures for an old Chevy?" I suddenly wished I still had the secondhand Chevette my mom and dad had bought me as my first car my junior year of high school.

She chuckled, though I sensed an undertone of sadness. "Not all old things are useless."

"I'm sorry. I didn't mean anything by it. It's just—"

Trudy cut off my apology with a wave of the hand. "It's nothing to apologize for."

A sudden thought hit me. Chick might have been killed for the car. Maybe whoever killed him figured the grieving widow would be only too happy to sell now that her husband was dead. Not only could she possibly use the money, but the car could hold bad memories for her.

I knew I wouldn't want to have to keep seeing, every day, the car that my husband had been found under, smushed like a bug. "Do you know who any of these men are who wanted to buy the El Morocco?"

"Sorry, no." Trudy Sherman called to the hound dog, who was sniffing around my van. Princess loped back to her mistress and scooted back inside the shop.

I went to my van and pulled open the door. "Would you mind if I come by the house sometime?" I explained how I'd bought a bird print from her husband. "I was thinking I might like to purchase some more."

"Of course."

I slid behind the wheel and stuck the key in the ignition. "I don't suppose you have any"—I wriggled my fingers in the air—"sense of who might have murdered Chick?"

She managed a smile. "Everybody thinks that if you have the gift, you will be rich and have all the answers."

I shrugged. "It doesn't work that way?"

"The truth is, the gift does not work on oneself. I can only share with others. And I am happy to do this." She moved closer and motioned for me to extend my hand.

So far, I'd been the one sharing—twenty dollars—with her.

I looked at my hand a moment, then hesitantly complied.

She took it in her fingers and turned it over, palm up, nodded in silence a moment, then turned it over to peer some more at the back of it. Finally, she let go of my hand.

I pulled my hand back inside the van. "Well?"

"Goodbye, Ms. Simms." With those words said, she turned and walked away. I noticed yellow leather moccasins on her feet with tiny tassels on the back.

"Aren't you going to tell me my fortune?" For twenty bucks I ought to get more than a cheap wooden statue that was probably made in China.

"Sorry, no." She closed the door behind her.

I had no choice but to start my van. I drove back to town slowly and pensively. I didn't like one bit the way she'd said goodbye.

It had had such a ring of finality to it. And I wasn't ready yet for the big goodbye.

11

"And that's all you got out of her?" Kim said with disbelief. "A dusty old statue of the Lord of Death?"

"And it cost me twenty bucks."

"Twenty dollars? For this?" Kim shook her head. "For that money, she should have thrown in a free fortune."

I explained how Madame Trudy had taken one look at my palm and left me sitting in my van by the side of the road.

"That's weird."

"Tell me about it. The woman read my palm, then practically fled." I frowned at the memory. "It was as if she saw my future and couldn't get away from me fast enough."

Kim laughed. "Don't let her get to you. To know you is to love you."

"Thanks."

"Do you think she had anything to do with her husband's death?"

"She says she spent the night at her sister's house."

"Where does her sister live?" Kim settled onto the stool behind the counter and began flipping through the pages of a supply catalog.

"She didn't say and I forgot to ask. According to her, the police are going on the theory that Chick's death was a murder. If so, I expect they'll be taking a close look at Trudy's movements. I'm still hoping that Chick's death was just what it looked like. A terrible accident." That would certainly be the best outcome for Paul.

"I suppose so."

Something in Kim's tone made me suspicious. "What? Have you heard anything? Did Dan tell you something?"

Kim stopped her page turning. "You won't tell him I told you?"

I shook my head quickly.

"Dan told me that the police are definitely treating Mr. Sherman's death as a murder. There was this blow to the back of the head, plus the jack thingamajig that had been holding up the car appeared to have been tampered with."

"That jibes with what Greeley said. Paul, too."

"Paul? What's he got to do with this?"

I hesitated. I had promised Paul that I would keep his involvement secret, at least for a couple of days. Kim was my best friend, but a promise was a promise. "He mentioned hearing something. I don't remember where." He had noticed the sheared pin on the car jack.

Kim wrinkled her nose as she picked up the statue and studied it some more. "This guy is almost as creepy as Robert LaChance. What are you going to do with it?"

"I was thinking it might look nice on the mantel over your fireplace," I teased. "Right next to your Miss Fall Festival crown and Real Estate Agent of the Year award."

"No, thanks." Kim balanced the red-suited skeleton on top of the cash register.

I snatched it up and went to place it behind the counter. "Let's not scare the customers away," I explained.

"That thing gives me the creeps," Esther cracked as she came down the stairs. She was dressed for work in an ankle-length plum skirt and Birds & Bees polo. Her store apron was clutched in her hand. "If I was you, I'd take out that devil and burn it in the yard."

"It's not a devil," Kim explained. "It's the Lord of Death."

"Mercy me!" cried Esther. "All the more reason to be rid of it."

"It's harmless, Esther. See?" I extended my hand.

"You keep that doll away from me."

Esther took a step back and glanced toward the front patch of lawn. "Uh-oh." Esther's eyes widened in fear.

"What's wrong?"

"Speaking of burning something out in the backyard." She tossed her apron on the counter and headed up the stairs. "I'm clocking out." She hollered as she climbed the steps, "I just remembered I left something baking in the oven."

Kim and I looked at each other and chuckled.

"Do you have any idea what's gotten into her?" asked Kim.

"No," I replied, "and I don't—" I froze. "Uh-oh."

"What? You too?"

Kim turned at the tinkle of bells indicating a customer coming into the shop. Only this wasn't a customer, it was Elizabeth Sudsbury. "Oh," Kim said on spying the svelte little woman. Mrs. Sudsbury spotted us at the counter and tapped our way on two-inch black heels. She was dressed in a gray tweed wool jacket and matching skirt. Her idea of comfort wear, no doubt. She wiped at the counter with a gloved hand, then settled her black leather purse atop it. "Ladies."

"Mrs. Sudsbury," I said with feigned delight. "How good to see you again."

"Hello, Mrs. Sudsbury," Kim added. "You're looking well."

The elderly matron of the Sudsbury clan tightened her lips. "And you, Miss Christy, you're looking . . ." She cleared her throat as she ran her eyes up and down the two of us. "Well . . . how is your mother, Miss Christy? I haven't seen her in simply ages."

"She's still in Florida. Enjoying the sunshine." Kim untied her apron and hung it on the hook behind the register. "It was really nice seeing you, Mrs. Sudsbury. I'm sorry I can't stay." She grabbed her handbag and coat.

"Where are you going?" I demanded. "I thought you were working today."

"I am." Kim wiggled her fingers goodbye. "At selling houses."

I frowned. "How about selling some birdhouses?"

"No can do. I'm showing a house this afternoon. People houses. You know how my boss, Mr. Belzer, gets." That said, Kim hustled out the back door. I only wished that I could join her.

I'd been deserted in the face of the enemy.

Mr. and Mrs. Sudsbury's son, Clay, was my age. As their only child, he was scion to the Sudsbury fortune. Clay had been chasing my skirt in high school and had finally built up the nerve to ask me out. He was handsome and charming and practically all the girls were drooling over him. Of course, I said yes—I'd been on pins and needles waiting for him to ask!

Mr. and Mrs. Sudsbury, when they caught wind of it, said NO. Clay canceled our date, telling me only that his mother and father had objected. I had already told Kim and the rest of my girlfriends about the pending date and was mortified. Maybe that was why I had impulsively agreed to go out on a date with Jerry Kennedy soon after.

Now Jerry was chief of police, Clay was a successful lawyer and member of the state legislature, and my life was for the birds.

No matter. I had my very own legal ace and he was all the man I wanted.

Elizabeth Sudsbury cleared her throat once more and I turned to face her, remembering to plaster a smile on my face as I did so.

"What is that thing?" Her eyes were glued to the Lord of Death.

"This? It's nothing." I tucked the statue on a shelf under the counter. "Is there something I can do for you, Mrs. Sudsbury?"

"I see you have a poster for the Fall Festival in your window."

"That's right," I was happy to reply.

"You know, many merchants have two posters." She held up two fingers.

"I have a second one here in the store." I stepped aside and pointed to the corkboard behind me. "See? This way, if customers miss it coming in, they'll see it when they pay."

Mrs. Sudsbury tilted her head to the left. "And if they buy nothing?"

I bit my tongue before I could say what I was thinking. "How about if I hang this second one on the inside of the door? That way people can't miss it."

"That would be an excellent idea."

"I'll get right on it." *Someday* . . . "Was there anything else? Were you interested in buying a bird feeder, perhaps?"

"Why would I want to do that?"

"So you can feed the birds. It's fun." Somehow I wasn't sure old Sudsy knew the meaning of the word.

"That's not why I'm here."

"Of course not." I waited to hear just why she had come. She certainly hadn't come to shoot the breeze. Sudsy and I didn't exactly travel in the same circles.

Mrs. Sudsbury slowly removed her gloves and limbered up her fingers. "My husband, Parker, as you may know, oversees the car and tractor portion of our Fall Festival. He tells me your friends . . ." She paused, unlatched her purse, and drew out a small spiral notebook. "A Paul Anderson and Derek Harlan are planning to enter an automobile in the car show."

"That's right. Is there a problem?"

She shook her head. "No. No problem. However, they have not

submitted a photo of the car with their entry fee and application. It is a requirement. We cannot have just any car in the show. It is essential that the committee approve each vehicle. I enquired next door at the biergarten. Mr. Anderson was nowhere to be found."

There was a committee approving the cars that could participate in the car and tractor show? "Did you ask Derek?"

"His office is closed today."

"Of course, today is a court day."

"And he wasn't in at all yesterday. What sort of practice is he running?"

I ignored the question. "I'll be sure to let Derek and Paul know that they need to submit a photo of the car."

"Thank you." She snapped her purse shut. "Normally, Parker would handle such matters himself, but he has been busy since the tragedy."

"Tragedy?"

"Our cousin died suddenly and Parker is assisting."

"I'm terribly sorry to hear that, Mrs. Sudsbury. My condolences." I wrung my hands and felt a sudden remorse for her loss. Sudsy and I may not have been best of friends, but it's always hard to lose someone close. "Was your cousin local?"

"To be precise," Mrs. Sudsbury began dryly, "James was Parker's cousin, not mine." She flicked her eyes at me as she pulled her gray gloves back over her pale fingers. "Except by marriage."

"James Sudsbury." I followed the woman to the door. "The name doesn't ring a bell."

"James Sherman," Mrs. Sudsbury corrected.

I froze. "Chick Sherman?"

"That's correct." She made a sour face. "Chick was the name most called him by." She clearly didn't like it. "You knew him?"

"I-I'm the one who found his body." I gripped her forearm and only let go when I saw the icy stare she was giving me. "Sorry."

"Yes, I remember now. Chief Kennedy mentioned that James had been discovered by a woman who'd been wandering about where she shouldn't."

I felt my face go pink.

She looked up at me with cold gray eyes. Her long lashes looked as phony as a four-dollar owl decoy. "Perhaps that will be a lesson to you."

With that, she pulled open the door and exited. A waft of cool fall air washed over me and I shivered.

I wasn't sure if I'd been threatened or chastened.

I watched as Sudsy marched down the street, past the biergarten to the next corner. A pearly white and teal antique automobile sat idling at the curb. She stood at the curb while a tall gentleman in a brown suit opened the driver's-side door, hurried over to her side, and held the passenger door open for her.

Sudsy entered the car. The driver muttered a few words to her, then closed the passenger door. He loped around the big car, got behind the wheel, and drove off.

I had a hunch that was the car Floyd and Karl had been talking about yesterday morning. I'd seen it, or a car similar to it, out by the Sherman place.

I reached into the pocket of my jeans for my phone to take a picture. Then I realized: I had no phone.

12

I planned to spend the rest of the day in the store with Esther, who'd returned the minute Sudsy had left, dealing with the customers and stocking shelves. Trying not to think about yesterday.

The store phone rang as I was unpacking a spotting scope, and I answered. It was Derek.

"Hi, Amy. I heard what happened last night from Paul and wanted to make sure you are okay."

I smiled at the sound of his voice. "Yes, I'm fine. It's terrible about Chick Sherman though." I explained how I'd spoken with Chick's widow. "At least there were no children involved."

"I don't know about that," Derek replied through the phone.

"What do you mean?"

"Having children around is a wonderful thing. With her husband gone, she would have at least had their children to solace her. I'm blessed to have Maeve in my life."

"Of course. I didn't mean it like that. I only meant that losing a father would have been hard on his children, too, if he'd had any."

"How is his wife taking it?"

I thought about the question. "It's hard to say. She's . . ." I paused. "Different."

"Different how?"

"She's a fortune-teller, for one thing."

Derek's laughter spilled through the wires. "You aren't a believer?"

"I wouldn't say that. There's just something odd about the woman."

"Like what?"

"Like she foisted a statue of Baron Samedi on me."

"Who?"

"The Lord of Death." I described the little doll to Derek's titters of amusement. "There's also something strange going on at that house. I'd bet on it. And Kim told me that Dan told her that the police are treating Chick Sherman's death as a murder."

I heard Derek exhale heavily. "Paul said as much."

"How did he sound?"

"Paul?" I sensed that Derek was surprised by my question. "Okay, I guess. Why?"

"Did he seem troubled at all?"

"No," Derek said slowly. "Should he be? What aren't you telling me, Amy?"

"Nothing," I said quickly.

"I'm dropping Maeve off at her mom's around six. How about if I pick you up after, for dinner? We can talk more then."

"Sounds good."

"Great. I have a surprise for you."

"What sort of a surprise?" I wasn't sure I was ready for any more surprises but was hoping for the best.

"You'll see. I've got to run. I'm taking Maeve to the matinée, but I'll come by your place around seven."

"It's a date. Call me on the store phone when you get here. My phone's out of order."

"That explains why my other calls to you went unanswered," Derek replied. "I thought you were avoiding me."

"Never." In the background, I heard Maeve calling for her father and we rang off.

I couldn't get Chick Sherman's death off my mind. Accident or murder? Like the police, my bet was on murder, but I knew there was no sense getting carried away until I knew for certain one way or the other.

I did do some online snooping. The Audubon print I'd bought at the Shermans' home-based thrift and antique shop might have been more valuable than I'd suspected. There was a good chance it was worth many times over the ten dollars I'd paid for it.

"Look here," I said, sliding the laptop over so Esther could get a look. We were behind the sales counter, alone in the store. It was near closing time. I was looking at a list of auction prices for similar Audubon illustrations. "Some of these plates are selling for upward of six hundred dollars. This one went for over a thousand."

Esther chuckled. "Yeah, I see that. Too bad you lost yours."

I frowned. "Yeah. And it isn't lost. I've simply misplaced it. " I turned my head side to side, knowing full well it was futile. "It has to be here somewhere."

"Now that you know how much it's worth, what are you going to do when you find it? Sell it?"

"No. I suppose I should return it."

"Return it?!" Esther jumped off her stool. "Why would you do that?"

"Because I wouldn't feel right keeping it. Not after learning how valuable it might be."

"But Trudy Sherman sold it to you!"

"Actually, it was her husband who sold it. And he's dead. I feel sorry for her."

"If you say so. Me," Esther said, studying the screen, "I'd sell it and take me a nice vacation somewhere."

"A vacation, eh? Where would you go?"

Esther thought long and hard. "I have no idea." She blinked. The realization seemed to perturb her. "Hey, look." She poked a sharp fingernail at the screen. "Too bad you don't have some of those books."

"What books?" I squinted at the tiny print on the screen.

"Those."

I looked at the auction-house listing. It was for a tattered, leather-bound set of Audubon's *Birds of America*.

My eyes grew. "I think I saw a set of books like that for sale in the Shermans' house."

"It says here this set sold for thirty-six thousand dollars," read Esther. She turned to me. I smelled peppermint candy. I was pretty sure she sucked on the hard candies to mask the distinct scent of tobacco on her breath. "How much is Trudy asking for her set?"

I closed my eyes. "One hundred dollars."

"Whoa. What do you say we put in fifty each and buy it?"

"We don't know for sure that the books and art that Trudy has are worth more than she's asking."

Could the books and other artwork in the Shermans' house be

worth a small fortune? Trudy Sherman had already told me about the six-figure offers they'd received for Chick's El Morocco. Could Trudy be sitting on a gold mine? If so, did she know it?

"I'm willing to take a chance if you are. What do you think, Amy?"

"I think I need to have another word with Trudy Sherman."

Steve Dykstra walked in the door carrying a green canvas tote with OTELIA'S CHOCOLATES printed on its sides. "Hello, ladies," he said, swinging the empty bag at his side. "Otelia sent me over for some bird food." He was dressed in chinos and a black fleece jacket over a flamingo-pink turtleneck.

"Again?" quipped Esther.

"Help yourself, Steve," I called. "Let me know if you need help."

"Don't worry, Otelia gave me a list." He waved a piece of paper that he pulled from the pocket of his fleece jacket. "The woman doesn't trust me to tie my own shoes, bless her heart."

Esther worked her hard candy across her teeth. "Weren't you just in buying seed for that woman?"

Steve smiled as he sauntered over to the bins along the front of the store. "What can I say? You've got the woman hooked on all this bird stuff, Amy."

He grabbed a stainless steel scoop and lifted the hinged acrylic top off the bin of safflower seeds. "Otelia's added two feeders behind the store." He shoveled seed into the bag, closed the bin, then moved on to the millet.

"I know, I sold them to her," I answered, my eyes still on the laptop screen. "Along with the three she's already got hanging from her balcony."

Steve chuckled. "I think she feeds her birds better than she feeds me."

"It doesn't appear to me that you've missed too many meals," Esther said with a twinkle in her eye.

"Yeah, yeah. I can't argue with you there, Esther." Steve patted his belly.

"I heard about Chick Sherman," he said as he settled his seed-filled tote onto the scale that hung by a chain from the ceiling. "Such a shame. Now I suppose the world will never see that car he was working on." He gazed at me inquisitively. "I don't suppose you got a look at it, Amy? I heard you were the one who found his body in his workshop."

"Sorry," I said, looking up from the computer. "It was covered in a shroud."

"Too bad." Steve dropped the bag on the sales counter beside me. "Three pounds, two ounces."

Esther did some math on a scratch pad and pounded the keys of the register.

"What's that you're looking at?" Steve squinted at the laptop screen.

I turned it so he could see. "I'm looking up the prices of Audubon bird prints."

Steve's eyes ran along the page. "They aren't cheap, are they? Don't tell me you're thinking of buying?"

Esther rang the register and handed Steve his change from the twenty-dollar bill he'd forked over. "If she's smart, she'll think of selling." She turned her eyes on me, her voice firm as she said, "For top dollar."

I turned the screen back to me. "We'll see, Esther. We'll see."

"Good luck either way," replied Steve, hefting his bag in his hand. "I've been buying and selling cars practically my whole life, and if there's one thing I've learned, it's that it's all in the timing."

I closed the lid to the laptop. "Speaking of timing, who's your guess for who might have murdered Chick Sherman?"

"Murdered?" Steve dropped his sack back on the counter. "I thought he had an accident!"

"The police are pretty certain it's murder." Esther made clubbing motions with her hands.

"Esther," I said. "Must you?"

"What? It's true, isn't it?"

"Is it?" Steve's mouth hung open.

"I'm afraid so."

"So it wasn't an accident? His car didn't fall on him like I heard?"

"Oh, it fell on him, all right," put in Esther.

"Andrew Greeley says there's a wound consistent with a blow to the back of the head that's inconsistent with the injuries Chick would have sustained if the jack failed and the car fell on him."

"Have the police talked to the wife?" asked Steve.

"Trudy? I'm sure they have. Why?"

"Because it's most always the wife," shot Esther. "Or the husband. Live together long enough, one is bound to want to kill the other."

I looked at Esther in wonder. I didn't know if she'd ever been married. She kept her personal life private. Maybe I needed to check her closet for a dead body. Then again, maybe I didn't want to know . . .

"I appreciate your opinion, Esther," I said, keeping my voice even, "but Trudy was visiting her sister at the time of her husband's death."

"Are you sure about that?" asked Steve.

The corners of my mouth turned up. "No, actually, I'm not." I'd simply taken her word for it. "Why would she lie?"

"Because she killed her husband? Duh." Esther shook her head at me.

I was saved from having to listen to any more from her by the appearance of a customer. I pointed to the opening door and Esther went into attack mode. For a little old lady, she could move like an Olympic sprinter when she wanted to.

Steve shouldered his bag. "I'd better get this back to Otelia. Don't want our little feathered friends to starve, do we?"

I held him back. "Before you go, what can you tell me about the Sudsburys?" They'd always been a close-knit family, never telling more than they wanted known.

Steve thought a minute. "I can't tell you much about Mrs. Sudsbury. I avoid her like the plague. Her husband, Parker, he's a good guy. A bit out of my league, but he comes down and hangs with us at the triple C sometimes."

"The triple C?"

"The Ruby Lake Classic Car Club. We meet down at the gas station once a month on Tuesday mornings around nine." He grinned. "Coffee, donuts, and car talk."

"And Parker attends?" It didn't seem quite like his cup of tea.

"Not often, but now and again. Loves his cars." Steve winked at me. "We're all nothing but a bunch of petrol-heads at heart. In Parker's case, I think he also likes to get away from the missus for a bit."

I couldn't blame the man for that. "Did you know that Parker and Chick Sherman were related?"

"Sure." Steve shrugged as if to say it was old news.

"Did Chick ever come to your car club?"

Steve was smiling at the very idea. "Not a chance. Number one, Parker and Chick couldn't stand one another. Number two, Chick wasn't much of a joiner."

"Why didn't the two men like one another?"

Steve shrugged once more. "They were different as night and day, despite their blood. Plus, Parker was angry with Chick for all the money he'd cost him over the years. I can't blame him. He poured a lot of money into Chick and his schemes and never got so much as a nickel back."

"I can see that might have made Parker angry."

Steve grinned ear to ear. "Not half as mad as Parker said it made his wife."

"Then why did he keep investing?"

Steve twisted his lip. "Family. You're stuck with 'em." With that, Steve said goodbye and Esther returned to the counter with her shell-shocked-appearing customer in tow. I predicted a double-digit sale.

Yes, you were stuck with them—unless you murdered them.

Derek telephoned upstairs to tell me he'd arrived and was waiting outside. "I'll be right down," I said. "Mom," I called toward my mother's room, "Derek's here. I'm leaving!"

"Have a nice time, dear."

"I will. You too!" Mom was going to be playing cards with Derek's father, Ben, and another couple. I grabbed my cream-colored fleece jacket and hurried downstairs and out the door.

Derek sat at the curb, but he wasn't in the car I had been expecting. I stared in wonder. "You got the carburetor in?"

"Yes." I could see the surprise on Derek's face. "How did you know about that?"

I stepped back and admired the car. The Impala looked pretty good with the top down. The car was white with a red stripe running along the side and had a red and white leather interior.

The whitewall tires were spotless, a far cry from the grime that had covered the tires and wheels, the entire car, when the guys had hauled it into town on a flatbed truck.

A northern mockingbird in the tree outside my window called out. Across the street, another answered.

I leaned in and kissed Derek. "I missed you."

"You too." Derek pulled me closer and we kissed once more. When I opened my eyes, he was looking at me. "Like her?"

"It's beautiful."

"Thanks." Derek ran his hand along the edge of the door. "She still needs a lot of work, but at least she's presentable for the parade."

I nodded. Any car or tractor older than 1981 was eligible for the car and tractor show and parade. A handful of ribbons would be given out to the best in several categories. Derek and Paul had explained those categories to me, but the information had gone in one ear and out the proverbial other. If cars had wings and feathers, maybe then I'd care.

The Chevy Impala had belonged to Paul's dad. He had kept the vehicle in a garage behind his house in Indiana, unused and neglected for years. While plenty of rust patches and dings remained, it was still a thing of beauty. I thumped the solid door with the palm of my hand. "They don't make them like this anymore."

"They sure don't." There was pride in Derek's voice. "Hop in. I'm starved."

I climbed inside, slid across the leather bench seat, and enjoyed the warmth of Derek's arms folding around me. He looked handsome in his gray wool sports coat and matching slacks and cream-colored turtleneck shirt. I was glad I'd worn my nicest red dress and gold locket.

"Are you sure you're okay? I've heard some pretty gruesome stories about how you found Chick Sherman squashed like a bug under some car of his in his workshop."

"It wasn't quite as gruesome as all that," I answered, as Derek put the car in gear. "But it was spooky."

"I'll bet." Derek turned the key in the ignition and the engine rumbled to life. The mockingbirds whistled in agitation. "Do you mind if we keep the top down? I know it's cold, but the sky's so clear . . ."

I patted his arm. "Don't worry. I'm fine." We were only going across the street to Lake House anyway. "The engine sounds good," I said. "This carburetor you installed, isn't it the one that Chick Sherman was rebuilding for you?"

"That's right." Derek eased the big car into the lot and came to a halt in a space near the docks. "How did you know?"

"Paul told me he was doing the work for you guys." And I had told him not to do anything—like install potential evidence in a murder investigation in the engine of his car—until he heard back from me. I was going to murder him the next time I saw him. And possibly the next time after that, just for good measure. "Where is Paul, anyway?"

"The biergarten, I guess. He asked me to bring the car by. Since we're all but done with the work, and the festival is just around the corner, he wants to keep it close to home now."

"He's about finished, all right," I muttered as Derek came around to open my door for me.

"What's that?"

"Nothing." What was Paul thinking, installing that carburetor? It had been found at a crime scene. Was he concealing evidence? Trying to keep it close to home where he could keep an eye on it?

We were escorted by a hostess in a sleek black dress to a table for two near the stone fireplace. Derek ordered a bottle of wine and we enjoyed it while watching the flames flicker and dance.

I looked over the thick vellum menu and chose the lasagna and a salad. Derek ordered the eggplant.

"Has Paul been acting strange at all?" I asked as we waited for our entrées. The salads had arrived and I drizzled a small amount of raspberry dressing over mine.

"Strange how?" Puzzlement showed on Derek's face, the candle between us flickering shadows across his firm chin. If I wasn't careful, he'd be thinking that I was acting strangely myself.

Strange like in he just murdered somebody, was what I wanted to say. Instead I said, "Nervous. Edgy, maybe?"

Derek worked his jaw. "Not more than usual, I'd say." He played with his napkin. "He has been worried about his business. Some of his equipment's been acting up." He picked up the wine bottle and topped off my glass.

I nodded. "I heard about that. Paul intimated that Chick Sherman was to blame."

"Apparently so. Paul wanted to sue the guy, but I told him it wasn't worth it and that he should try to work things out. He still talked about filing in small claims court though. He'd shelled out thousands and wasn't happy."

"Sounds like a mess."

"I told him that's what happens when you hire an amateur." Derek smiled at me across the table. "Paul's learned his lesson. Besides, Sherman did a great job on the carburetor rebuild. Say what you want about the guy, he knew his stuff when it came to cars."

Except not to get crushed underneath one. "Paul picked up the carburetor, didn't he?" I asked casually. "I'll bet he was one of the last people to see Chick Sherman alive."

Derek took a drink before answering. "Yep. He got the text from Chick and headed over pretty quickly afterward. If he'd stuck around, maybe he could have prevented the murder." He stabbed at a radish in his salad bowl. "Paul mentioned that the police asked him about that."

"Oh?"

"Yeah. It seems Paul's cell phone was the last number that Sherman dialed before he was killed."

I nodded. That jibed with what Paul had said about getting a message from the man. "So Paul talked to the police?"

"He said Chief Kennedy stopped in to see him at the biergarten. He was particularly interested in the heated argument that he'd heard Paul and Chick had. I can understand the chief's questions, but what about you? Why all the questions, Amy?" Derek suddenly leaned back in his chair and tilted his head. "Amy, you can't possibly think that Paul is involved in any way with Chick Sherman's death?"

"No," I answered quickly. "Of course not. I'm only concerned that the police might think he is."

"Why would they? Chick called Paul to tell him the carburetor was ready. He picked it up." Derek reached for his napkin. "End of story."

"And their fight?"

Derek waved my question away. "Two guys having a heated exchange over some faulty equipment. No big deal."

"And the two of you installed the carburetor earlier today." My mind was swirling with questions. I studied my glass. No answers were to be found.

"No, I had Maeve, remember? Paul did the work himself. Then he called me and asked me to drive the car back here. Maeve's mom gave me a ride out to Paul's house."

"How nice of her." I tried to keep the ice from my voice.

Derek was saved from responding because we were interrupted by the server, who set two hot dishes before us.

"I just remembered. Mrs. Sudsbury came in the store today. She said you and Paul forgot to send in a photograph of your car with your application for the festival."

Derek frowned. "No, I'm sure we did. I took the picture myself."

"That's funny."

Derek shrugged. "I'll give Parker a call. I'm sure we'll get it straightened out."

Halfway through my lasagna, I said, "You know, I was doing some research online this afternoon." I had explained earlier how I'd bought the Audubon sketch from the Shermans' shop. "That sketch I bought, if it's authentic, could be worth as much as a thousand dollars. Maybe more."

Derek whistled softly. "You don't say. You mean there are other people out there who are as crazy about birds as you are and would be willing to spend that much on a picture of titmice?" He was grinning.

"Very funny." I pushed my plate away and indicated for the waiter to take it away before I finished the entire thing. "There were dozens of other Audubon prints at the Sherman house. Some books and things, too. I think that they could be worth a bundle."

Derek wasted no time polishing off everything on his plate. "How big a bundle are we talking?"

"Esther saw a set of Audubon books advertised on the website we were looking at that had sold for thirty-six thousand dollars."

"Wow."

"And I think I saw a set that looked just like it at their house. I'm going try to take a second look tomorrow."

"So the Shermans were sitting on a small gold mine."

"Maybe a big one," I conjectured. "Trudy Sherman told me Chick had been offered six figures for that car he was found under."

"The El Morocco." Derek must have noticed my surprise. "Paul told me. That is a valuable car."

"I'll say. The odd thing is, the price on the print I bought was only ten dollars."

"So? Maybe it isn't as valuable as you think it is. Maybe it's a cheap copy."

I frowned. "You're right. I suppose it could be."

"Why not find somebody to appraise it for you?"

"That's a good idea," I said. "The problem is, I can't find it. I hope no one walked off with it."

"I'm sure it simply got misplaced. It'll turn up. When it does, get it checked out." Derek waved to the waiter. "Could we see the dessert menu, please?"

"Oh, no," I protested.

"Come on, a chocolate soufflé or a slice of cheesecake never hurt anybody."

I acquiesced. When a man's right, he's right. I excused myself to go to the ladies' room.

As I worked my way to the restrooms near the kitchen, I spotted a young couple near the window. They looked familiar. The young man had long, stringy hair that hung below his shoulders. There was a small silver stud below his lower lip. The young girl with him looked about his age, which I guesstimated as early twenties.

She was rather pretty, in a simple white frock with a few wrinkles in it and tan leather moccasins. The boy wore baggy jeans and a raspberry-red sweater with a denim jacket. He'd rolled the jacket's sleeves up to his elbows.

Large, thick steaks sat atop each plate and they ate like ravenous crows, barely saying a word, enjoying their meat, which from here looked quite pink and rare. Equally large baked potatoes soaking in butter and chives sat beside the steaks, with several stalks of asparagus between them.

An open bottle of domestic sparkling wine sat in an ice bucket on a tray at the edge of the table. Both glasses bubbled with golden liquid.

I stood riveted, trying to remember how I knew them. A woman bumped my arm. "Sorry," she said as she passed.

I rubbed my elbow. Now I remembered. This was the young couple selling at the side of the road near the Shermans' homestead. "How odd," I muttered, wondering how they could afford such an expensive dinner.

When I returned to the table, I told Derek about it. He glanced over his shoulder and looked at them quickly. "Maybe they had a good day and are splurging."

"Maybe."

"Do you know who they are?"

"I haven't a clue. Don't you think it's strange that they should be hawking stuff at the side of the very road that leads to Chick Sherman's house?"

Derek looked amused. "Not really. I'm sure the Shermans aren't the only people who live out that way."

"No," I replied. "But I'll bet Chick is the only person down that road who's been murdered lately."

13

I never did like coincidences and I hadn't liked the one last night. How could a couple of kids selling odds and ends at the side of the road one day, be dining on steaks the next?

First things first, however. I wanted a word with that miscreant, Paul. I showered, dressed, breakfasted with Mom, then went down one flight of stairs and banged on Paul's door. Prepared for battle.

There was no answer.

I pressed my ear to the door. Not a sound. Either he was feigning absence or he was really out. "The big chicken," I muttered, vowing to catch him yet.

I went downstairs and up the sidewalk to Brewer's Biergarten. I rattled the locked door but nobody came. If anybody was there at that early hour, they'd be in back.

It was my day off. Kim was coming in to watch the store with Mom and Esther. I returned to Birds & Bees, dropped the ever-grimacing Lord of Death in my purse, and went out again.

I passed Kim's car coming in, stuck my hand out the window, smiled and waved. "Perfect," I said to myself.

I drove by Kim's Craftsman-style bungalow, pulled up the drive to the back, and turned off the ignition. For as long as she'd had the house, Kim had kept a spare key under a glazed flowerpot off the back porch. I tipped the five-gallon pot and picked up the key. I blew off the dirt and stuck the key in the lock of the kitchen door.

I knew there was no one home, so I didn't bother calling out. I crossed to the living room, pulled open my purse, and set the Lord of Death in a place of honor on the mantel. "Welcome to your new home," I said, patting his little red top-hatted head.

I smiled as I locked up behind myself and returned the key to the ground beneath the flowerpot.

The next thing I did was stop at the electronics shop for a new phone. Though the salesman looked at me with disdain, I opted for the cheapest model they had.

I returned home. Cousin Riley had come by and I was instructing him on what needed to be done to the front flower beds. Mom watched from the porch. I hoped she'd keep an eye on him, but mostly she simply doted on him. She'd brought out a pitcher of ice-cold lemonade that my cousin was draining in a furious fashion.

Riley's mother is my Aunt Betty. Aunty Betty and Mom are twins. Riley's a twin, too. His sister is Rhonda. Riley's hair is black and wavy. Rhonda's is dark brown these days and she favors the fifties bouffant look. Both have hazel eyes. Rhonda works at Spring Beauty, a local salon. Riley works around town as a jack-of-all-trades. He's never held a steady job.

It was handy having him around to maintain the house and grounds. When you've got a big old house built in the late eighteen hundreds, there's always something in need of propping up or mending. I often wondered if I hadn't made a mistake in buying the drafty old place instead of opting for some sleek, modern space in one of the new buildings around town. But there was something special and homey about the Queen Anne Victorian–style house that made me feel comfortable, despite its constant need for attention.

"Don't worry, Amy." Riley wiped his arm across his forehead. He looked like a scarecrow in a floppy pair of blue jeans and a red and black flannel shirt. "Once I've cleared out the beds, I'll take the truck down to the farmer's market and get everything on this list."

"Thanks." I'd given Riley a handwritten list of plantings that would work well this time of year. Plus, I wanted to give the yard a spot of color.

"Don't forget about the Birds and Brewsmobile, Riley," called Mom from the porch. "You promised to give the roof a fresh coat of paint."

"I won't," replied my cousin.

"Wonderful. I have to finish another couple batches of bird bars, and I think Paul has quite a few supplies to go in yet, too. I hope we have room for everything."

"He already told me about it, Aunt Barbara. Chick Sherman was supposed to help him install the taps and lines, but I suppose it's up to us now."

"You?" I gaped at Riley. "What do you know about installing beverage equipment? Won't it involve a bit of plumbing and electrical?"

Riley shrugged. "We'll figure it out. How hard can it be?"

"Speaking of Paul," I said, "have either of you seen him this morning?"

"I saw him drive off early in his camper," Riley offered.

"Rats, I was hoping for a word with him."

Mom fluffed my hair. "What about you, dear? Did Aaron bring those brand-new birdhouses he promised you?"

"He's planning on bringing them by today." I'd been out to his farm with Tiffany and seen a couple of samples of his latest birdhouses. They were charming, a real step above the plain-Jane boxes on my shelves. I had high hopes that they'd do well with the tourists.

"Are you going to wear the cap?" Cousin Riley teased.

I pulled a face. The cap in question was a hideous orange hen sitting on a nest. The whole thing was sewn together out of batting, fake fur, and plastic feathers. One of Paul's waitresses had designed and built the thing. Did I mention it was hideous? She'd crafted Paul a giant beer stein resting on a Brewer's Biergarten coaster. Paul swore he was going to wear his while he worked the festival. I swore I was not going to wear mine. "Not on your life."

"Not on your life what?"

I spun around. Paul Anderson stood on the sidewalk, his hands in his back pockets. "We were just discussing those goofy caps of yours."

"Trust me," said Paul, sauntering up to the picket fence edging the sidewalk. "It's great marketing."

"Trust me," I answered, stepping closer, "it's not happening."

Paul tilted his head and smiled. "I'll tell you what. How about a friendly bet?"

I stared him down. "I'm listening."

"Well . . ." Paul scratched his cheek. "How about we see who sells the most."

"Beer over birdseed?" I shook my head. "Not a chance. Nothing says festival like beer."

"Okay, then . . ." Paul pursed his lips and looked upward. "How about—"

"Hey, I know," said Cousin Riley, snapping his fingers.

"What?" we turned and asked in unison.

"We'll see who can collect the most money for charity. We'll put out two jars. You can each pick your charity, and at the end of the day, whoever collects the most is the winner."

Paul and I studied one another.

"I like it!" called Mom. "And all the money goes to charity. That's a wonderful idea." She gave Riley a loving pat on the shoulder.

Riley beamed like a happy puppy. "Amy, if you win, Paul enters the Fall Festival Queen contest."

"What?" Paul took a step backward, slipped off the sidewalk, and almost got clipped by a passing station wagon before catching himself. The wagon's driver honked and sped away.

"In a gown," Riley added for good measure.

I grinned. "That I've got to see!"

Mom laughed loud and hard.

Paul looked aghast. He narrowed his eyes toward Riley. "And what happens to her," he said, pointing to me, "if—I mean, when—I win?"

Riley curled his fingers under his lower lip. "Amy, if you lose . . ." He left me hanging a moment.

"Spill it already, Riley!" I snapped.

"You enter the contest wearing the chicken hat—"

Paul snorted and my mother keeled over in a laughing fit.

"And a pair of overalls."

Paul snorted once more.

"You can borrow a pair of mine." Riley was beaming.

I shook my head.

"What's wrong, Simms? Are you *chicken*?" Paul cocked his arms and flapped his elbows.

"How old are you, five?" I said.

Paul extended his hand over the picket fence toward me.

"Fine," I said. "It's a bet."

"The winner has to wear the chicken hat, or gown," Riley said, turning his eyes on Paul, "for the rest of the day. And the two of you can't tell anyone about the bet. It might spoil things, unduly influence folks."

Mom agreed.

Paul let go of my hand. "I can't wait to see you up on stage, Amy. Don't worry, I'll take plenty of pictures."

"Ha-ha." I leaned closer. "I need to talk to you about you-know-what."

"Sorry, I've got a new assistant brewmaster and I've got to show him the ropes." He waved goodbye to my mom. "Catch you later, Mrs. Simms. Riley, I'm counting on you to help me sort things out in the brewery."

"I've got you covered," Riley promised, though I for one had limited confidence in him.

"Are you going to have the Birds and Brewsmobile ready to go Friday night, Riley?" Mom inquired after Paul had returned to the biergarten.

"You have my word, Aunt Barbara. I'd like to haul her down early Saturday." He knuckle-punched me in the arm. Not hard, just enough to show he loved me—at least, so he always claimed. "Get you a good spot."

I drew my brows together. "It was my understanding that we had a reserved space."

"Nope." Riley smiled. "First-come, first-served. But don't you worry, I plan on getting there before the first rooster crows." He hitched up his blue jeans. "I've got to get the JD downtown. The kids are decorating her for the parade."

I nodded. Cousin Riley always drove his vintage John Deere tractor in the car and tractor parade leading up to the crowning of the Fall Festival Queen. After her coronation, she was paraded once around the town square on a float that the middle-schoolers decorated and Riley slowly pulled along with his tractor.

"I was hoping for a spot between town hall and TOTS." The Theater on the Square, or TOTS, was our community theater. There was also a nice parking lot on the side. Space was tight downtown at the best of times. During the festival days, between the vendors, the visitors, and the sections that the town roped off for public services, there wouldn't be an inch to spare.

Riley shook his head in the negative. "No can do, Amy. Don't you remember? TOTS is where all the cars and tractors have to stage before the judging and parade."

I sighed. "Right." I had forgotten. "I was hoping for someplace expansive enough to set up the trailer and have room for Roland and his birds."

"You actually talked Roland into returning?" Riley looked at me in disbelief.

Roland Ibarra runs the Raptor Rescue Ranch near Morganton. Last time I'd seen him, he'd vowed never to return.

Previously, I'd invited him to Birds & Bees for our grand opening celebration, and things hadn't gone to plan. Roscoe, his beloved peregrine falcon, had gotten spooked in the store and had fled through the door that had carelessly been left open. When Roscoe flew the coop, so did half my customers. I couldn't blame them. Roscoe had put on quite a show, even if it wasn't the one his trainer had carefully planned.

It hadn't helped that a delirious redhead kept yelling that the falcon had scalped her. I'd had to give her a brand-new bird feeder and a ten-pound bag of seed to calm her down and keep her from filing a lawsuit.

It had taken hours on the phone with Roland over the past week to get him to agree to a return visit. I was hoping the birds he was promising to bring would draw festival-goers to our Birds & Brews-mobile. I also wanted to make sure the trained birds had plenty of space to maneuver.

"It wasn't easy. Roland warned me to be sure we don't set up near the fried turkey stand."

Riley laughed. "I'll do my best." He leaned against his shovel. "Not that you can blame a falcon for wanting some of that delicious turkey." His shovel got more use as a crutch than it did a gardening tool. "But in the end it's all up to Sudsbury."

"You mean Parker? I heard that he's in charge of the car and tractor show. What would he care about where the vendors set up?"

"Parker does handle the cars and he is the lead judge," Cousin Riley explained. "But it's Mrs. Sudsbury who runs the show down to the minutest detail."

Somehow I wasn't surprised. "Did you know that Chick Sherman was related to the Sudsburys?"

"You don't say? No, I had no idea." Riley shifted the shovel to his left armpit and leaned in. "Chick never mentioned anything like that to me." He tilted his head back. "You'd never guess they were related, would you?" He chuckled. "The Sudsburys and Shermans don't seem at all alike."

"Considering the Sudsburys' country club lifestyle and Trudy and Chick Sherman's eccentric existence, I couldn't agree more. Did you know Chick well?"

"No." Riley sighed. "A real shame he died the way he did." He looked up and down the busy sidewalk as if to see who might be listening before saying, "I'll bet it was them kids that did it."

"Did what?"

"Killed him, of course."

"You think Chick Sherman was murdered? I don't believe the police have said so conclusively yet, although they seem to be leaning that way."

"It was murder, all right."

"What makes you so sure?" Cousin Riley could have some wacky ideas, so I was prepared for the best of them.

"Old Chick was careful. The man knew what he was doing around the garage. The way I hear it, he was supposed to have been killed when the El Morocco fell on him."

"That's right. I saw the body and the car myself." I shivered at the memory. "The jack failed." At least that was one theory.

"Chick built most of his own gear. He wouldn't have gone under that car if there was a chance that jack was defective." Cousin Riley rolled his tongue over his upper lip. "Hey, Aunt Barbara!" he shouted. "How about some lemonade?"

"Coming, dear." Mom rose, poured a generous serving of lemonade, and carried it down to my cousin.

"Thanks, ma'am." He chugged it down at a gulp. "I was telling Amy that I'll bet it was those kids that killed old Chick."

"Kids?" asked my mother.

I frowned. "Yes, exactly what kids are you talking about? The Shermans don't have any kids."

Cousin Riley shrugged. "I know that. It was just a couple of kids. Scruffy looking. I saw them snooping around Chick's yard the other morning."

"Was one a young man, early twenties? And a girl about the same age?"

"That sounds about right."

"Do you know their names or where they live?"

"Not a clue."

I turned to my mother. "I don't suppose you know who they might be?"

Mom shook her head. "Sorry, dear."

"What were you doing out at his place?" I asked Cousin Riley.

"Chick was sharpening the blades on the tiller for me. He's good and he's cheap. I warned Chick that those two looked like they'd take anything that wasn't tied down, but he told me not to worry about them."

"And now he's dead."

Riley removed his cap and held it over his heart. "Rest his soul."

"To hear his wife, Trudy, tell it, her husband's soul isn't resting at all."

Riley squinted at me. "It isn't?" He scratched the top of his head, then plopped his cap back over his hair. "What's it doing exactly?"

"Probably trying to find his killer. Or," I said, unable to resist, "maybe he's looking for someone to haunt . . ."

"Amy!" scolded my mother.

"I wouldn't put it past him," Riley said. "I'd be haunting folks, too, if somebody took me before my time."

"We still don't know for sure that Mr. Sherman was murdered," I reminded him.

Riley handed his empty glass back to my mother. "Like I told you, I can't see Chick sliding under a car if he had any doubt at all about his equipment. Besides, to hear Mr. Greeley tell it, there isn't much doubt." He stabbed at the ground with the shovel. If he wasn't careful, he'd soon be doing some actual work. "No doubt at all. At least not in his mind."

"You spoke to Greeley?"

"Sure. I did some work for Greeley early this morning." Among his various work about town, Cousin Riley mowed the lawn out at Eternal Harmony once a week.

"What exactly did Greeley say?"

Riley tilted his head to the sky and gathered up his memories. "He said that Chick was likely dead or at least unconscious before he was crushed by his car."

I nodded. That jibed with what Mrs. Sudsbury said she'd been told by the police. It also matched Paul's suspicions and what everybody else was telling me. I needed to have a word with Greeley to confirm that it couldn't have been Paul's carburetor that had been used to strike Chick Sherman down.

I winked at Mom as I warned Cousin Riley to keep one eye open for ghosts, and left him to mull over my words.

14

I'd spent the day running errands, working in the store, trying to catch a minute alone with Paul, and failing to meet with the coroner. My lack of success wasn't doing much for my mood, so it wasn't surprising that I was knocking rather loudly on Paul's door once again—just as I had done to no avail that morning.

I knocked a second time, then a third. I had already tried the biergarten, and the staff said he was home. His vehicle in the lot seemed to confirm that.

I pressed my ear to the door—this was getting to be a habit. I thought I heard a cough, so I banged on the door again.

After some rustling noises and a lot of muffled cursing, Paul answered the door and peered out at me through bloodshot eyes. "Oh, it's you."

I looked him up and down. His face was haggard and unshaven. He looked slovenly in a faded blue-and-black checked bathrobe that was frayed at the sleeves. "Nice robe. Can I come in?"

"It's the crack of dawn."

"It's the crack of six o'clock, Paul," I replied. "In the evening."

Paul stepped away from the door. "Is it?" He rubbed his face. "Okay, sure. Come on in." He squeezed his head between his hands a moment. "What's up?" He padded off to the tiny galley kitchen. "Let me start the coffee."

I waited at the counter, arms crossed, while Paul went through the motions of loading up his coffee machine. He scooped several oversize tablespoons of ground coffee into the bowels of the machine and added water. A moment later the machine was hissing like an angry squirrel.

"I've been waiting to get you alone all day."

"It's been a rough one." Paul handed me a relatively clean mug and I carried my coffee to the window and looked out over the street.

Paul slumped into an aged blue recliner that faced the television. He smelled of beer.

Several chickadees weaved in and out of the branches just out of reach. These were Carolina chickadees, with distinctive black caps and bibs and white-sided faces. In the fall, they tended to flock together. Hopping spryly from branch to branch, they were no doubt searching for insects. It was suppertime. Before long, the insects would all but disappear for the winter and seeds and berries would become the mainstay of their winter diet.

I heard Paul yawn behind me as if to get my attention. I took a bracing sip of the strong, black brew. It wasn't bad. The man had been haphazard in his approach. Why didn't my coffee taste this good?

"You lied to me," I said, moving closer and setting my cup down on a coffee table littered with sports magazines and empty beer glasses. Several crusts of pizza held place of honor on a pale green plastic plate that hung over the edge of the table, ready to fall at a moment's notice.

Paul sat straighter. "What are you talking about?"

"We had a deal. You came to me asking for help."

"Yeah." Paul dumped some cream from a pint container into his coffee. "Thanks."

"Thanks? Last night Derek told me what you did."

Paul gazed across the tiny apartment at me, all innocence. "What did I do?"

"You installed the carburetor you found in Chick Sherman's workshop." I paced the rug. "You were supposed to give me a couple of days to look into things for you." I spun on him. "You practically begged me!"

"In the first place," said Paul, looked affronted, "I did not lie to you."

"You lied to the police."

"I did not!" He rubbed his unshaven face. "I told them I went by Chick's place, picked up the carburetor, and left."

I made a face.

"What? Technically, it's not a lie."

"You're almost as bad as Craig. The two of you are like peas in a proverbial amoral pod. No wonder you're friends."

"Hey, that's not fair!" Paul protested.

Silence filled the small, stale space. I crossed to the window and opened it, or at least tried to. "This thing's stuck."

"Talk to my landlord," quipped Paul.

I ignored the remark and banged hard on the sash. Finally, the window gave. I pushed it upward and a rush of cool air swept through—along with several leaves and a small spider that had been resting on the ledge.

"Hey!" shouted Paul, lifting his legs off the floor. "Now look what you've done, Simms! Get that thing out of here!"

"Good grief." I picked up one of the brown maple leaves that had skittered in and coaxed the spider onto it. As much as I was tempted to hold the arthropod under Paul's nose, I instead released it back outdoors.

"It wouldn't hurt if you'd spring for some window screens." Paul settled his bare feet back on the rug and picked up his coffee cup.

I pulled a face. "I'll get right on that." I downed my coffee and headed for the door. "Right after I get done clearing you of murder charges."

Paul rose and followed me to the door. "Come on, Amy. You know I didn't kill anybody."

"Maybe not." I turned and we stood nose to nose. "Why didn't you tell me you were threatening to take Sherman to court over the money you'd paid him?"

He shrugged. "It didn't seem important."

"Please. You can do better than that. And what on earth possessed you to install that carburetor when you know it might be evidence?"

It was his turn to pull a face and he did. "You saw it. It was clean. I couldn't see the harm. I wanted to get the car done."

"Do you know how that makes you look? First, you argue with Sherman in front of witnesses, then you're possibly the last one to see him alive—"

"Except the killer," Paul was quick to interject.

I was having none of it. "—and then you tamper with evidence!" I threw open the door and stormed out.

"Where are you going?" Paul hollered from the doorway.

I stopped at the stairs and turned on my heels. "To find out who killed Chick Sherman!" I shouted.

"Thanks, Amy," Paul said, lowering his chin. "Really, I appreciate it." His hand hung onto the doorknob.

"Don't thank me," I growled. "I'm not doing this for you. I'm doing it for me. Keeping you out of jail," I said, pointing my finger at him, "is the only way I can win our little bet. And I am so looking forward to seeing you in a dress!"

I took the first two steps, then paused and said over my shoulder, "Practice your curtsy, Paul, because you're going to need it!"

I grabbed the keys to the minivan and drove toward the edge of town. When I'd stopped in earlier, Mr. Greeley's assistant had told me he'd be back in the evening in preparation for a viewing. She insisted it would be okay if I stopped by beforehand.

Greeley's Mortuary sat on one corner of a tree-shaded block with a church at the opposite end. The cemetery sat between the church and the funeral home, a colonial-style redbrick building with white Grecian columns. Greeley's hearse sat to one side of the circular drive. I eased up behind it and stepped out. A line of vehicles, each with a single white carnation on its windshield, stood at the curb.

I found Andrew Greeley in his private office at the left side of the facility. "Good evening, Mr. Greeley." The place gave me the creeps and I hoped to get in and out as fast as possible.

He looked at me from over the screen of his computer. "Ms. Simms." He motioned for me to enter. "I suppose you're here about Mr. Sherman. My receptionist told me you might be stopping by."

"Yes, I was wondering—"

Mr. Greeley held up his hand. "I know what you are wondering." He took a moment before answering. "Chick was clobbered with a long, sharp object." He held up two bent fingers. "Twice. That is what you wanted to know, isn't it?"

"Yes. Twice?"

"Bang! Bang!" Greeley slammed his fist against his desk then locked his eyes on me. "Twice."

"Whether the car killed him or he was killed with something prior to being crushed under it, you can be assured of one thing, Ms. Simms. James Sherman did not die of natural causes." Greeley shook his head side to side as if to punctuate his remark. "Somebody helped him cross to the other side."

I gulped. "With something like a carburetor?" To tell the truth, if I hadn't seen one the other night in Paul's camper, I wouldn't have known what the devil one looked like, let alone if it would have made a possible murder weapon.

Greeley looked at me like I had sprouted two more heads—and one of them was ostrich. "What's that supposed to mean?"

"Never mind. So this long, sharp object—that's what killed him?"

"Maybe, maybe not. I expect it knocked him unconscious at the very least."

Cousin Riley had said as much. "Any idea what this object might be?"

Greeley laced his fingers and appeared to give the question some thought. Finally, he spoke. "There are many, many objects lying around out there at the Sherman place. You were there. You saw it yourself.

"That barn workshop alone is full of tools. One of the officers noticed that the tire iron was missing from the trunk. When asked about it, Trudy Sherman believed there had been one there previously. She indicated that her husband liked everything just so and liked to keep a spare and a jack in the car at all times. The spare and jack were there. The tire iron was not."

"So that's what was used to kill Chick or knock him out?"

"Maybe. It might have been something like a tire iron or even a farming implement. And that's what I told Chief Kennedy. I expect they'll be turning the house, the barn, and the yard itself upside down, looking for the tire iron and anything else that might have been used in the crime."

"The killer might have taken the implement with him or her. It could be long gone or they might have wiped it clean."

"Even if the killer attempted to wipe the item clean, there are bound to be traces of blood and skin and the like. If it's there, I expect they'll find it."

Good luck, I thought. "As you suggested, there's enough junk out there to keep the entire police force looking for a lifetime."

"That's not my problem." Greeley fiddled with an expensive-looking black and gold fountain pen. "The man's skull was a mess. I'm not sure if we'll ever know for certain if it was the sharp object that killed him or the car that was dropped on his face afterward. It'll take a keener eye than mine to even hazard a better guess. The body has been sent to county for a complete autopsy."

I grimaced. Greeley painted an ugly picture.

After a night filled with ugly dreams, I was back on the road, more determined than ever to get some answers.

I cranked up the volume to *My Fair Lady* and the heat inside the Kia as I drove off toward the Sherman homestead. Madame Trudy's little house at the side of the road looked empty, so I drove on. There was no sign of the two kids I'd seen the day of Chick Sherman's murder and again the other night at the Lake House restaurant.

To the tune of Colonel Pickering singing "You Did It," I slowed the van and came to a stop near a small wood with a stream running along the roadside. Though the dear colonel was singing about something altogether different, it made me wonder all the more who did it. Who killed Chick Sherman? And why?

If I knew the answer to that, I'd be singing, too.

I exited the van and went around to the back, where I kept a small canvas waist pack in which I kept an extra pair of binoculars, a field guide to the birds of North Carolina, a bottle of water, and a snack bar.

I'd dressed sensibly in blue jeans, a cable-knit sweater, and a fleece jacket. I lifted my jacket and clipped the pack to my waist after removing the binoculars and hanging them by their nylon strap around my neck. I'd worn my sturdy over-the-ankle hiking boots.

Testing the door to be sure I'd locked up, I picked my way across the stream by stepping on half-submerged stones. I climbed through the mud on the other side and headed into the woods after taking my bearings. If I was right, the Sherman place was about a half mile to the northeast of me.

The sky was gray and it was a cheerless afternoon. At the high-pitched sound of a chickadee calling *chickadee-dee-dee, chickadee-dee-dee!* I paused and trained my eyes on the nearest clump of trees. Midway up a thick branch, I spotted my vocalist. It was a Carolina chickadee. After a moment, a second bird joined him.

I lowered my binoculars and marched on. I followed a narrow deer track that seemed to be leading in the direction I wanted to go. A slow-moving wisp of white smoke a few hundred yards away caused me to stop. I pulled out the binoculars and studied the small clearing.

A ring of stones encircled a low flame. To the left of the fire, a two-toned domed tent sat between a pair of tall pines. The upper half of the tent was olive green and the bottom was taupe colored. If it hadn't been for the rising smoke, I would have missed it.

A red sleeping bag hung over the lower branch of one of the pines. There was no sign of the campers who'd pitched the tent. I moved on. After fifteen minutes of marching, I spotted the Sherman house through a break in the trees.

Lifting my binoculars to my eyes, I studied the house from the side. I hadn't been around this side previously. This part of the overgrown and weed-infested yard, like every other, was cluttered with rusted car parts and every assortment of items, like a flea market gone awry. A white refrigerator, missing its door, rested on its side, its insides filled with pine needles and brown leaves.

Looking at the house, it was impossible to tell if anyone was home. I walked up to the house, rounded the corner, and neared the front porch.

A tall, thin man stood on the front porch watching my approach. He must have been close to six and a half feet tall.

"Hello." I stopped in my tracks. "Who are you?" I called.

A pair of intelligent gray eyes took me in. "Parker Sudsbury," he said evenly. "And you?" His thinning silver hair swept back from his ruddy face. His teeth were straight and narrow.

"Amy Simms." I unzipped my jacket and tucked my binoculars inside. This was the first time I was meeting the elusive Parker Sudsbury, half of the duo that had forbidden their son from dating me. If my name stirred up any memory of the incident, his face wasn't revealing it. "I understand Chick was your cousin. I'm very sorry for your loss."

Parker nodded but said nothing. He leaned over the rail and looked down on me. "You haven't explained what you're doing here." He wore a baggy brown coat and khakis.

"I came to see Trudy."

"She's not here." His finely manicured hands clutched the wooden rail.

I frowned. "Do you know when she'll be back? I told her there were a few items I was interested in."

"She's staying with her sister. The police were here earlier and she didn't want to be present."

"The police?" Again?

"A couple of officers and Chief Kennedy. They were here with a dog sniffing around."

"Did they find anything?"

Parker smiled at the question. "A lot of junk."

Not surprising. You could hardly take a step around the Sherman place without hitting some so-called junk. Then again, some of that junk might be as valuable as precious jewels. "Would it be okay if I went inside and had a look around?"

Parker Sudsbury turned his head and gazed in the front window a moment before replying. "I suppose that will be all right. I just stopped by to check on the place." He motioned for me to come up.

I climbed the short set of steps to the porch, nodded and entered the house. Everything looked pretty much the same as the last time I'd been there. Not that anything less than the effects of a hurricane would have been evident in this cramped and cluttered space. There was no sign of the hound, Princess.

I wandered up the narrow aisles, working my way toward the Audubon collection.

"If there's anything you're interested in purchasing, make a note of it. I'll see that Trudy gets your list and gets back to you."

"That would be fine," I said, though the man's presence left me feeling uneasy. What was it about him that created such a sense of discomfort? Was it those inscrutable eyes or the stiffness of his manner?

Parker Sudsbury followed me at a distance. "Do you mind telling me how you got here? I don't see a car, young lady."

I turned and smiled politely. "I parked down the road a bit and walked up." I pulled my binoculars back out of my jacket and lifted them. "I'm a bird-watcher and like to take every opportunity I get."

I lowered the binoculars and left my jacket unzipped. "You never know what you might discover."

Parker looked at me oddly. "And did you discover anything of interest?"

"Not yet." I turned my attention to the Audubon prints. "There seem to be fewer than I remember." The few that were left didn't seem anywhere near the quality of the others I had seen the other day. The five remaining pieces were cheap copies, nothing at all like the delicately colored drawing I'd bought of the chickadees.

He shrugged.

I studied the shelf where I'd seen the red leather, seven-volume set of James J. Audubon's *Birds of America*. There was a hole where the volumes had sat. Nothing but a layer of dust along the edge of the wooden shelf showed that some books had once occupied the space. I turned to Parker. "They're gone," I said.

"What's gone?"

"The books." I ran my fingers through the dusty line at the lip of the shelf. "They were right here. And most of the sketches."

"So?"

"So it was a seven-book set of Audubon's *Birds of America*. I saw them here the last time I was out here. They were right here. And the sketches were right here." My eyes darted left and right, up and down. "I know they were."

He sounded rather stoic, but I noticed a distinct twitch in the corner of his right eye. "What did these books look like?"

"They were red leather, quite old, with gold lettering. They could be quite valuable."

"Maybe Trudy or Chick moved them," Parker said smoothly. He'd come up closer, blocking me in the narrow makeshift aisle. I smelled the woodsy scent of his cologne, noticed the wide pores of his round nose. "Or someone might have purchased them."

I took a step back, pressing against the bookshelf. "I suppose." I took a step sideways and touched his arm. "Excuse me. I'll just look over here." Had someone bought them for the one-hundred-dollar asking price? If so, someone had made out like a bandit.

If I'd been a more suspicious person, I might have suspected Esther, but for all her faults, I knew she would never truly take advantage of someone—especially not to the tune of tens of thousands of dollars.

Parker hesitated, then moved to let me pass.

I scurried around the room. There was so much clutter, I didn't know if I'd ever find the books.

Parker continued to shadow me. "Was there something special about these books?"

"I'm not sure." I also wasn't sure how much I wanted to tell Parker Sudsbury. He might have been Chick Sherman's cousin, but he was a stranger to me. And an odd one at that.

"If you're interested in buying them, I'll inquire of Trudy when she returns. I'm sure if they are here, she'll know, and will be happy to sell them to you."

"Do you have any idea when that might be?"

"No." He shook his head once. "Not precisely. Chick's death has taken a toll on her." He extended his arm, indicating the front door.

I stifled a frown and followed him outdoors. "Where's Princess?"

"With Trudy." He pulled a ring of keys from his trouser pocket and jangled them loosely for a moment before locking the door behind us.

As I stepped off the porch, I noticed an automobile parked close along the opposite side of the house. It was the pearl white and teal car that Parker had chauffeured his wife, Sudsy, to Birds & Bees in.

"Nice car," I said.

The trunk hung open and I stepped closer, wanting to get a look. "In fact, it's the envy of everyone. At least my friends Karl and Floyd." I walked my fingers over the left front fender. "I saw you driving out this way the other day, or a car just like yours. And by the looks of it, I'd say there aren't many like it around Ruby Lake."

"There aren't." Before I could reach the trunk, Parker had taken several long strides and slammed it shut. He tossed the keys through the open driver's-side window, then stood beside me. He patted the hood lovingly as he might a child. "But so what if you did, Ms. Simms? The Apple Mountain Country Club is down that county road." He pointed "My house is, as well."

"Did you and Chick get along?"

His brow creased. "I find that an odd and, I might add, rude thing to ask, Ms. Simms."

"Sorry, I'm just trying to figure out who might have killed your cousin and why."

Parker smiled. "And why is that? To divert suspicion from yourself?" His smile grew, revealing long white teeth and a pink tongue.

Despite the chill, I felt my cheeks heat up. "What does that mean? Why would I be trying to divert suspicion from myself? I didn't kill Chick." I folded my arms over my chest. "I'm the one who found him."

"I know all about that," Parker said, pacing beside the car. "How you came to the house, spying on Chick."

"Spying?" I sputtered. "I never—"

Parker cut me off with a chop of his hand through the air. "Spying, Ms. Simms. Chick told me all about it. Trying to get a look at his car and his other inventions, no doubt." He shook his head in disgust. "You ought to be ashamed."

"I can assure you I did no such thing. I came out here to do some shopping."

He looked at me rather dubiously.

"In fact, I bought an Audubon print. That's why I came back today. I was hoping to buy some more." I drew myself up and adjusted my waist pack. "Do you really think I'd come back out here if I'd murdered your cousin?"

Parker shrugged and stroked his chin. "Perhaps. Perhaps to throw off suspicion, perhaps to see if you'd left behind any incriminating evidence."

"That's ridiculous! I barely knew Chick. Why would I kill him?"

Parker rolled his pink tongue across his upper lip. "Maybe Chick made a pass at you. You got angry," he speculated, "and grabbed the nearest thing at hand, whatever that might be."

"So then I killed him and dragged him under the El Morocco? That's ridiculous."

"Is it? To hear Trudy tell it, that's just what happened."

My eyes grew wide. "She said that? She said that she thought I murdered her husband?" I jammed my finger into my chest.

He lifted both shoulders. "I'm afraid so."

I shook my head. "I don't believe it." Trudy Sherman hadn't given me any indication at all that she suspected I might have been involved in her husband's death. If anything, she'd been rather gracious despite her grief.

"Why do you think she gave you the Lord of Death?"

I cringed. "You mean . . . ?"

A chill danced along my vertebrae.

Parker yanked open the car door and slid behind the wheel of the Bel Air. "Good afternoon, Ms. Simms."

I collected myself and hurried to the open window to confront Parker. "You're wrong," I said. "And what are you implying? Are you telling me that Chick had a history of accosting women?"

Parker turned the key in the ignition and the engine sprang to life. He moved the shifter into gear and lifted his foot from the brake. The car inched forward. "I'm merely saying my cousin liked to fiddle with more than cars."

The car shot forward another foot, then stopped. Parker looked back at me. "If you don't believe me, ask Sally Potts."

"Sally P—" There was no point finishing my sentence. Parker left me in a cloud of dust.

15

I watched the big old car and its nasty driver disappear, then walked over to the barn. The tattered remains of the yellow police tape dangled from one of the doors. A thick padlock held the two doors in place.

I couldn't have gotten inside if I wanted to. Nonetheless, I walked all the way around the barn workshop, hoping to find a secondary entrance. I did. It was a standard size door with no window. It, too, was locked.

Disgusted and getting colder and more hungry by the minute, I took my bearings and made my way back to the van, taking the same trail that I had followed out.

I stumbled along the narrow dirt path, my brain still bruised and swirling from my conversation with Parker Sudsbury. Who did he think he was to accuse me of murder?

The man was more likely to have killed Chick himself. They were family. What deeper connections did they have besides an evident love for antique automobiles?

Parker had the key to the Shermans' house. Despite what I'd heard, the two men couldn't have been all that estranged.

Just maybe Parker was close to Trudy and not Chick. That led to some interesting possibilities. And what, if anything, did Sally Potts have to do with Chick and his murder? She'd been to a few bird walks and was a quiet, unassuming woman. Was that modest exterior hiding a killer?

Deep in thought, I stumbled over a white-oak root that rose several inches out of the ground. I threw out my arms to keep from landing on my face. It still hurt like the dickens when I struck the earth, but at least I wasn't wearing rocks and soil for makeup.

I checked my hands for blood, found none, and wiped them against my jeans. The gray sky showed no signs of clearing and in a few hours dusk would be arriving. I stopped to check my bearings once again, thinking that I should have reached the stream, the road, and my car, in that order by now.

I hadn't.

I pulled my binoculars from my neck and shoved them back in my pack. As I did so, I noticed a puff of smoke to my left. I watched it for a moment. It could have been coming from the campsite I'd passed earlier.

I left the track and pushed my way through the undergrowth and low branches, keeping my eyes on the rising smoke. Soon I came within sight of the domed tent once again. It was definitely the tent I'd seen before. The red sleeping bag I'd noticed when I'd passed by earlier still hung from a low limb. It was odd finding the tent out here. I did not know who the land belonged to, but this was not a public campground.

As I came within a dozen yards of the campsite, I spotted two old bicycles, one red, one yellow. The yellow one lay on its side. The red bike was propped against a pine to the rear of the tent.

A yellow bedsheet lay atop a white one. Sandwiched in between were various items whose shapes were vague but appeared to be clothing, small appliances, and other seemingly random items.

Suddenly I knew whose camp this was. It had to belong to the young couple I'd first spotted selling at the side of the road and then again at the Lake House the night before, enjoying a fancy and expensive meal.

I stepped around a cluster of calf-high boulders and moved closer to the smoldering fire, which had been lit a mere two steps from the tent flap. "Hello," I called. "Is anybody here?" A dirty blue plastic cooler sat next to the tent along with two small folding chairs with metal frames and green canvas backs.

Muffled noises and whispers came from within the tent.

A moment later the flap fell open and a young woman crawled out. The first thing I noticed was the blue and green hair on the left side of her head. Definitely the same young couple. Her face was flushed and her hair was in a loose ponytail. She wore tight jeans and an oversize man's shirt of blue denim. She fastened the button on her jeans as she looked me over.

"Hello," she said, her voice soft and low. "Can I help you?"

"Hi, I got a little lost. I was bird-watching"—I patted my waist pack as evidence—"and seem to have misplaced my car."

The scraggly haired young man crawled out in a pair of dirty dungarees. He clutched a raspberry-red sweater in his hands and quickly drew it over his head, covering his thin, white chest. "What's up?" He nodded in my direction. "Who's she?"

I held out my hand to him. "I'm Amy. I was just telling your friend that I was out bird-watching."

The two looked at one another and shared a shrug. The young man stuck his hands deep in his pockets. His face had several days' growth of hair on it.

"And you are?" Up close, the young man appeared to have some Hispanic blood in him.

"Dom," the boy said rather grudgingly. "This is Tam."

I nodded. "Have you been camping here long?"

Dom narrowed his dark eyes at me. "Why? Is this your property?"

"No."

"Are you a cop?"

I forced a laugh. "Of course not." I unzipped my pack, revealing my binocs and birding guide. "Bird-watcher, see?"

He curled his lip. The woman moved to the cooler and removed a can of soda. I noticed a plastic bag with the Lake House restaurant's logo on it. Leftovers, no doubt. The girl pulled the tab of the can and took a sip.

"We've been here a week or two." Dom walked over to the girl and held out his hand. She gave him the can, he took a long pull, then returned it to her.

"Planning on staying long?"

"We'll see. Tam and me like to move around. See the sights." He turned to his young companion. "Isn't that right, babe?"

"That's right." She popped open one of the folding chairs and sat. Her feet were bare and she dug her toes into the earth.

"Speaking of seeing things, did you hear about the murder?"

"Murder?" asked Dom.

I looked back the way I'd come. "I don't mean to spook you, but it happened not far from here." The woods suddenly seemed such a gloomy, foreboding place.

"We can take care of ourselves." Dom appeared confident.

I turned my attention to the young woman. "Maybe you saw something?"

Dom eyed me in icy silence. Was he afraid of me or sullen by nature?

"Or heard something? It happened Tuesday night."

I waited a long time for an answer.

Finally, it was the girl who spoke. "We haven't seen anything." She smiled at me. "Lots of deer. And raccoons. They are terrible pests. Always trying to get into our food."

"I can imagine," I commiserated. I would not want to be camping out in these woods for some indeterminate amount of time, no matter what the season. I was very partial to firm mattresses. And soft pillows.

"If I catch one of the obnoxious critters," Dom said, "it is going to be our dinner."

In the unlikely event these two ever asked me to supper, I'd pass on the invitation.

"Speaking of dinner, I bet you enjoyed your steaks at the Lake House the other night. They're famous for them."

Dom's mouth twitched before he spoke. "I don't know what you're talking about. Steak!" He turned to his companion. "You hear that, babe? She thinks we're dining on steaks!" He slapped his leg. "You see how we're living out here? Do we look like we're dining on steak and potato dinners?" He shook his head. "That's a hoot. You're a hoot, lady."

There was no sense in arguing with him about what I had seen with my own eyes. He'd only continue to deny it. I made a mental note to check with the restaurant. Hopefully, there would be a credit card receipt to show they had been there.

Why were they lying to me? Did they have something to hide, or was it simply that they mistrusted me and wanted to protect their privacy? "My cousin tells me you were looking around the Shermans' yard last week. He said you were snooping."

"Your cousin doesn't sound very bright." Dom spat between his feet.

I couldn't argue with him there, but wasn't about to go down that road with him. Besides, when it comes to family, I always defend them. "He saw you both."

"We weren't snooping, we were poking," explained Tam. "Chick told us we could."

"That's right, we had permission. He gave us some stuff he thought we might be able to use. Like those chairs," he said, pointing to the folding chair that his girlfriend now occupied.

"How did you meet him?"

"We ran into him in the woods," explained Dom.

"He liked to walk out here with that hound of his," put in Tam. "He claimed it helped him to think through his problems."

I drew my brows together. "Problems? What kind of problems?"

"I don't know," said the girl. "Just problems. We've all got problems, right?"

"He was a nice enough sort. He asked where we were living and we showed him."

"That's when he said that if there was anything we needed and it was lying around his yard, that we should help ourselves." Tam leaned back in her chair and extended her legs, wiggled her toes.

I gave her answer some thought. Had she and Dom taken Chick's invitation a little too far? Had he caught them stealing, and when confronting them paid the ultimate price?

"You can ask him yourself. He didn't even charge us."

Either the two were playing dumb or they didn't know Chick Sherman was dead. "The man you're talking about is dead. Like I told you, there was a murder nearby. Somebody killed Chick Sherman, then tried to make it look like an accident." I watched them both carefully but neither so much as blinked.

"I told you this place wasn't safe," the girl said finally. She finished her soda and tossed the empty can in the ring of stones.

"Yeah," replied Dom. "Maybe we should be moving along. Robbery is one thing, but murder?" He shook his head. "That's a whole other thing."

"Robbery?"

"Somebody ransacked our campsite and—" Tam stopped when Dom chopped his hand in the air.

Whatever she had been about to say was lost forever. "I wouldn't leave without talking to the police, if I were you. They may want to interview you."

"What for?" Dom's dark brows bunched together.

"They're the police. That's what they do. The two of you may have seen or heard something and not recognized its significance." Or they were hiding something, because they were sure acting squirrelly.

"We haven't." Dom locked his arms across his chest. "I heard you tell Tam that you were lost." He grabbed me by the shoulder and turned me around. "There's a small road that the forestry service uses about fifty yards straight ahead. Turn right when you get there and that will take you back to the main road."

I took a few steps, then stopped. "One more thing," I said, though I knew for my own safety I probably shouldn't have. "Do either of you own a tire iron?"

"Tire iron?" The side of Dom's face twisted up. Tam had joined him and held his hand. "Lady, we don't even own a car."

16

I had no trouble finding the road that my new friend Dom had enlightened me about. It was nothing more than a couple of undulating rutted dirt tracks, half overgrown with weeds and prickly bushes. I followed it to the main road. If it hadn't been pointed out to me, I might never have known it existed.

And if one knew the track existed, it provided a short and discreet route to the Sherman homestead. It wasn't the best of roads, but even the Kia could have made it up and down without too much trouble.

Tired but determined, I followed the main road to the secondary road I had come in on and sometime later found my van right where I'd left it.

I'd never been so happy in my life to sit down. I unclasped my pack and threw it in the rear of the van, then climbed in the driver's side. I started the engine and cranked up the heater. I discovered a half-empty water bottle on the floor of the front passenger side that didn't look too nasty and drank gratefully. My lips were dry and cracked. I pulled a tube of lip balm from my purse and applied a generous coat.

As I did, a squarish maroon sedan rattled past me. I dropped my purse on the seat and studied the vehicle. Trudy Sherman was at the wheel, the dog, Princess, riding shotgun.

Trudy was driving with one hand on the wheel. In her other hand was a cell phone and she'd been deep in conversation with someone.

I put my van in gear and slowly followed as the sky grew grayer and darker.

Trudy had parked her Camry directly in front of the porch steps. She stood outside the car, bundled in a deep red shawl. Princess danced around the yard.

I eased to a stop behind the Camry and climbed out.

"Are you following me?" demanded Trudy.

"No, I was out bird-watching in the woods nearby. I saw you go by. I guess you didn't notice me. You were on the phone."

She tilted her head at me.

"I thought you didn't believe in cell phones. Didn't you say they caused some sort of disruption in the psychic waves?"

"Death requires change," Trudy said rather enigmatically.

"I wanted to see about buying the remainder of the Audubon prints."

"Audubon prints?" She dug around in the oversize woven tapestry purse on her left shoulder.

"Don't you remember? You husband sold me one the last time I was here. I was hoping to purchase more. And since I happened to see you passing by . . ." I shrugged and gave her my best *look how charming I am* smile.

She wasn't buying.

Trudy shook her head. A ring of keys, not unlike the set I'd seen Parker with earlier, hung from her finger. "I really must be going."

"But if I could just take a look—"

A small smile played across her face. "Some other time, perhaps." She called to the dog, who came quickly and climbed the porch steps. Princess sat at the door, wagging her tail.

"I understand."

Trudy turned toward the house.

"You know, some of those sketches might be quite valuable. You should be careful with them."

Trudy stopped and turned. "What exactly are you trying to say, Ms. Simms?"

"I have to admit, I came by the house earlier and Parker Sudsbury was here. He let me inside the house."

"And?"

"I didn't see any more of the Audubon sketches or the set of books that I saw the first time I was here."

"Why the profound interest in these things, Ms. Simms? Are you a collector? Do they hold some extraordinary significance to you?"

"No, but they may be quite valuable."

Trudy turned her back and trod up the wood steps to the porch. There, she stopped, trained her hypnotic eyes on me, and said, "Nothing is so valuable as life, Ms. Simms." She pulled her lips tight. "You should remember that."

I stood frozen in place as first Princess and then she disappeared into the house, closing the door behind them.

As worn out and hungry as I was, I was hungrier for answers. I drove past my house and kept on going until I reached the long, sloping drive that led to the sprawling acreage of Rolling Acres, the senior living facility where Karl and Floyd now lived.

When I'd first met Floyd Withers, he'd been recently widowed and living alone in the house that he and his wife had occupied throughout their married lives. Now she was gone and he had a one-bedroom condo in Rolling Acres' main building. Karl occupied a larger, two-bedroom bungalow on a separate section of the grounds called the West Village. There were three bungalows to each one-story brown brick building. Each bungalow had a private patio.

Though it was very nearly dark, both Karl and Floyd were outside in the parking lot, jackets zipped to their necks, hard at work on their newly purchased Chrysler.

I tooted the horn as I angled into the empty space beside them. I trained my headlights at the side of their car and rolled down my window. "Looking good, guys! But I think you could use some extra light!"

Karl, who'd had his head buried beneath the hood of the car and was fussing with the engine, looked up. He had a long yellow-handled screwdriver in his hand. "Hi, Amy. I'm giving Miss B a last-minute tune-up."

I turned off the ignition but left the headlights on. I climbed out and inspected the vehicle. "Miss B?"

Floyd poked his head up from inside. He had a damp white rag in his hand. "A car's got to have a name, Amy."

I laughed. "If you say so." I took a look back at my own sorry vehicle. I realized I had been neglecting the van. I couldn't remember the last time I'd washed it, vacuumed it, or even checked the air in the tires. And I had never even considered naming her.

"What brings you here, bird lady?" Karl wiped the length of his screwdriver with his shirttail.

I ran over my day with them, giving them the highlights of my talks with Parker Sudsbury, Trudy Sherman, and the two campers.

"You've been busy," Karl said. He had been fiddling with his engine as we talked. A table lamp sat precariously atop the engine block. An orange extension cord hung from the car, snaked over the lawn, and disappeared somewhere over the patio wall.

"Shouldn't you be using a flashlight?" I watched him and the table lamp anxiously. "Or one of those shop lights?"

"Nah," Karl grunted. "This is fine." He played with some thingamabobs and wires on the engine.

Floyd hopped out from the front passenger-side door. "I've got the interior polished up and ready to go." He wiped his face with the rag he'd been using on the leather interior. "I sure wish we had more time to work on her."

Karl stopped what he was doing. "Don't worry. We'll have all next year to work on her." He slapped the fender. "Miss B is really going to shine this time next year." He turned to Floyd. "Like I told you, this is a dry run."

"I know," replied Floyd. "All we want to do is be part of the parade."

"I'm surprised you were able to get in at the last minute. I've heard that Sudsy, that is, Mrs. Sudsbury, can be really strict about who gets in. Especially latecomers."

"I told you not to worry. Nobody says no to Karl Vogel." Karl winked at me.

"Besides," Floyd added, "she said there had been a cancellation."

"Lucky for you."

"No luck necessary," protested Karl. He shoved the screwdriver inside his jacket pocket and laid his hands on the hood of the car.

He released the rod holding it up and started to pull the hood down.

"Whoa!" I said as I grabbed for the table lamp before it became a casualty of his carelessness.

"Careful," warned Karl. "You almost got your hands chopped off."

I stifled a response as I set the lamp on the blacktop and unplugged it from the extension cord before there were any further mishaps. "Have you heard anything from Jerry that might lead you to think that he's closing in on Chick's killer, Karl?" Karl had been the chief up until he retired, and Jerry had been chief of police ever since. Jerry relied on Karl for his expertise in all police-related matters.

Something for which I was sure the Town of Ruby Lake was grateful.

"Not so much. Jerry tells me they had the dog out sniffing around the Sherman property, and the dog and the officers with him came up empty." Karl started wrapping the extension cord around his arm. "They are pretty sure he was struck pretty good on the back of the head. Probably killed him."

"And then they laid him under the car." I shivered at the cold-bloodedness of the act.

"Who would do such a thing?" Floyd said. He had walked to the patio and unplugged the other end of the cord. He held it out to Karl, who took it and tied it through the cord held now between his palm and his elbow.

"Probably a man," Karl said.

"What makes you say that?" I asked.

"Chick wasn't a little guy."

I nodded. I'd seen him up close and personal. "You're saying a man because it would have been hard for a woman to drag him under the car."

Karl shrugged. "Hard but not impossible."

"Do you think Trudy could have done it?"

"You think gypsy lady did it?" Karl asked.

I tossed my hands in frustration. "Honestly, I have no idea."

Karl chuckled. "That makes you and Kennedy even."

"I did notice at the Shermans' house today that some Audubon books and sketches that I had seen the day of Chick's murder were no longer there."

"Did you tell Jerry that?" Karl looked intrigued.

I pushed out my lip. "Come to think of it, no."

"Sounds like you'd better. You had better tell him about those two youngsters you say are camping in the woods out near there, too."

I frowned. "That's what Derek said."

"Smart man." Karl tossed the cord over his shoulder.

"I like him," said Floyd.

"Me too," I said with a grin. I thought about what Parker Suds-bury had hinted at concerning Chick Sherman and Sally Potts. "Remember Sally Potts?"

"Sally Potts. Sally Potts." Karl repeated the name over and over as if to stir up distant memories. "Can't say as I do, Simms."

"I do," Floyd said. "She went on that bird walk with us, right? Red hair? Green eyes?"

"That's her," I answered.

"You're losing it, Karl," Floyd said. "Why do you ask, Amy?"

"Parker Sudsbury suggested that Chick Sherman and her might have been involved."

Floyd's head jerked. "I don't think so. I don't know her well, but I've seen her in church."

"Is there a Mr. Potts?" Sally had come to a couple of bird walks but never said much and had always come alone.

"I don't know. Sorry."

"Don't worry about it. It's probably nothing. Parker also suggested that I might have killed Mr. Sherman myself if he made a pass at me."

"That's preposterous!" Karl snorted.

"I never did like those Sudsburys," Floyd said.

"I'm beginning to like them less and less myself. You don't suppose Parker killed his cousin, do you, Karl?"

Karl ran his hand along his collar. "What would be the motive? It can't be money. The Sudsburys have plenty."

I shrugged helplessly. "I should add that Parker also told me that Trudy thinks I killed her husband."

Floyd gasped. "Parker Sudsbury needs to learn to hold his tongue."

"If he doesn't," Karl said, picking up his tool box in his free hand, "somebody might just cut it out for him one of these days." He glanced at the darkening sky. "Lock up Miss B, would you, Floyd?"

"Sure thing. Coming in for a drink, Amy?" Floyd extracted a car key from his pocket.

"Yeah, come on in, Simms. We'll order up a pizza and play some poker. What do you say, nickel ante?"

"No. Thank you, but I can't. It's been a long day." I'd also been talked into playing poker once before with Karl and some of his cronies living at Rolling Acres. Those nickels had turned into a twenty-dollar loss for me. "Besides," I said, turning to the van, "I think my headlights are beginning to dim." My headlights had been aiming at the Chrysler 300's middle; now they were drooping nearer the lower frame.

Floyd pulled at his mustache. "I hope you've got enough juice left to start her."

"No worries if you don't." Karl patted Miss B's roof. "This Chrysler could jump up a Saturn five rocket."

I got behind the wheel and turned the key. Nothing.

"Give it a minute and try again," suggested Floyd.

I did. After a minute, I crossed my fingers and turned the key and the engine sprang to life. I pushed my head out the window and waved. "I'll see you boys there tomorrow!"

"Count on it!" called Karl.

And I was.

What I hadn't been counting on was the Lord of Death following me there.

17

I returned home. Birds & Bees was closed. I climbed the stairs, wishing, not for the first time, that I could afford an elevator. I knocked on Paul's door, but he wasn't answering. He was either next door at the biergarten or still in avoid-Amy mode.

I keyed the door to my apartment and was welcomed with the mouthwatering aroma of chicken potpie. "Hi, Mom."

My mother stood in the kitchen, wearing a black knit dress and white apron. "Where have you been? Dinner is almost ready."

"Sorry," I said. "Do I have time to shower?" I went to the kitchen and kissed her cheek.

"We'll make time." Mom gave me a gentle shove toward the bathroom. "Besides, we're still waiting on Ben and Derek."

"Oh?" I called from the bathroom door. "A double date, eh?"

Mom smiled. "I suppose you could call it that."

I took a shower then dressed in a nice pair of slacks and a blue sweater that I'd bought weeks ago but had yet to wear. Tonight was the night.

When I returned to the living room, Ben and Derek were already there, seated at the bar across from the stove, drinks in hand.

Derek rose and kissed me. "You look nice." He took a sniff. "Smell nice, too."

"Thanks," I said, feeling my cheeks go pink. "Actually, it's Mom's perfume."

"I thought something smelled familiar," Ben quipped.

"Hello, Ben. Good to see you again." Derek's father, Ben, was a suave, sixtyish gentleman with rich black and silver hair and a sturdy Roman nose. Though Derek and his daughter, Maeve, shared blue eyes, Ben's were brown.

I pulled up an extra barstool we kept in the corner of the kitchen and joined them.

Mom peeked in the oven to check on the potpie.

"I had no idea you were coming," I said. Derek reached for the bottle of red wine on the counter and poured me a glass as I talked. "Not that I'm not delighted to see you."

I squeezed Derek's warm neck. He wore a pair of brown pants and an ecru long-sleeved Henley-style shirt. Ben was wearing gray trousers and a white turtleneck sweater.

"Barbara has asked me to help sell her delicious Barbara's Bird Bars at the festival," explained Ben.

"Delicious?" I said. "How would you know, have you tasted one?" I'd accidentally tasted an earlier version of Mom's homemade bird-food bar and *delicious* was not the word that came to my mind.

Ben chuckled and took a sip of his wine. "Delicious is what I'm going to tell everyone. Your mother has asked me to hand out samples on a tray outside the trailer."

"Samples? Mom, what are you thinking? What if people actually think they are for humans and try to eat them?"

Mom frowned. "I hadn't thought about that. Maybe it isn't such a good idea . . ." She looked at Ben for an answer.

"Don't worry, Barbara. I'll warn everyone that these are for their backyard birds, not themselves."

"That reminds me," I said. "You guys don't have even a single bird feeder at your place."

"That's true," Ben said. "I ought to have a feeder in the yard." He chuckled. "I don't know why I hadn't thought about it sooner."

I patted his knee. "Come by the store and pick one up. My treat."

"I couldn't," protested Ben with a wave of his hands. "I always pay for what I get."

"Then consider it payment for working for Mom tomorrow." I winked at my mother. "We Simms women always pay for what we get."

"That's the truth," Mom said, her back to us as she carefully pulled the chicken potpie from the oven. "Dinner is served. Everybody to the table."

As we headed to our seats, I pulled Derek aside. "Don't worry, I'll get you a feeder, too."

"Where would I put it?" he protested. "Are you forgetting that I live in a second-floor apartment above the law office?" He laughed as he pulled out my chair. "I don't even have a balcony."

"I've got you covered," I explained, taking my seat. "I'll get you a window feeder."

"Window feeder?"

"It's got little suction cups. All you have to do is fill it and stick it to the glass."

Derek sat down beside me, a dubious look on his face.

"Don't worry," I said. "You can handle it." I took his hand. "And if you play your cards right, I might just come by once a week with free refills."

"Now that I can handle." Derek leaned forward and kissed my nose. I blushed.

"How's the investigation going, Amy?" Ben asked as he folded his napkin across his lap. Mom moved around the table serving up steaming portions of potpie. I would have helped, but Mom was in her element and takes great joy in serving others.

"Investigation?" I said, leaning back as Mom shoveled a man-sized portion onto my dinner plate. "Wow, that's a lot, Mom."

"I've seen you eat more, young lady."

"Mom," I complained. I felt my cheeks heat up.

Derek laughed but then quieted down. "Sorry," he said with a smile plastered on his adorable face. "I was laughing with you, not at you."

I pulled a face. "A likely story."

"How *is* the investigation coming?" Derek pushed his fork into the tip of a wedge of potpie almost, but not quite, as large as my own.

"What investigation are you guys talking about?" I asked.

Mom settled in the empty seat nearest the window and beamed when Ben told her how delicious dinner was. "I'm sure they're talking about how you're looking into the unfortunate death of Chick Sherman, dear."

I dropped my fork and swiveled my head at Derek and his dad. "What makes you think that?"

Derek and his father exchanged a look. "What else would you be doing?" Derek said. "You're hardly ever in your store—"

"Don't I know it," muttered my mother.

"Not helping," I quipped back at her.

"So what else could you be doing?" continued Derek.

I folded my arms over my chest. "For your information, I was out bird-watching this afternoon."

"Really?" Derek asked. "Where did you go? Did you spot any interesting species?"

"Out near the lumber yard. There are some nice, secluded forests there. When are we going to get you out bird-watching?"

"I'd like that," Derek said. "Maybe when work calms down."

I leveled my eyes at him. "You've been saying that for weeks."

"The lumber yard?" Ben squinted his eyes at me. "Isn't that out near the Sherman house?"

Derek chuckled.

"Maybe," I muttered.

"Maybe?" Derek chided.

"Okay, fine." I jammed my fork into my potpie and pulled out a hunk of potato and carrot. "I wanted to take a look around."

"Did you find anything?" Mom asked.

"There's a creepy couple living in a tent not far from the Sherman house. You remember, Mom, the young man and woman that Riley was talking about?"

"Yes, I remember. Riley was of the opinion that they might have murdered Mr. Sherman."

Ben looked at my mom, then turned to me. "Really? You spoke with them, Amy? What's your opinion in the matter?"

I gave the question some serious thought. "Maybe. They might have murdered him. At first they denied knowing him, but later admitted to not only knowing him but claiming that he'd given them some things."

"Such as?"

"Some old folding chairs."

"Hardly something worth murdering over, even if he asked for them back." Derek rose, crossed to the counter, and returned with the wine. He refilled our glasses.

"I agree. But there are a lot more valuable things, probably more valuable than anyone, including the Shermans, was aware of, in that house."

"Like those Audubon sketches and books you were telling me about?" Derek returned to his seat and didn't say no when my mother offered him seconds on the chicken potpie.

"That's right." I settled my elbows on the table. "And when I talked to Trudy Sherman about them—"

"You talked to Trudy?" interjected Mom.

"Yes." I explained how I'd spotted her driving home and stopped to have a chat with her.

"It doesn't sound like she was very friendly," Ben said.

"She has just lost her husband," Mom said. "And in such a brutal fashion."

Ben squeezed Mom's hand. "You're right, Barbara."

"Did Trudy tell you anything that might suggest that she knows who her husband's killer could be?" Derek asked.

"No." I shook my head. "And when I asked her about the sketches, she pretty much told me to mind my own business."

"Perhaps that's not a bad idea," Derek said. "There's somebody very dangerous loose out there. If they think you're getting close to finding them out . . ." He left the thought unspoken. We all knew what he meant.

"I know, but I promised—"

"Promised what?" Derek looked at me carefully.

"I promise I'll be careful." I'd almost blurted out that I'd promised Paul I'd look into the matter.

Derek leaned back and tilted his head.

"Parker Sudsbury was there at the house, too," I added, trying to move the subject off what I had almost let slip.

"At the Sherman house?" Ben asked.

"Yes. He let me inside. And guess what?"

"What?" Ben said.

"Practically all of the Audubon sketches were gone. The books, too."

"That is odd," my mother said, still working on her first small sliver of potpie.

"Maybe, maybe not," Derek said. "Somebody could have moved them or bought them."

"That's what Parker suggested, but I think Parker might have taken them himself. The trunk of his car was open and when I tried to take a look inside, he practically slammed it shut in my face." The more I thought about it, the more certain I was. "Think about it. He had keys and probably knows his way around his cousin's place. That gives him means and opportunity."

"The only thing missing is motive," Derek said. "Any theories why Parker would murder Chick?"

"I can think of a few," I said. The problem was, none of them were all that good. "Money, maybe?"

"Why would Parker Sudsbury murder his cousin over money?" Ben said, his voice filled with doubt. "The Sudsburys are quite well-to-do. I hardly can consider that he might be stealing from his dead cousin."

"What if Parker was having an affair with Trudy?" I blurted out.

"Amy!" my mother looked shocked.

"What?" I said from across the table. "It's possible, isn't it?"

"I suppose." Mom quickly polished off her remaining potpie and went to the fridge for the pumpkin cheesecake she'd made us for dessert.

"But it doesn't explain what happened to the Audubon stuff," Derek said.

Ben placed his chin on his hand. "How valuable are we talking, Amy?"

I told him what I had discovered on the internet about the potential prices of the books and sketches.

"Of course, that's if it's all authentic," Derek added.

I nodded. "Yes, if they are authentic." I frowned. "If I had my sketch, I could at least get that one appraised. That would tell us something." It would tell me whether I was on the right track on figuring out why Chick Sherman was killed.

If I were as clairvoyant as Trudy Sherman claimed to be, I might have known where that sketch was and when it would be discovered.

"Somebody should talk to those kids you saw in the woods," Mom suggested.

Derek nodded. "You should let Chief Kennedy know about them."

"Are you sure you can't do it?" I begged.

"Why me?"

"Because he'll take the lead more seriously coming from you." I rubbed his forearm through the shirt. "You know how Jerry feels about me."

"Sorry," Derek said with a shake of the head. "But you're the one who talked to them. He'll want to hear what you have to say."

I pulled a face. "Fine," I said. I reached for the plate of cheese-cake that Mom was sliding under Derek's nose. "But no cheesecake for you!" I stuck my tongue out at him.

Before I knew what was happening, Mom snatched the big hunk of cheesecake she had just served me and handed it to Derek.

Derek grinned and dug in with his dessert fork. "Thanks, Barbara."

"Yeah," I said out of the side of my mouth. "Thanks, Mom."

Mom chuckled. "Any time, dear."

As Mom offered me up a slice of cheesecake, I thought about all the suspects I had uncovered. "Dom and Tam, Trudy Sherman, and Parker Sudsbury." I ticked them off on my fingers. "I suppose I should include Paul, but he seemed more like a patsy than a killer."

"Paul?" Derek said with amazement.

"Why would you suspect Paul, Amy?" asked my mother, also surprised.

I couldn't tell them everything, but I could tell them what they already knew. "He was the last person to see Chick Sherman alive. Except for the killer."

Ben pointed his dessert fork at me. "That's correct. Except for the killer."

"My money is on Parker Sudsbury. I may not have it all figured out yet but, if you ask me, he's behind this. And I'm going to be keeping a close eye on him at the festival tomorrow."

18

Cousin Riley wrapped his hands around the travel mug I'd pre-pared for him. His faded green John Deere tractor idled like a snoring lion beside us. It was a 1943 model with a hand starter, and Riley was inordinately proud of it. He'd had it for about five years now and kept it out at his mother's house. Aunt Betty's house sits on twenty acres at the edge of town.

Paul yawned as he loaded the last of the kegs in the trailer. "Take it easy driving downtown, Riley." He cast a loving look at the Birds & Brewsmobile. "Let's get her there in one piece."

"Don't worry," promised Riley, sliding open the little doohickey atop the cup to take a sip of strong black coffee. "We'll get her there." He turned to me. "You ready, Amy?"

"Ready as I'll ever be." I pulled the collar of my coat up around my neck and wished I'd worn a thicker shirt underneath the sweater that was underneath my fleece coat. Because I'd be at the festival on business, I'd chosen my khaki slacks and a raven-black Birds & Bees–logoed long-sleeve polo. Thankfully, the temperature was pre-dicted to rise into the upper fifties once the sun decided to join us. Hopefully, I wouldn't freeze.

Personally, the sun couldn't come soon enough for me. I loved looking at stars as much as the next person, but that didn't mean I wanted to wake up with them.

"Are you sure we have everything?" I asked them both once more.

"Stop fretting, Amy," said Riley. "Whatever we lack, Rhonda will bring by later when she comes with my pickup. She and Aunt Bar-bara already made arrangements."

I smothered a yawn and hopped onto the secondary tractor seat that Riley had rigged up to the right and slightly behind the tractor's attached seat. My makeshift seat was nothing more than a spare tractor seat that Riley had bought at a flea market. Chick Sherman had made him a quick-release catch for the springy seat because Cousin Rhonda liked to ride around with Riley sometimes. Now it was my turn.

There was barely room for my butt on the seat, which was itself nothing more than a hard, cold, green spoon. I moved up and down tentatively, testing the seat's safety. I had no faith that it would hold my weight or hold up long enough to get us downtown.

"Are you sure about this?" I did not want to get mangled beneath the tractor's gigantic tires. "Doesn't this thing have seat belts?"

Cousin Riley ignored me. He climbed behind the wheel, took his own seat, and shifted the behemoth into gear. "Hold on tight!" he hollered as we lurched forward with the Birds & Brewsmobile in tow.

It took us about twenty-five loud and tooth-rattling minutes to reach the square. "Brilliant," I said as Riley maneuvered our trailer up against the curb, directly on the square and right across the street from the Theater on the Square. This was nearly the perfect location and we were one of the first vendors to set up.

I jumped down. Never had I been more grateful to be on solid, unmoving ground. My legs wouldn't stop shaking. I rubbed my hands up and down my thighs.

Riley killed the motor and I reveled in the relative silence. "Look good, Amy?"

"Looks perfect. Thanks, Riley." I walked with him to the back of the trailer and we started undoing the hitch and leveling the Birds & Brewsmobile. I looked across the street to the nearly empty parking lot. "What time does Parker Sudsbury get here?"

"Parker?" Riley pulled off his gloves. "Around nine, I suppose. He comes in early to check in the cars. His wife drives in separately. She usually has breakfast with some of the sponsors first."

I digested the information. From our location, I'd have a good view of Parker Sudsbury and his activities. The streets surrounding the town square were closed to motorized traffic for the event, except for registered participants.

Mom would be coming by later. Kim would be left alone in the store for the afternoon because Esther was attending the festival as well, to my surprise. More surprising was that Karl and Floyd were picking her up for the occasion.

Paul said he had business to attend to and would get to the square in time for serving beer, which wasn't allowed before noon. Mom and I would be selling all things bird related, including her Barbara's Bird Bars, once we opened around tenish, maybe sooner if the crowds picked up early. Ben was still promising to come by and shill for my mother, bless his heart.

Derek was attending the festival with Maeve, so I knew I'd be seeing him sooner or later. I only hoped he wouldn't be seeing me wearing my cousin's overalls and a chicken hat.

Speaking of which, after setting up the trailer, I pulled out two large glass jars that had once held pickles and placed them on each end of the flip-down sales counter. Mom had made labels for each, one for me and one for Paul. My charity was a honey-bee conservancy group. Paul's money was pegged to go to the local food bank.

Afterward, I treated my cousin to breakfast and we waited for the festival to get started.

"Say, Amy, did you hear about Esther?"

"What about her?" I asked as the waitress at Coffee and Tea House brought our scones and coffees.

"She says she's thinking of moving to Rolling Acres." Riley poured a gallon of cream into his mug, followed by a ton and a half of sugar. How he was able to defy physics that way, I had no idea.

"Really? She told you that?" My heart quickened and my brain filled with colored party balloons.

"Says she's thinking about it." Riley drank.

I lifted my cup. Esther moving out was certainly something worth thinking about . . .

As the day warmed up, I was able to remove my jacket and hang it up inside our trailer. Cousin Riley had left to set up for the car and tractor parade. I could see him rubbing down his tractor in the TOTS parking lot across the street. Parker Sudsbury stood in a tweed jacket, matching tweed cap, and brown trousers. He clutched a clipboard in his hand and kept referring to it as he talked to various gentlemen and one or two ladies who had cars or tractors showing in the parade.

Among them, I spotted Andrew Greeley's mile-long hearse. He'd been taking part in the parade for as long as anybody could remember. Some folks thought it a bit ghoulish to have a hearse parading in a festival, but nobody dared tell him that.

Aaron Maddley was there with his truck. The old workhorse looked far spiffier than I'd ever seen it. He must have spent dozens of hours doting over it. Dan Sutton was a few rows over, running a red rag over the top of his Trans Am.

I also noticed Gertrude "Gertie" Hammer leaning against the front fender of her pride and joy, an Oldsmobile Delta 88. Gertie was sort of the town curmudgeon. I had no scientific proof, but I was pretty certain she was older than the mountains. I'd bought my house from her. At the time, she thought she'd gotten the better of me but, ever since, she'd been wanting it back.

I think it irked her that I was making a go of the place. I considered us even—I'd inherited Esther from Gertie.

"Hungry?"

I turned. Derek stood there. He was wearing comfortable blue jeans, hiking boots, and a gray hoodie under which a blue tee peeked. He had an order of apple fries in one hand and an apple margarita in the other.

"Derek! How did you find me?" I'd had little hope of seeing him. The crowds were thick as flies on a wet horse, as my aunt would say.

Derek goggled at the Birds & Brewsmobile. "Are you kidding? Who can miss a giant red birdhouse?"

He was right. And Paul had really been right about the drawing power of the hokey trailer. I said a silent prayer to the man who'd been responsible for its initial creation. Without him, there would be no Birds & Brewsmobile. And now there was no him . . .

Derek laid a hand on my shoulder. It was the hand holding the aromatic apple fries. "You okay?"

"What, yeah?" I ran my fingers through my hair even as I took in a whiff of fried heaven. "Fine."

"These are for you."

"Bless you." I snatched an apple fry from the paper tube and popped it in my mouth. Then I relieved him of his load. "Thanks."

The deep-fried apple treats were cut into the shape of a French fry, rolled in cornstarch, deep-fried, then sprinkled with cinnamon and sugar.

Derek appeared amused. "It was either the French fries or the fried okra. I seem to have made the right choice."

"A better way to get a daily serving of fruit has yet to be invented." I grabbed another couple of fries and washed them down with a sip of margarita. "I was famished."

Derek kissed me and I spilled the margarita on his arm. He laughed and brushed away the green slush.

"Sorry." I helped him wipe up with a napkin I grabbed from the stainless steel dispenser on the counter of the Birds & Brewsmobile.

"No problem." He kissed me again and stole a couple of fries. "How's your day going?" He swiveled his head around the crowd. "I don't see my dad. Is he here?"

I nodded and arched up on my tiptoes. "He's here somewhere." I scanned the thick sea of heads.

"I sent him for some more packages of sunflower seeds!" Mom called from within our trailer.

Derek waved. "Hi, Barbara."

"Hello, Derek." She rested her hands on the counter and leaned out. "Where's your daughter?"

"Maeve's with her mother." He pushed up the left sleeve of his hoodie and looked at his watch. "I'm supposed to meet up with them in a few minutes."

I walked with him to the counter and offered Mom an apple fry. I knew she wouldn't like the margarita. She wasn't much of a drinker except for wine. Paul had insisted she try one of his beers and, to her consternation, hadn't been able to stop burping.

"Can I bring you anything, Barbara?" Derek inquired.

"No, thanks. I'm good. Ben promised to bring us sandwiches."

"Not too tired?" I asked.

My mother shook her head and pointed. "I've got the stool Paul brought if I need to get off my feet."

Paul had been thoughtful enough to bring the padded barstool over from his biergarten for Mom's comfort. "Where is Paul? Shouldn't he be helping you?" His colorful beer-stein-and-coaster cap sat at the end of the counter. I was surprised he hadn't sent over any extra help from the biergarten.

"He said he was going to fetch some more cases and another keg," Mom answered. She moved to talk to a customer. "Rhonda's pitching in, too."

I didn't see my cousin Rhonda anywhere. "What time is she coming?"

"She's already here. She left to help Paul."

I couldn't help frowning. Rhonda should have been here, not out assisting Paul, a fully capable, able-bodied man. I hoped she returned soon. It was going to be a long day and Mom was going to need all the help she could get, including me.

I noticed we'd already sold several of Aaron Maddley's bird-houses, and Mom's bird bars seemed to be selling like hotcakes, which was heartening. It was great to see my mother have a new interest in life. Making and selling the bars had given her something to look forward to in her retirement. Of course, spending time with Ben Harlan also seemed to be having a beneficial effect on her.

"I'll be by later," Derek said. "For the parade."

"Aren't you riding in the Impala with Paul?"

"No. Paul can handle it. I promised Maeve I'd watch the parade with her."

"Okay, have fun." I watched Derek disappear into the crowd and couldn't help feeling a small pang that we wouldn't be spending this lovely afternoon together.

I felt a jab in the ribs and turned. Kim had shown up. "Hey!"

"What are you doing here?" I asked. She wasn't in her Birds & Bees shirt or khaki slacks. She wore an open denim jacket, jeans, and a V-necked orange tee. Her yellow hair blew in the breeze. "Is something wrong at the store?"

"Wrong? No, of course not. It's the big day. I wanted to see who gets crowned Miss Fall Festival Queen." She tugged my sleeve. "Do you think Jerry's daughter will win? What about Derek's daughter? What's her name? Maeve?"

"Yes, Maeve."

"That's right." Kim did a three-sixty spin, taking in the festival. "Did she enter?"

"No, I don't think so." I grabbed Kim's arms and held her in place. "But what are you doing here? Who's watching Birds and Bees?"

Kim looked at me like I'd asked what color the sky was. "It's closed."

"What?" I let go of her arms.

"The store is closed, Amy." She giggled and waved.

I turned to see what she was looking at. It wasn't a what. It was a who. A who named Dan Sutton.

"You closed Birds and Bees?"

"You told me to." Kim said hello to Dan and gave him a quick embrace.

"Hi, Amy."

"Hello, Dan. Aren't you supposed to be getting ready for the parade?"

"I've got a few minutes. I thought I'd enjoy them with Kim."

"You're so cute." She pecked him on the cheek.

I returned my attention to my partner. "Kim, you closed Birds and Bees?" I repeated my question, hoping maybe this time I would get an answer.

"Yep, just like you told me to." Kim looked at Dan and rolled her eyes.

"No," I said slowly. "What I told you was to be sure you locked up when you left."

The corners of her lips perked up. "And I did!" she said brightly.

"Fine," I sighed, recognizing that I'd lost the battle. "Go. Have fun."

Kim grabbed a handful of my fries. "We will."

"Take care," I said to Dan, making shooing motions with my hands. "She's all yours!" It wouldn't kill the bottom line for the store to be closed for the rest of the afternoon.

Kim departed hand in hand with Dan.

I went inside the Birds & Brewsmobile to lend my mother a hand. The Lord of Death sat on the ledge above the sink. "What's that doing here?" I asked Mom.

Mom took a look to see what I was talking about. "I don't know. What is it doing here?"

"Don't look at me." Rhonda appeared in the narrow doorway of the trailer. "I don't have a clue." She dropped a case of beer on the floor. She wore a rose print, knee-length knit dress. Her thick brown hair was arranged in a fifties-style bouffant.

"Huh." I picked him up by the base. "The last time I saw you, you were on Kim's mantel."

"Be right back!" Rhonda said, stepping back outside.

"Where are you going now?" I cried.

"One more trip!" she explained. "I'll be right back!"

"Where's Paul?"

Rhonda paused and did a half turn. "I don't know. He left his camper before I did. I thought he'd be back here by now."

I unpacked the beer and stuck as much as I could in the small refrigerator. I had insisted that Paul disinfect the pint-sized appliance before the event, and he had. Thank goodness.

Through the window of the Birds & Brewsmobile, I spied Derek to the left of a small crowd gathered around the queue for the cups-and-saucers ride. The cups looked like strawberries and the saucers had been designed to look like the stems.

He was talking to Amy-the-ex, who held Maeve's hand. She was the girl's mother and Maeve looked content. I found myself smiling despite the animosity that Derek's ex had for me.

Besides, if it hadn't been for her moving to Ruby Lake, it was quite possible that Derek never would have moved up himself. Ben had been living here for several years. Derek had only recently moved to town when his ex and daughter did.

Why the woman had chosen Ruby Lake, I didn't know. I had heard she was from Delray Beach, Florida. So why had she chosen our little home in western Carolina over sunny south Florida?

Maybe it was because Maeve's grandfather was here.

I rubbed my chin. And maybe she figured if she moved here, then Derek would follow, lured by the draw of his daughter and his father.

I could only wonder.

Officer Pratt strutted by in uniform, apparently on foot patrol. Keeping the crowds safe from overexuberant festival goers.

A man in suspenders, using a bullhorn, announced that the parade would be starting in an hour. There was no sign of Parker, but I knew he had to be around here someplace. I had seen his wife, Sudsy, pass by with a small throng of country club friends. She'd looked with distaste at the Birds & Brewsmobile, then continued on.

As soon as I could get away, I was going to have a word with her husband. I wanted some straight answers for a change. His answers the other day had been as crooked as the Blue Ridge Parkway winding its way through the Smokies.

19

I checked my watch. Roland should have been here already, setting up for his raptor show. I was expecting we'd draw quite a crowd.

As if soaring in on wings, Roland Ibarra swept toward the Birds & Brewsmobile like a bird that had mistaken it for the giant red birdhouse that it had been designed to resemble.

"Whoa! Hold on there!" I cried, holding on to him by his shirt. The heavyset young man wore a baggy black sweatshirt and black denim jeans. In his hand, he held a peregrine falcon who clung to the elbow-length black leather glove on Roland's right hand. The bird's sharp talons sank deep into the worn leather.

"Hello, Amy." Roland brushed a lock of black hair from his eyes. "Sorry I'm late."

"Don't apologize. You're not late." I double-checked my watch. "But you're not early either. I'd like to get started as soon as you're ready so we don't butt up to the parade."

Roland nodded. "No problem." He handed me a glove that had been tucked into his belt. "Here."

"What's this for?"

"I need you to hold on to Roscoe while I go get the rest of the birds."

I backed away from him. "Oh no, you don't." I waved my hand at him. "I'm not holding Roscoe."

He pulled a face. "You've got to, Amy. I have to get the rest of the birds." He looked at me sternly. "Some of the other birds are afraid of him."

"I'm more than a little afraid of him myself!" I took another step back. The bird's striking blue-black wings glistened in the sunlight.

"Put on the glove. Please?"

"Where's your assistant?"

"She couldn't make it. She's down with the flu."

"And she's too sick to help with a couple of birds?"

Roland tilted his head at me. "I can't have the birds around sick people. Come on," he urged. "Put on the glove."

"I'm supposed to be helping my mother in the trailer."

"Don't worry, I've got it, dear!" Mom cried over the heads of a couple young men ordering brews. "And, look, here comes Rhonda!"

Good grief. Sometimes my mother was no help at all. "Fine." I twisted my lips and took the glove, against my better judgment. The glove went easily over my hand and was, in fact, far too large for me. I jiggled my hand and the leather glove wobbled loosely. "He better not bite my nose off."

"Tsk-tsk. Roscoe hasn't bitten anybody's nose off in over a week now."

I gasped, my fingers flying to my nostrils.

"It's a joke, Amy."

"It had better be." I cringed as Roland coaxed the bird from his arm to mine.

"There, see? Nothing to it." Roland stroked the bird's head. "I'll be right back."

I moved very carefully to the side of the trailer, wanting to keep Roscoe calm and out of the sight of the festival-goers. If anything spooked him, I feared it would be the devil to hold him in place despite the leather strap attached to his left foot.

I waited with bated breath while Roland made not one but two trips back to his van around the corner. Each time, he brought a caged specimen for the show, including a buzzard, a northern goshawk, an osprey, and a barn owl. In between, my mother hand-fed Roscoe bits of her homemade bird bars. There was still no sign of Paul, so Mom was busy helping to sell Birds & Bees products and pouring plastic cups of beer. Fortunately, Rhonda arrived, tied on a half apron, and pitched in behind the counter.

"Careful," I warned. "Don't let Roscoe eat too much, Mom. He needs his appetite for the show." Twirling a rope in the air with a hunk of raw meat attached to it was one of the best things about Roland's raptor show. It was breathtaking to watch the bird take sight of its prey and swoop in for the proverbial kill.

"That's the last of it," said Roland. "Man, it's crowded out here."

"Sure," I quipped, looking over the caged birds. "Owls and buzzards you bring in cages, but killer peregrine falcons you stroll around with on your arm."

Roland pulled his teeth across his lower lip. "This better go as smoothly as you promised." He looked worriedly at the vendor stall next to us: DEEP-FRIED TURKEY DELITE. "That's exactly what I didn't want."

"Sorry, but don't worry," I vowed. "Nothing can go wrong this time."

I cleared some space near the front of the trailer and urged people to move back and give Roland some room to work his magic. I'd erected an easel with a poster on it advertising the bird show, so a good crowd had already gathered.

"Whenever you're ready, Roland." I waved with my free hand. "Here, take Roscoe."

"In a minute, Amy." Roland squatted and reached for the barn owl, who hopped about inside his two-foot square cage. "I like to start small. Plus, the kids and the parents love seeing the owl up close."

"Okay," I said with a frown. Roscoe wasn't looking happy, and nervously balanced on one foot then the other.

I watched Roland cup the bird in his hands. "Aren't you afraid it will fly away?"

"Wendy is a rescue bird, like all the rest. Her wings were damaged when she was young. She can't fly." He held the bird up and walked to the front of the trailer. A large group had gathered in a semicircle around us, leaving approximately ten feet of open space for Roland and his bird show.

I stood nervously to his right, waiting for his signal to hand him Roscoe. From over the heads of the crowd, I noticed movement in the TOTS parking lot. Were the cars and tractors getting ready to line up for the parade and display already?

Riley sat atop his John Deere, looking proud as a rooster beside about a dozen other tractors of all shapes, sizes, and vintages.

Sure enough, a number of vehicles were starting to line up earlier than I had expected. The crowd pressed closer toward us to make room for the cars and tractors that were now working their way out of the parking lot and into the street. Once all the cars were lined up on

Lake Shore Drive, they would parade once around the town square. There, the drivers would park their vehicles, as instructed, in the street in front of the stage that had been erected for the weekend.

The stage was used for the musical acts, the announcement of the winner of the various ribbons for the car and tractor portion of the festivities, and the highlight of the evening—the crowning of this year's Miss Fall Festival Queen.

Andrew Greeley eased by right behind the bright red antique fire truck owned by the town. Gertie Hammer was directly behind him. There was still no sign of Paul and his Impala. The massive Chrysler 300B that Karl and Floyd had recently purchased soon followed. Karl was at the wheel. Floyd sat near the window on the opposite side.

I squinted. Was that Esther sitting between them?

I noticed a bit of smoke coming from under the sides of the hood of their car. I waved with my free hand. Karl waved back and blasted his horn. Roscoe jumped. "Whoa, bird!' I cooed. "Calm down."

Karl waved again and gunned the engine, a big grin on his face. He was like a kid with a new toy.

Unfortunately, this toy was in trouble.

Smoke began billowing from under the hood and soon obscured the entire front of the car, including the windshield. People started shouting. Karl and Floyd were shouting at each other. Esther had half risen from the bench seat and was clutching her head in her hands.

I struggled to hold Roscoe in my grip.

Suddenly, there was a sound like several gunshots in quick succession and then a sharp crack like firecrackers exploding. Flames leapt from the front of Floyd and Karl's automobile. People were screaming and shouting now.

Roscoe tugged, surprising me. I accidentally let go of the leather strap. The falcon shot into the air above the crowd. My hands dropped to my side as I bent my head skyward. The too-big glove slid off my arm.

More screams filled my ears as I watched the bird climb ever higher, then veer across the street toward a cluster of trees at the rear of the TOTS parking lot.

"Roland!" I hollered madly. "Roscoe's loose!" I spun around.

"So is Wendy!" Roland blurted. "Look out! Look out, everybody!"

Roland had dropped to his knees in the street. "Wendy! Wendy!" He looked anxiously among the sea of legs and feet. "Careful you don't step on her! Careful!" He shot an accusatory look at me. "This is a bird catastrophe, Amy!" He glanced at the sky and moaned, "Poor Wendy. Poor Roscoe."

Oh, no! Poor little Wendy the owl was about to be crushed underfoot. And the peregrine falcon had gotten loose on my watch . . .

Again.

I glanced upward at Roscoe's shrinking profile, then dropped to the ground beside Roland.

"You stay here and take care of Wendy and the others!" I hollered. "I've got this, Roland!"

"Here!" blurted Roland, clearly upset, eyes bulging and nostrils flaring in anger. "Take this!" He thrust his extra leather glove at me.

"Thanks!" I pushed through the crowd, detoured to the turkey cart, and stuck my hand in the metal tray. "Pay you later!" I cried even as I turned and sprinted across the street toward the community theater parking lot.

I ran top speed after the raptor, armed with nothing more than a hot fried turkey leg and the leather handler's glove that Roland had tossed in my face.

I was prepared for battle and I *would* be taking prisoners. And this prisoner had a name, and that name was Roscoe. Most of the cars had left the lot, so I had a clear shot to the trees near the back of the building.

Out of the corner of my eye, I saw Parker Sudsbury near the far end of the building. He appeared to be arguing with someone whose identity was shielded by the large trash bin. His antique car stood near him. Several other vehicles, including Paul's, sat nearby. There was no sign of Sudsbury's wife. He could have been arguing with her, though by everything I'd heard, they seemed to get along as well as any married couple.

When I was done with the raptor, I'd start in on Parker Sudsbury.

The falcon screeched at me. I looked up and scanned the oaks. "There you are!" He sat on a high branch of the middle tree. "Come on, Roscoe," I purred. "Lunch time!" I waved the turkey leg in the air.

Nothing.

I brought the hunk of meat to my nose and sniffed. "Mmm, good." I glanced up. Nothing. Not a peep. He merely twitched his head side to side.

"Take a bite!"

I jerked and turned around. The crowd had followed me across the street. Many had cell phones in their hands. "Are you taking pictures?!"

One beefy man shook his head, his eyes studying his phone as he said, "Not me, I'm shooting a video. Wait until I post this online!" He waved at me. "Go ahead, take a bite, lady!"

"Yeah, you can do it! Come on!" chanted several others in the crowd.

I turned my attention back to the bird and took a bite. "Mmm, yummy. Want some, Roscoe?" It really was quite delicious. I lifted the turkey toward the tree.

Roscoe fluttered his wings.

"Everything under control here?" I heard a voice yell.

I turned and watched Officer Pratt come jogging up. He held an aluminum-handled fishing net in his hands. I felt a jerk. Roscoe had landed atop the turkey leg and was pecking furiously at the cooked flesh.

"Be still," cautioned Officer Pratt. I nodded, keeping my arm stiff and still as I could considering my nerves were shot, as he lowered the green netting gently over Roscoe.

I closed my eyes for a moment, and breathed a sigh of relief. I decided right then and there to forgive Officer Pratt for manhandling me and trying to cuff my hands behind my back like a common criminal.

I handed the netted bird to Officer Pratt.

"You okay?" Concern showed in his eyes.

I nodded. "I just need to sit down a minute. How's Wendy?"

"Wendy?" Officer Pratt's eyes were on Roscoe who, despite being netted, seemed content to nibble on the turkey leg.

"The little owl."

"She's back in her cage."

"Good." I glanced down the alleyway. Parker Sudsbury and his car were gone. My eyes fell on the bicycle rack against the side of the theater. Among the cluster of bikes, two stood out: one red, one yellow. That could only mean that Dom and Tam, my camping friends, were here at the festival.

That meant that all my suspects were here together in one place. I had already seen Trudy Sherman when Riley and I were walking back from breakfast. She had set up a small booth near Jessamine's Kitchen, where she was offering up her fortune-telling skills.

"Come on," Officer Pratt said, moving slowly. "I'll take you back. You really don't look so good."

I walked across the street with Officer Pratt.

Floyd and Karl's big Chrysler had broken down in the middle of the road. A couple of fireman had popped the hood and extinguished the fire. A tow truck had been called in to haul it away to the garage.

Karl scratched his head. "I don't understand it. I tuned Miss B up myself just last night."

Two firemen hovered nearby, sticking around to make sure the fire was completely out. The tow-truck driver hitched a chain to the back bumper of the sad-looking vehicle.

Floyd chuckled. He didn't seem too perturbed by their troubles. Floyd was that kind of guy—most things rolled off his shoulders. Esther clung to his arm.

"Yes, and that might just explain it." Floyd sighed. "I guess we're out of the parade though." The blackened hood of the Chrysler pretty much made that clear.

"Don't worry," I said, giving them each a pat on the back. "There's always next year."

Both men agreed.

"Hey!" Esther tugged hard at the sleeve of my coat. "Your birdhouse is on fire!"

"My what?"

"The Birds and Brewsmobile!"

I turned quickly, my eyes widening as I took in the growing flames licking their way up the tall red roof. "Mom and Rhonda are in there!"

I started running.

20

The firemen who'd been minding Karl and Floyd's Chrysler came running up right behind me.

The flames ran up the backside of the trailer. The door hung open and black smoke obscured the view. There was no sign of Mom or Rhonda. "Mom! I'm coming!" I streaked for the open door.

A muscular fireman held me back, lifting me off my feet. He handed me off to Officer Pratt. I struggled against his arms, which were wrapped around my waist, as effective as a jungle python. "Let me go!" I kicked at him. I was about to unforgive him for handcuffing me the other night.

"Ouch!" Officer Pratt hollered and dropped me.

I surged forward. This time it was Derek who stopped me. "Relax, Amy." He held me in his arms. "Barbara and Rhonda are fine."

"You can't know that!" I pushed my hands against his chest in a futile attempt to free myself.

"Yes, I can," he said softly. He gripped my head gently in his hands and forced me to turn. Mom and Rhonda stood to one side along with the gathered crowd being kept away by the fire brigade and Officers Pratt and Sutton.

They appeared stunned.

Derek walked me over to my cousin and mother. "What happened?" I cried with relief, taking Mom's hand in mine. They both looked perfectly fine. Thank goodness. "Are you okay?"

"Me and Aunt Barbara are fine." Rhonda ran her hands through her bouffant. "I don't know what happened. Do you, Aunt Barbara?"

Mom shook her head. "Not a clue. I am so sorry, dear." She shook her head as she looked at the soot-smudged trailer.

"I'm afraid your mom and I got distracted," confessed Rhonda. "I mean, what with everything going on."

"I'm just glad the two of you are okay. I'd say we're done selling for the day though." I watched as one of the firemen blasted foam at the remaining flames along the bottom of the door. He set the extinguisher on the ground and he and his companion went inside to take a look around. The fire chief, Jefferson McLamb, showed up soon after.

The fire chief was a stocky man in his fifties, with silvery hair. His eyebrows, by contrast, were as dark as charcoal briquettes. He didn't look happy as he talked to his crew.

He glanced over at me, nodded, then approached. "You're the owner of this trailer, young lady?"

I said that I was. "Can you tell me what happened, Chief?"

He tipped back his fire hat, exposing a line of perspiration. "My guess is that the fire was caused by peanut oil and gasoline." He shook his head in disgust. "You got lots of smoke but not too much damage. You're lucky."

"Peanut oil? We don't do any cooking, let alone with cooking oil. And we don't use gasoline."

"I'd better get back to it. We'll look your trailer over with a fine-tooth comb, but we might never know who did it. I hate to admit it, I like to think our town is above such things, but it could have been a prank. You know how kids can be."

"Thanks, Chief." Over his shoulder, I noticed Trudy Sherman standing stoically near the mailbox on the sidewalk, watching.

I looked at my damp and dirty Birds & Brewsmobile. Officers Pratt and Sutton stood outside it and were conferring with the firefighters.

Kim ran over to my side. "What do you think happened?"

I repeated what Chief McLamb had told me.

"I suppose McLamb could be right. It might have been kids."

Had it been a prank? A warning?

Or would we find out it had simply been Cousin Riley's amateurish electrical work?

Mom and Rhonda joined me. I told them what I'd already told Kim. There was no sign of Roland Ibarra or his birds. "Where's Roland?"

"He packed up and left while you were talking to the fire chief," Mom explained.

"He didn't appear happy," added Cousin Rhonda.

"I'm just glad his birds are okay." I'd been scared to death Wendy was going to be crushed underfoot.

"Yes." Mom wrapped her arms around me. "They're all safe and sound."

"Including Roscoe?" I hadn't had a chance to take a close look at him.

"Apparently. He was chomping quite contentedly on that turkey leg even as Roland carried him off."

"Turkey leg!" I ran to the vendor beside me. Several plastic jugs of peanut oil were lined up beneath a table away from the fryer. Now I knew where the oil had come from. The gasoline could have come from anywhere.

"Sorry about your birdhouse, ma'am," replied the teenager manning the turkey fryer.

"Thanks. I owe you for the turkey leg. How much?"

"Six dollars, ma'am."

I realized I didn't have my purse with me. "I'll be right back."

Derek tapped my shoulder. "You okay?"

"Hi. I need to get my wallet. I owe this nice young man for a turkey leg."

Derek chuckled and reached for his billfold in his back pocket. "My treat." He handed the young man a ten-dollar bill and told him to keep the change.

"Fire Chief McLamb said the fire was likely caused by a combination of peanut oil and gasoline."

"That's sick."

"Yeah." The question was: Who was sick enough to have perpetrated the crime? "I don't think this was a mere prank." I turned to the turkey-leg vendor. "I don't suppose you saw anything or anybody around my trailer that shouldn't have been there?"

"Sorry, ma'am," he said with a shrug of his narrow shoulders. The boy was very skinny. Apparently he didn't indulge in fried turkey legs too often himself. "But when all the commotion across the street started, I'm afraid I wasn't paying much attention."

I grinned at him. "I don't blame you." Mom and Rhonda had said the same thing.

"You won't tell my boss, Mr. Nattering, will you?"

Derek and I promised not to.

"If this was a prank, I hope they catch whoever did it. They've done some serious property damage and somebody could have been hurt." There was a hard edge to Derek's voice that I hadn't heard before.

He squeezed my hand. "Riley's going to haul the trailer away after the parade. I'm sorry. Fortunately, the trailer was insured. But Paul's going to take it hard when he finds out."

"Where is Paul?"

"Setting up for the parade. Once the cars are lined up, he said he'll have some time to come by and help." He took a look at the Birds & Brewsmobile. "Not that there's much to do now."

"Are they really planning on still holding the parade? I mean, after Karl and Floyd's car self-destructing and now this." I indicated the ruined Birds & Brewsmobile.

Derek shrugged. "Like they say, the show must go on. I haven't heard anything about it being cancelled."

He was right. Already the crowds that had gathered to witness all the excitement were moving on to other things.

"Sudsy and her husband would probably insist it continue even if the whole town was on fire," I quipped.

"Hey, wait!" called the young man at the turkey stand. He waved a pair of shiny tongs in the air.

"Yes?" I called back.

"Right after all the commotion started and you grabbed that turkey leg from me, I remember I did have a couple of customers. Maybe they saw something."

"Do you remember what they looked like?"

He frowned. "Not really. I see a lot of people at these things. It's tough to remember one from the other." He tilted his head. "Only I do remember the girl. Her hair was sort of funny colored."

"Funny colored?"

"Yeah, you know," he answered. "Like two different colors."

Bells went off in my brain. "Like blue and green? Over on this side of her head?" I patted the left side of my hair.

"Yeah." He pointed the tongs at me. "You got it."

"Thanks," Derek said. "You know them, Amy?" he asked as we moved closer to the others. Kim, Mom, Ben, and Rhonda were huddled together. Dan and Officer Reynolds had joined them. Ben held Mom's elbow as if to comfort her or prop her up.

"It sounds like my two camping friends from the woods near Chick Sherman's house."

"Interesting."

"Very," I agreed. Did they have a hankering for fried turkey, or mayhem and murder?

We all stood around helplessly as the police and fire department finished up their tasks. Surprisingly, there was no sign of Chief Kennedy. "Where's Jerry?" I asked.

Dan answered. "He's with his wife and daughter. The chief said not to disturb him unless it was really necessary. I told him we'd let him know if we needed him."

"We've got this," Officer Reynolds said, sticking his thumbs in his belt.

Officer Pratt pushed through the crowd and joined us.

"Thanks again for helping with Roscoe," I said.

"No problem. I was just seeing to it that Mr. Ibarra was able to get out okay. Traffic is a mess."

"Did he say anything about me?"

Officer Pratt literally guffawed. "Ma'am, he had a lot to say about you." His eyes twinkled in Officers Sutton and Reynolds's direction.

I felt my face heat up. I was spared any further embarrassment by the return of Fire Chief McLamb.

"It's all yours now," Fire Chief McLamb said with a nod. "I'll let you know if we learn anything further, but I wouldn't hold my breath if I was you."

Derek got a text. "It's from Paul. He wants me to come by. You going to be okay? I'll be back as soon as I can."

I promised I would and watched him disappear into the sea of strangers. I peeked inside the trailer. It was a mess and I was in no mood to face it.

The Lord of Death sat unharmed on the ledge above the sink. How had he managed to avoid the flames?

If his presence was an omen, it wasn't a good one.

I lowered the shutters and locked the door, though I knew it was useless. The damage had already been done.

21

"Come on," said Mom, helping me down the step at the rear of the trailer. "I know what will cheer you up."

"What's that?"

"We haven't checked to see who's won the contest."

"But the jars—"

"Don't worry, Rhonda and I saved them." She pointed to the patch of grass beneath a tree where the two glass jars lay nestled against each other.

I started to say that the day wasn't over, but it clearly was for us. "Shouldn't we wait for Paul?"

"Here he comes now." Mom pointed as Paul lumbered across the lawn at an angle behind city hall. There was a big brown sack in his left hand.

"You're just in time," my mother said.

"I came just as soon as I heard!" Paul panted and doubled over. He dropped the bag on the lawn near Kim's feet.

"Where's Derek?"

Paul looked over his shoulder. "I don't know. I texted him, but then I heard somebody say that it was the Birds and Brewsmobile that was on fire so I ran right over."

"I'm sure he'll be back soon, once he sees you aren't with the Impala."

"I'll text him anyway." Paul dug out his phone and shot Derek a quick text. There was a responding beep. Paul nodded. "He says he's on his way back."

"Come on," insisted Mom. She settled herself on the lawn. "I want to see who's won."

"But the trailer?" Paul pointed at his prized Birds & Brewsmobile, looking forlorn and lifeless now.

"There's nothing to be done for it now," Kim said. She was alone again. Dan had gone off with Officer Reynolds. She was going to somehow blame me for spoiling her date, I just knew it.

Mom nodded to Rhonda. "Grab a jar."

I knew what Mom was trying to do. She was trying to distract me from what had happened. It was half working.

We added up the loot behind the Birds & Brewsmobile, out of the wind and the curious eyes of festival goers.

"My, but everyone was very generous," noted my mother as she patiently counted the bills. "Paul," she said, shoving a pile of bills and change back into his jar, "that's two hundred thirty-seven dollars and seventy-nine cents."

"Awesome!" He rubbed his hands together with glee as he eyed my smaller pile.

I squirmed on my butt on the hard ground as Mom slowly counted my pile. "Amy." Mom had dumped my charitable take for the day in her apron and scooped it up and dropped it back inside my jar. She handed me the jar.

"Yes. Tell me, Mom."

"Yes, Barbara," said Paul, "don't keep us waiting."

"Amy—" Mother started to rise and I helped her. I set my jar on the grass. "You collected two hundred thirty-nine dollars and—"

I didn't wait for my mother to finish. "Sorry, Paul." I beamed, though we both knew full well that I was anything but sorry. I was sure the smile plastered on my face underscored the fact. "It looks like I beat you by two dollars."

I patted his arm in consolation. "It seems you'll be playing dress-up today. I hope you have a nice pair of heels to go with your gown." I flicked a lock of hair at the side of his head. "And you might want to get your hair done."

Paul uttered a few oaths that weren't worth repeating.

"Hey, guys." Derek appeared from nowhere. Cousin Riley was with him. Derek pulled out his wallet and dropped a five-spot in Paul's jar. "How's it—"

"No, don't!" I lunged for him.

"—going?" I tumbled into Derek. He caught me in his arms and kissed me hard.

Paul laughed. "Who's laughing now?" he bragged. "Oh, wait, it's me!" I gave him the evil eye.

Paul couldn't wipe the smug look from his face. I felt like helping him do it but resisted. "Have you got those overalls and work boots ready, Riley?"

"In the bed of my pickup around the corner," Cousin Riley answered, rather unhelpfully in my opinion.

"Great." Paul dug into the rumpled brown grocery sack he was carrying. "Because I've got your crown right here."

I looked in horror at the hen-and-nest monstrosity one of his employees had created. "Was she drunk when she made that?" I gasped.

Riley snickered and I gave him a warning look.

Steve Dykstra sauntered up. "Give me a beer," he said, looking rather parched and disheveled. He tossed a five in my open jar.

"I'm sorry," Mom started to say, "but I'm afraid we're—"

"Bingo!" I jumped in the air.

"Hey, no!" Paul grabbed at me. "Wait! It's over." He was violently crossing his arms back and forth one atop the other. "Over. The bet was over. I won."

Derek's mouth hung open. "Would somebody please tell me what you two are carrying on about?"

"Paul and Amy had a little bet going," explained my mother.

"And it was over," insisted Paul. "Right, Riley? Rhonda?"

Rhonda took a sudden interest in her bright pink fingernails. Riley opened his mouth, but no words came out. I'd trained them well.

"Ben," Paul pleaded. "You're a lawyer. Say something!"

Ben smiled. "I'm afraid this isn't my area of expertise. Derek?"

"Oh no you don't!" Derek waved his hands in the air and took a step back. "I'm pleading the Fifth!"

Paul cursed.

"Such language," I said, shaking my head at him. "And with ladies present." I picked up the lid to one of the jars and used it to screw Paul's shut. "Sorry, but it's not over until it's over, Paul." I twisted the second lid securely onto my jar. "And now," I said, waving the sealed jar in his face, "it's over."

"What's going on?" asked Steve, looking rather befuddled. "Did I miss something?"

I patted him on the back. "On the contrary, Steve. You were just in time." His back was damp. "Nice shirt." If you liked looking like a lawn flamingo.

"I'll go get the dress." Rhonda rose and smoothed her clothing.

Paul groaned.

I urged Rhonda to hurry back, and she did. She had her high school prom dress on a hanger. It was hideous and pink, with a pink chiffon corsage in the center of its cleavage.

She handed it to me and I handed it to Paul. "The portable restrooms are right over there." A bank of them sat outside the town hall.

"This is so unfair." Paul looked as aghast at the sight of Rhonda's old dress as I had the first time I'd seen her in it.

"A bet's a bet," I insisted.

Paul snatched the dress from my hand. "I can't believe it. I'm going to have to stand next to the Impala dressed like this in front of the judges!" His head shook violently side to side. "What are they going to think?"

Derek laughed. "They'll probably think you're trying to sway them with your beauty." He tilted his head. "You should have shaved first though." He ran his hand along his own chin. "You've got a bit of five o'clock shadow showing there, Paul."

Paul turned his back and stormed off.

"Don't forget the shoes!" Rhonda called sweetly. "I picked up pair for you at thrift store. I didn't know your size so I picked the largest they had. I hope they fit!"

Paul froze, balled up his fists, and turned. Rhonda held out the fuchsia heels. To his credit, Paul took them without protest.

"For the record," Derek said, holding my hand as we followed Paul, "you dodged a bullet. I saw that ridiculous outfit you were going to have to wear."

He was right and I knew it.

In a couple of minutes, Paul popped out in Rhonda's prom dress. On him it looked even worse than it had on her. Mom and Ben had already headed across the square to the stage for the judging of the cars and tractors and the Miss Fall Festival Queen competition to follow. Riley had promised to come back with the John Deere for the

Birds & Brewsmobile as soon as the show was over and haul it to the lot behind Birds & Bees and Brewer's Biergarten, where it would be available if the fire or police personnel wanted to revisit it and investigate further.

It was beginning to cool down, and Derek offered me his hoodie. My jacket had been ruined in the fire. Cousins Rhonda and Riley were going to await the judging beside the John Deere. Kim tagged along with us.

After several tentative steps, Paul had given up trying to walk in the heels and crossed the grass barefoot.

We arrived at the broad lawn in front of the portable stage that had been erected for the weekend. The tractors were grouped together, but the cars were arranged by decade.

Paul and the Impala had ended up near the front of the line. Knowing Paul, he'd probably planned it that way and cut in somehow. I was surprised that he didn't have big Brewer's Biergarten signs on each car door. Paul was all about marketing.

Paul stood beside the open driver's door with his arms folded across his chest. The look on his face dared anybody to make fun of him.

We stood at the edge of the crowd and watched as judges, identified by their bright orange vests, moved among the vehicles one at a time.

Elizabeth Sudsbury was on stage with a small group of intimates, along with Mayor Mac MacDonald and several other town officials. Jerry Kennedy had come in his uniform and was sitting in one of the white folding chairs that had been arranged in front of the stage. His wife, Sharon, and daughter, Cassandra, flanked him.

"Where's Parker?" I asked Derek. "I thought he was head judge?"

"He is." Derek's eyes scanned the crowd. "He must be here somewhere. He wouldn't miss this."

I scanned the throng, too, looking for Trudy Sherman, Dom and Tam—I still didn't know what their last names were—and the elusive Parker Sudsbury.

The judges approached the white Impala, clipboards in hand, and began moving around the vehicle, though two of the judges seemed far more curious about Paul than they were the car.

Derek chuckled. "You're enjoying this, aren't you?"

I squeezed his hand. "More than I ever thought I'd enjoy any car and tractor show."

After several minutes of moving around the shiny car and pointing at the tires, examining the red and white leather interior like it was a space-shuttle preflight check, one of the judges said something to Paul and he reached inside the car and popped the hood. He propped it open and the judges took their time looking around—though what they found interesting in there, I couldn't imagine.

Satisfied, one of the judges waved for Paul to latch the hood, which he did. Then they had him start the car up, turn the signals and headlights on and off, then shut the car down again.

Finally, they moved around to the rear, and by the motion of his arm, I could tell that the judge beside him was asking him to open the trunk.

Paul hesitated, then hobbled over, glaring my way as he did so. I wiggled my fingers at him and smiled even as I reached for my cell phone to take a few pictures.

"This is just too good," Derek muttered while shooting video with his phone.

Paul popped open the trunk. He bobbled and fell backward into the arms of an openmouthed judge. The judge's clipboard slipped from his hand to the ground.

"What's wrong with Paul?" I asked.

"I don't know." Derek lowered his phone.

The other judges had converged on the trunk and all were staring inside. One judge, a portly gentleman in jeans, a blue chambray shirt and orange vest, waved furiously. "Chief Kennedy! Chief Kennedy!"

Paul clutched the rear fender for support.

"Come on!" Derek pushed me forward. We raced to the car.

"Stand back!" ordered one of the judges, holding his clipboard up like a shield.

"What is it?" demanded Derek.

I shoved between Derek and the judge.

And screamed.

Parker Sudsbury lay folded up inside the trunk like a big toy doll. And, like a toy doll, he was very much dead.

Chief Kennedy rose from his seat and pushed his way through the swelling crowd gathered in the street.

Jerry stopped in front of Paul's Impala and gawped. "Parker Sudsbury."

A scream came from nearby and Elizabeth "Sudsy" Sudsbury

surged forward, eyes lit with fear and disbelief. I pulled her back. "Elizabeth, Elizabeth," I called as she fought against me. "There's nothing you can do."

"Parker!" Sudsy broke loose and shot past me.

Jerry allowed Parker's wife a brief look, then escorted her to the curb and ordered her to sit. Jerry's wife sat with her.

Jerry pulled out his phone and called for backup. In a matter of seconds, Officers Pratt and Reynolds, who were on duty at the fair and in uniform, were on the scene. Dan Sutton arrived soon after.

"Everybody make some room!" hollered Jerry.

Emmett Lancaster and his wife, Belle, stood several yards away. His wife had a big, fancy camera slung around her neck and was capturing the scene, which seemed rather in bad taste if not downright morbid.

Andrew Greeley, who had been sitting parade-ready in his nearby hearse, hurried over as well. He peered down into the open trunk.

"Well?" Jerry tipped back his cap.

Derek was huddled on the far side of the car, deep in conversation with an ashen-faced Paul. He looked like he was having trouble standing, let alone comprehending what was happening.

The side of Parker's head was red, his hair matted with blood. "Unless I'm mistaken," said Greeley, "that there is your murder weapon."

He pointed to a black tire iron on which even I could see traces of skin and hair.

Jerry whistled through his teeth. He snapped his fingers and held out his right hand. Officer Pratt handed him a pair of nitrile gloves. He put them on.

"A tire iron? Isn't that a bit cliché?" I asked. "Besides, doesn't practically every car have a tire iron?"

"Yep. Most do," agreed Jerry. "Though nowadays some of the new cars have no spare and no jack or tire iron of any sort." He didn't sound as though he liked the idea. "The problem we have here is that Mr. Anderson's trunk has two."

"Two?"

Jerry held a tire iron in each gloved hand. "Two tire irons."

One was black and the other gray, but indeed there were two tire irons. The black one looked clean, but the gray looked like it had been used on Parker Sudsbury before he'd been ignominiously placed in the car's trunk.

Parker's wife sobbed in the background. In the distance, I heard the approach of the ambulance. Moments later, its flashing lights were visible above the parting crowd.

"Make way, everyone! Clear the street!" ordered Officer Reynolds.

I looked at Paul. What was going on?

"If I'm not mistaken," Jerry said, "I think we just might have found the murder weapon that was used on Chick Sherman, too."

"Jerry, you don't know that for sure," I argued.

"This one's got the victim's hair and blood stains on it. Right, Greeley?"

Andrew Greeley nodded. "It would appear so."

Trudy Sherman's face stood out in the crowd. She had a blue scarf wrapped around her head.

Jerry pulled himself up to his full height. "Paul Anderson, you are under arrest for the murders of Chick Sherman and Parker Suds-bury."

"I didn't do anything!" Paul protested.

"I saw him arguing with Mr. Sudsbury outside TOTS!" Trudy shouted.

Jerry nodded. "Interesting."

"I was never arguing with Parker. I sold him a case of beer!" Paul exclaimed.

"You know the way to the police station, Larry." Chief Kennedy turned his back on the officer. "I'll meet you down there just as soon as I finish up here."

Officer Reynolds held out his handcuffs and Paul reluctantly extended his hands.

Derek hugged me. "What a mess."

"Can't you do something?"

"I keep telling you all, I am not a criminal attorney." Derek scrubbed his hands over his face. "Though sometimes I think I should be, the way things are going around here."

Seeing Paul, dressed clumsily in my Cousin Rhonda's pink high school prom gown, being led into the back of a police cruiser, would have been funny under other circumstances—any other circumstances . . . but murder.

22

I sat on the edge of my bed with my laptop warm against my thighs. Nothing that had happened yesterday—all week for that matter—had made any sense. Now Paul was in jail, accused of murdering not one but two men.

I really needed to hurry up and figure out what was going on. If I didn't get Paul out of jail soon, Jerry would see to it that he was tried and convicted. A vicious killer would go free.

To top it off, as Paul had warned me, my ex-boyfriend Craig would be coming to run the biergarten. Craig had already called once from Raleigh last night. He sounded panicky and nervous, not only about his friend and business partner but the business itself.

I told him not to get so worked up and that everything would work out. I also told him never to call me again.

I yawned. Karl had promised to text me if he heard anything from Jerry. Derek had promised to go down to the police station and see what he could learn. But after a long, restless night, I had checked my cell phone and emails. Nothing.

I had scoured the internet for information on Sally Potts and come up empty-handed. Whatever Parker Sudsbury had been implying about her might go unresolved, now that he was dead. I had not uncovered a hint of scandal or news of any kind.

As for the Lancasters, from what little I had learned searching the web, they were just what they appeared to be. A couple from the eastern part of the state with a fondness for antique automobiles.

That left Trudy Sherman and the young couple, Tam and Dom. I threw on a pair of jeans, a white tee, and a UNC-Chapel Hill sweatshirt.

I left my bedroom. I was alone in the apartment. Mom's bedroom door was ajar, sunlight spilling in through the open curtains. I laced up my hiking boots in anticipation of traipsing out to Tam and Dom's campsite. I grabbed my purse and keys and left the apartment.

I heard voices in the store and hurried down, curious. Kim, Esther, and my mother stood behind the sales counter. All were dressed for business. Their eyes were latched on a computer tablet propped up beside the credit card scanner.

"What are you all doing down here so early?"

"Getting ready to open." Kim adjusted her store apron.

"Are you forgetting? It's Sunday, we don't open until noon. It's barely eight thirty."

"That's what I tried to tell them," complained Esther. "But here I am. Who can sleep with all that commotion, anyway?" She shook her head. "Not me, that's who." She had a mug of coffee in one hand and a cherry Danish in the other.

"Just look at all those people!" Kim pointed to the front of the store.

"What the—" I did a double take. "What are all those people doing here?" A crowd had amassed on the front porch. Several cold noses pressed against the glass.

"Are you kidding?" Kim said rather breathlessly. "Haven't you looked at your computer?"

"Yes, but—"

"You've gone viral!" Kim gushed excitedly. "You are the Wild Turkey Woman of Birds and Buzzards!"

Kim grabbed the tablet and held it to my nose.

I moved her arm back so I could see. A video was running in a loop. In it, a crazy woman was seen running across the street waving a fried turkey leg overhead and yelling at a bird.

I groaned.

"There's more," Esther said, rather unhelpfully. "This site has a compilation of a whole bunch of videos that folks shot with their mobile phones."

I looked at the crazy woman on the screen. It couldn't be me.

But it was.

For all the world to see.

And I wasn't just clutching a fried turkey leg, I ran like a turkey.

"Isn't it amazing?" Kim asked with glee. "Over thirty thousand hits, already."

Sure enough, the caption below the moving picture read: *Wild Turkey Woman of Birds and Buzzards.*

"They got the name of the store wrong," I said, wondering how my mouth had gotten so dry.

"Who cares?" Esther quipped, taking a big bite of her Danish. "They found the place, didn't they?" Her eyes narrowed on the crowd as she chewed. "Maybe I should be working on commission."

I heard dollar signs in those words. I tapped the screen with my finger as another video, from a slightly different perspective but showing an equally ridiculous woman running ungracefully across the screen, played. "And Roscoe is a peregrine falcon, not a buzzard." I knew it was useless to point out but felt it needed to be said.

"Again," said Esther, "who cares?" She rubbed her now empty hands together. "They're here and I'll bet they are ready to buy. That's what counts. "Let them in, Barbara."

"Ready, dear?" Mom asked.

I braved a glance at the crowd outside, then turned and walked to the back door in a foggy daze.

Kim came running after me. "Amy, where are you going?"

"To the police station." I didn't bother to turn around. I opened the back door and felt the cool morning air wash over me. A trio of crows in a tall pine called out good morning. Maybe it was for them. For me, not so much.

"But all those people!" Kim yelled from the door. "They're here to see you!"

Ignoring Kim's pleas, I hopped in the van and started out. I glanced at the lot I shared with Brewer's Biergarten. There was no sign of Paul's Impala or his camper. Not that I had been expecting to see either.

Both would have been impounded.

Turning onto Lake Shore Drive, I saw Otelia and Steve standing outside the chocolate shop. Otelia turned at the sound to my approach and waved. Steve wore a loose-fitting denim jacket, orange flannel shirt, and jeans. Otelia wore black slacks and a puffy black coat.

I waved back and pulled to the side of the road. I rolled down the passenger-side window and stretched across. "Good morning. Everything okay?"

"Yes, I locked my keys in the shop." The chocolatier smiled as she shrugged. "It's a good thing I've got Steve."

As if on cue, Steve jostled the glass door. "Got it!"

"Great." Otelia reached backwards and patted Steve on the shoulder. "You were at the festival yesterday, Amy. Is it true that Parker Sudsbury is dead?"

"Yes."

Steve lowered his head and thrust his hands deep in his jacket pockets. "Such a shame. I had no idea. I noticed the commotion but couldn't get close enough to see what was going on. It wasn't until later that we both learned what happened. I heard all kinds of crazy rumors flying around."

Otelia was nodding. "The woman on the radio said that Chief Kennedy has locked up Paul Anderson for the crime. Is that true?"

"I'm afraid that's right, too. I was just on my way to the police station."

"How about some coffee first?" Steve asked, his arm around Otelia.

"Yes," agreed Otelia. "Come on in for some coffee and chocolate. You look like you could use it."

I hesitated. I wanted to check on Paul and see if there was anything new in the case. I also wanted to tell Jerry that he should look into whomever I had seen arguing with Parker behind the theater. I was also going to insist that he have a strong word with those two campers.

"I have yesterday's leftover fudge—dark chocolate with coconut, raisins, and walnuts. It's practically a health bar."

Steve patted his belly and chuckled. "That's what the dear lady tells me, but results would suggest otherwise." He winked my way. "What can I say? I'm addicted to fudge. Beats cigars, right?"

"Amen to that." Otelia joined him in laughter.

"Fine. How can I resist? But only for a minute." I parallel parked in front of the store and followed them inside. The sweet smell of chocolate hung in the air.

"Come around back," Otelia said, shrugging off her coat to reveal a black blouse. She hung the coat on a hook in the storeroom. There was a small black refrigerator nestled in a nook between boxes of supplies. A coffee machine sat atop the fridge.

Steve urged me to sit at a small vinyl-topped folding table that sat between two rows of metal shelving. Otelia measured several scoops of ground coffee into the top of the pot, added some water from a plastic liter-sized bottle, and flicked the machine on.

"I'll be right back." Otelia went out front to the sales area and returned a minute later with several generous slices of fudge on paper plates.

Steve reached behind and grabbed three forks from a plastic cup on the shelf. "Breakfast of kings!"

Breakfast of calories and cavities was probably more like it, but I dug in with gusto.

"You must be pretty unhappy about the car show getting cancelled," I began.

"Not half as unhappy as Paul Anderson."

"Besides," Otelia said, "Steve wasn't able to show his car, after all."

Steve's lips tightened and his cheeks wrinkled. "Nope. Can you believe it, Amy? I keep that car in tiptop shape and then the day of the show I go out to start her up and nothing." He shook his head. "The darn thing wouldn't start at all. I spent hours trying, too."

"Tell me about it." Otelia rolled her eyes. "You should have heard him, Amy. Such language!"

"Can we please change the subject?" Steve asked with a smile.

"Fine, but it's going to cost you." Otelia tore off a chunk of Steve's fudge with her fingers, having finished her own. "Steve was telling me about those Audubon sketches and books that have gone missing." She licked her fingers. "If I had known Trudy Sherman was selling such expensive things at bargain prices, I'd have been a customer myself."

"She couldn't have known how valuable they were," I said. I looked down at my plate, surprised to see that my fudge was gone. "But I think that Parker Sudsbury knew." I explained how I'd caught him at the Sherman house and how I'd discovered the rest of the Audubon collectibles missing.

"That's weird," said Otelia.

"If Parker took them," Steve said, nibbling slowly at the edge of his fudge, "why is he dead?"

"And who has them now?"

I sighed and lifted my coffee mug. I'd opted to forego the sugar since there'd be plenty of that in the fudge. "I wish I knew."

"Do you think Paul Anderson is the killer?" Steve inquired.

"He is a newcomer," Otelia added. "I mean, I hate to be judgmental, but what do we really know about him?"

I gave the questions some thought. "I don't believe he's the killer.

He just seems to have been in the wrong place at the wrong time." I sipped slowly. "And now someone seems to be setting him up to take the fall."

"If not him, who?" Steve pressed.

"Your guess is as good as mine. Do either of you know a young couple named Tam and Dom?"

Otelia shook her head. "I've never heard of them, you?" she asked, turning to Steve.

"Nope. Why do you ask, Amy?"

I explained how I'd discovered them camping out near the Sherman place. "There's something suspicious about them. Not to mention, they spent a lot of money on a meal at the Lake House the other night, and they don't strike me as a pair with money to spare on steak dinners."

Steve gnawed at his lip. "Is that so unusual? Maybe you should ask them about it."

"I tried, but they didn't exactly give me a straight answer. I called Tiffany. She has a friend on the waitstaff at Lake House. Her friend did some digging and it turns out they paid cash for their meal, so I couldn't even get a last name for either of them like I'd been hoping."

"Tell Chief Kennedy about it," suggested Steve. "If anybody can get them to talk, it'll be him."

"I plan to."

"How about Sally Potts?" I asked, grasping at straws.

Otelia's eyes snapped toward Steve, then looked off into space, not that there was much in the crowded storeroom. "What about her?"

"Parker told me some rather disturbing information about her and Chick."

"Disturbing?" Steve repeated. "Disturbing how?"

"He suggested the two of them were having an affair."

Steve smiled. "I think Sally would be surprised to hear that."

"So do I," Otelia agreed.

I frowned. "I thought so, too. But why would he lie about a thing like that?"

"Who knows?" Steve said.

Only Parker himself would have known the answer to that question and perhaps many others, and now that he was dead, those answers might never come to light.

"You've had some dealings with Parker, Steve. Any idea who might want him dead?" Otelia asked her boyfriend.

Steve tipped his chair back on two legs, bumping the shelf behind. "He was a little out of my social league, if you know what I mean. I work in a gas station and Parker had investments that worked for him."

"But you socialized with him at that classic car club of yours," Otelia said.

"True. But Parker wasn't a regular. No"—he shook his head—"I can't imagine anyone wanting him dead any more than I can imagine how he ended up in the trunk of Paul's Impala. Unless . . ." His voice trailed off.

"Unless what?" I leaned toward him.

"Unless Parker was having an affair with Chick's wife."

"What?" gasped Otelia, clearly shocked.

"Bear with me. Suppose Parker was having an affair with Trudy. Chick finds out and confronts Parker, but Parker comes out the victor."

"That makes sense," I said. It matched one of my own theories. I motioned with my hand. "Go on."

"Suppose then that Trudy finds out that Parker has murdered her husband and decides that she's going to avenge him."

Otelia's brows drew together. "But you're saying she was having an affair with Parker. Why would she then kill him for getting rid of her husband?"

Steve shrugged. "Chick was still her husband. There are all kinds of marriages in this world. She might not have minded having an affair with her husband's cousin, but might not have taken too kindly to that same cousin killing him."

I chewed my lower lip.

Steve lowered his chin. "I guess it does sound stupid . . ."

"On the contrary," I said. I reached across the table and hugged him. "Steve, you are a genius!"

He reddened. "I like to think so."

"Oh, dear, Amy. Now look what you've done." She shook her head in mock despair and chuckled. "There'll be no living with him now."

Steve rose and pushed back his chair. "Well, sorry to leave you lovely ladies, but I'd better get to work." He leaned over and kissed Otelia's cheek. "I'll bring back the minivan around three. Are we still on for our bird walk?"

"Bird walk?" I asked.

"Steve and I are going for a walk out near Wilson's Pond." She rubbed Steve's hand.

"It's supposed to be a good time of year to see a variety of species there."

I made a face. "I wish I could get Derek half as interested in bird-watching."

"Steve wasn't much into the hobby when we met, but he's become quite the aficionado. I even bought him a bird feeder for his house."

I remembered. It was one of those big, heavy-duty jobs with a thick plexi tube and hard steel mesh to keep the squirrels out.

"What can I say?" Steve zipped up his jacket. "I'm hooked on birds, like I'm hooked on you."

"Oh, Steve." Otelia blushed and stood. I joined them as they started toward the back door.

"A buddy of mine said he saw some wild turkeys. Of course, he was hunting them." Steve grabbed a set of keys from a hook next to the door and winked at Otelia. "The only shooting we'll be doing is with our cameras."

"Excuse me?" I eyed them warily. Wild turkeys and cameras? In one sentence? Was this their not-so-subtle way of letting me know that they knew about the Wild Turkey Woman of Birds and Buzzards?

"Is something wrong?" Otelia blinked innocently.

"No." I looked at them carefully for signs of subterfuge or hints of mockery and saw none. "I guess not."

I said goodbye to Otelia and exited out the back with Steve. He hopped in the Otelia's Chocolates minivan, painted a dark chocolate brown, and drove off. I walked around to the street and climbed in the Kia.

All that talk about turkeys still smarted.

23

I went to the police station as I originally had planned. When I got there, the place was in an uproar. That uproar was caused by Emmett and Belle Lancaster.

"I don't understand." Emmett and his wife had their backs to me, but I'd have recognized them anywhere. "Your chief of police is arrogant and stubborn. Why won't he listen to me?" Mr. Lancaster banged his fist down on Officer Sutton's desk.

Dan bent sideways and tilted his chin at me while Emmett Lancaster railed on.

Chief Kennedy swaggered in from the back, where the cells and interrogation room were located. He had a can of soda in his hand. My mom's friend Anita Brown, who worked as the dispatcher, sat at her desk. She was on the phone.

I hurried to Jerry's desk. He scowled as I approached. He took his seat behind the desk and set the can down at the edge. "What do you want, Simms? I've kind of got my hands full here."

I sat down across from him, uninvited. "So I see. How is Mrs. Sudsbury holding up?"

The chief looked drawn and tired. He was unshaven. "About as well as anyone who's lost her husband, let alone had him found in front of practically the whole town, stuffed in the trunk of a car. Her son is driving over from Wake Forest."

"Clay?"

"That's right." A smile began to form on Jerry's face. "Didn't you used to have a thing for him in high school?"

"No." I felt my forehead heat up like a billboard announcing what a big, fat liar I was.

"No? Because I'm pretty sure—"

"I can only imagine what Mrs. Sudsbury is going through," I interrupted. Jerry painted a not-so-pretty picture. No matter what my and Sudsy's differences, I felt for her. "What are you doing about all these murders? Do you really think Paul is guilty? Do you believe Parker and Chick's deaths are related because—"

Jerry's hand went up like a stop sign. "I've been busy collecting clues and interviewing suspects and witnesses," he shot back. "Unlike what you seem to think, I'm not just sitting on my thumbs, Simms!"

"Okay, okay." I rested my elbows on my thighs. "Do you want to hear my ideas?"

"No, I do not want to hear your ideas. There's enough on my plate as is. Now, today, on top of this mess, I've got the Fall Festival Queen competition and my wedding to get to."

"You haven't cancelled?"

Jerry's lips turned down. "Cassie will be sorely disappointed if I cancel the Miss Fall Festival Queen competition, and Sandra will have my head if I postpone our vow renewal."

I heard shouting from the front and twisted my neck in the direction of Dan's desk. "What's his problem?" I said, meaning Emmett Lancaster, since he was the one doing the shouting.

"His problem"—Jerry rose, thumping his palms down on his desk—"is that he wants to file a complaint against Mr. Hernando!" Jerry leaned so far he was practically in my lap as he bellowed, "But I keep telling him, there isn't a single Hernando in the entire town!"

Emmett and Belle turned as one. "Hernando swindled me!" he bellowed back. "I gave that man ten thousand dollars and he never showed up!"

I arched a brow at Jerry as he waved his hand at Lancaster and fell back into his swivel chair. "The fool never should have sent the man a cashier's check," Jerry muttered. "And now he wants me to do something about it." He shoved a pile of papers across his desk in frustration.

"Can't you trace the check?"

Jerry pulled a face. "It was a cashier's check and it wasn't cashed in Ruby Lake, I can tell you that. I looked into it." Jerry gnawed at his cheek.

"Whose address was it mailed to?"

"Do you think I didn't think of that?" Jerry snarled. "It was delivered to a house on Sandburg Lane—an empty house."

"Then why did the post office deliver it to an empty house?"

"Ask the post office that, Simms." He pointed to the door. "Now, if you don't mind." There was no question in his tone.

Emmett stormed to Jerry's desk. Apparently the man had absolutely no fear of the law. "Your deputy is useless. All he does is keep asking the same questions over and over."

"He ain't a deputy," Jerry replied. "He's an officer of the law."

"Well, he's useless," repeated Emmett.

"Now, Em." Belle tugged at her husband's sleeve. "I'm sure the nice police will do all they can." She turned to Jerry. "If only you could locate the automobile we bought. That would be something."

"Look, like I said before, there probably was no automobile." He propped his elbows on his desk and glared at her husband. "Just like there is no Mr. Hernando!" He snatched the can of soda at the corner of his desk and popped it open with unwarranted violence.

"What kind of car was it, Mr. Lancaster?"

"What?"

"What car had you arranged to buy from this Mr. Hernando?"

"What? And have you buy it from under me?"

"I'm only trying to help."

"Tell them, Em," Belle urged.

Emmett Lancaster hesitated, just as he had the day I'd first seen him at Jessamine's Kitchen. Finally, he capitulated. "I guess I might as well tell you. I mean, what's the harm." His voice was laced with defeat. "I'll probably never see it now."

"I'm sorry, Em." Belle wrapped an arm around his waist.

"It was an El Morocco." Emmett looked at his wife as he said it.

"Chick's car?" I gasped.

"What?" Jerry shot to attention, spilling his cola, which went cascading over the desk only to be absorbed by the paperwork scattered atop it.

"Are you saying you were buying Chick Sherman's El Morocco?" I asked. The one Chick had been found crushed beneath, I left unsaid.

Emmett scolded. "No. I don't know any Chick Sherman. At least, not until I read about the murder. I'm saying I came to buy the El Morocco, *my* El Morocco, from Mr. Hernando."

"Could there be a second El Morocco?" I asked.

"Not very likely," Emmett said firmly. "You have no idea how rare a vehicle it is."

My mind was reeling. Had Chick Sherman been Mr. Hernando? Had he scammed the Lancasters, taking their money under false pretenses, having never intended to sell them his precious car?

Jerry looked at the Lancasters with renewed interest. "Have a seat, Mr. Lancaster. You, too, Mrs. Lancaster." He motioned to the visitors' chairs, one of which I currently occupied. "Goodbye, Simms."

I rose begrudgingly and yanked my purse over my shoulder. "What about Paul?"

"Paul's in good hands." Jerry smiled enigmatically.

"What is that supposed to mean?"

Jerry slid open the low-slung cabinet behind him and laid a large print over his blotter. "Does this look familiar to you, Simms?"

"My Audubon sketch!" I cried. There they were, my three lovely pairs of birds. Very valuable birds quite possibly. "Where did you get that?" I pointed.

"We found it in Paul Anderson's apartment."

"His apartment?"

"Under the mattress."

"But I don't understand—"

"A dead body in his trunk, along with a murder weapon. Anderson was seen by witnesses arguing with Chick before he was killed." Jerry waved his fingers at me. "Goodbye, Simms."

"What about the second tire iron in the trunk of the Impala?"

Jerry motioned to someone across the office. A moment later I felt a gentle yet firm hand on my right shoulder.

"Time to leave now, Amy."

I turned. It was Officer Dan Sutton.

"Was it the tire iron that killed Chick? Were there any fingerprints on it?" I said over my shoulder as Dan showed me the door.

"What about the fire at the Birds and Brewsmobile?" I shouted desperately. Every eye in the police station was on me. "I think somebody set that fire on purpose as a warning to me to stay out of the investigation!"

Dan opened the door as Jerry shouted at me, "If you're smart, you'll heed them!" He pointed his fist at Dan. "Get her out of here, Dan."

Dan nodded. "Sorry, Amy." He closed the door to the station in my face.

"I know." I hurried to the van. Maybe Jerry wouldn't talk to me, but I wasn't going to give up until somebody did.

Sally Potts worked at Pressed to Thrill, the local dry cleaners, and it wasn't far from the police station. Not wanting to go in empty-handed, I grabbed some old clothes from the back of the van—some sweats, socks, and blankets that had gathered there from previous hikes. I'd been meaning to get them cleaned anyway, so now was the perfect time.

I parked in the lot on the side of the cleaners. Sally Potts was at the front counter and she was alone. "Hi, Sally," I said, clutching my precarious bundle as I pushed through the door. "I brought you a load."

Sally popped her gum. "Dump it here. I'll write you up." She reached under the counter and brought out a big nylon sack. "Here, it's on the house. Next time you won't have to carry all your dirty laundry around loose."

"Thanks." I took the navy bag. "Speaking of dirty laundry, I suppose you heard what happened to Parker Sudsbury."

Sally tongued her gum, spearmint by the smell of it, as she wrote out my ticket with a black pencil. "Yes. It's all the customers are talking about today."

"Did you know he was related to Chick Sherman?"

"Yes, I believe I did." Sally looked up from her writing. "Why do you ask?"

"Well . . ." I drummed my fingers on the counter. "There's no real tactful way to say this, so I'll just blurt it out, if you don't mind."

Sally crossed her arms and studied me. "Go ahead." She was wearing a white turtleneck with a slender gold chain and a red skirt that clashed with her hair.

"Before he died, Parker told me that you and Chick were having an affair."

Sally said nothing for a moment, glancing out the street at a passing bus. Then she laughed. "That's preposterous."

"So you didn't know Parker?"

Sally scooped my dirty clothing off the counter and into a wire basket. "Of course, I knew him. I know his wife, too. I was their housekeeper for all of five years." She tore the bottom off the ticket and handed it to me.

"Oh. I didn't realize." I dropped the stub in my purse. "I can't imagine why he would say such a horrible thing."

"Not to speak ill of the dead," Sally began, "but Parker Sudsbury had a way of deflecting attention from himself to others."

"But why you?"

Sally gave the question some thought. "As I told you, I worked for him and his wife for a number of years—I couldn't wait to get away and was glad when this job opened up. You can't imagine what it's like working for the Sudsburys."

I managed a small smile. "As a matter of fact, I can."

"Anyway, my name might have been the first name that came to his mind."

That made sense of a sort.

"Thank you, Sally." I balled up the laundry bag she'd given me. "I'm sorry for all the questions and I do hope that you'll come on more of our bird walks."

Sally smiled. "I'd love to." She popped her gum rapidly. "I thought it would be uncomfortable with Otelia and Steve along, but it worked out okay."

"Is there some problem with Otelia and Steve?" They seemed like a lovely pair.

"No, nothing like that. Steve and I dated for a bit. I wasn't sure how Otelia would take it. He's a sweet man, but she can have him."

I wasn't surprised. Ruby Lake was a small town, and Sally and Steve were approximately the same age. "Not your type?"

"I can't tolerate a man with vices. Now, his is chocolate."

"And cars."

Sally rolled her eyes. "Yeah, him and that car."

"Sounds like he's found the right partner," I remarked.

"Bless them both. I hear you might have, too. That Derek Harlan is easy on the eyes."

"That he is. What about you? Have you found anyone special?"

"Ruby Lake is chock full of healthy men." Sally grinned and stuck a strand of red hair behind her ear. "Let's just say I'm exploring my options."

I laughed and left her to explore to her heart's content while I went on a search for answers.

24

My next stop was the campsite where I'd found Tam and Dom. I drove down the rutted track and parked close to where I remembered the remote site being located. But as I parked and dove through the woods on foot, I saw no sign of the green-domed tent. After wandering for several minutes, I found a clearing that looked familiar. I squeezed around some boulders.

Bingo. This was the spot.

Except that the tent and everything else was gone.

All that remained were the two old folding chairs that they claimed Chick had given them, a couple of empty energy-drink cans, and the ring of the campfire. I kicked my toe through the ashes.

Something shiny and gold caught my eye. I picked it up and rubbed it off. It was a lighter. I gave the mechanism a flick. Empty.

I shoved the lighter in my pocket and headed in the direction of the Sherman house.

Trudy Sherman sat on the porch in a rocker. Princess sat on the boards beside her. Princess ran to greet me. I patted her head and stepped onto the porch.

"What do you want, Ms. Simms?"

A cigarette smoldered in her right hand. She took a puff and tossed it over the rail.

"You know those things can kill you."

Trudy looked at me darkly. "Death seems to be quite common these days." She looked up at me, locking me in those haunting eyes of hers. "What's one more?"

"Why did you give me that Baron Samedi doll, the Lord of Death?"

"Because you looked like you could use it." Trudy grinned. "And because I could use twenty dollars."

"Do you really think I killed your husband?"

"Why would I think that?"

"I don't know, but that's what Parker told me."

"Parker's dead."

"Were you having an affair with him?"

"No," she answered quickly and matter-of-factly.

"Was your husband selling the El Morocco?"

"Selling?"

"Yes." Princess rubbed against my leg and I patted her sleek back. "To a Mr. and Mrs. Lancaster."

She shook her head slowly. "I've never heard of them. And Chick would have told me if he had intended to sell his car."

A gust of wind shot across the yard and an eerie sound filled the air. Princess ignored it but I couldn't. "What is that?"

Trudy grinned. "Chick's Aeolian flute. He built it himself." She pulled another cigarette from the pack in her frock and lit it with a match. "It's on the other side of those trees." She pointed to a stand of pines.

I nodded. "Thank goodness, I thought it was—"

"Ghosts?" The cigarette between her lips bounced as she spoke.

"Yes." The Aeolian flute's eerie sound came from the wind blowing across it. Only, now that I knew what it was, it wasn't so eerie at all. In fact, it was rather soothing.

Trudy leaned back in her chair and rocked, smoke trailing up her face.

"Do you think Chick and Parker might have fought? Could Parker have murdered Chick?"

Trudy planted her feet on the ground. "No. They were more than cousins, they were partners. Parker financed all of Chick's projects."

I tilted my head and looked across toward the barn. "Yes, but if those projects lost money, might Parker have gotten angry enough to commit murder?"

"Never," replied Trudy. "It would have solved nothing. And it wouldn't have gotten him his money back."

"What will you do now?"

"Chick will be buried here. This was his home."

"So you'll be staying?"

Trudy shrugged once more and her gaze faded into the distance. I left her that way.

*   *   *

I hiked back to the van, detouring first to Tam and Dom's camp-site, hoping against hope that they might have returned. Of course, they had not.

I started up the van and bounced slowly back to the main road, wondering where to go next. I noticed the fuel gauge was slow. Ne-smith's Gas Station was only a couple of miles up the road.

I decided to gas up. Mr. Nesmith, the owner, might have noticed the young couple. My guess was that they would have stuck to the main road. If they had gone left, they would have ridden their bikes past the gas station.

I pulled up to the bank of empty pumps, exited the van, and walked to the pump. I slid the nozzle into the gas tank as Gordon Ne-smith sauntered over. "Good morning, Mr. Nesmith."

"Good morning, Ms. Simms." Nesmith wore his usual outfit, a gray one-piece coverall with blue pinstripes. A blue fleece vest kept him warm. With his long nose, brown eyes, and small, rounded head, he reminded me of a mourning dove. His tendency to whistle and his short legs only added to the similarities he shared with the graceful bird.

"Terrible about what happened to Parker Sudsbury, isn't it?" I said, one eye on the gas pump meter.

"Yep. Sure is. Chick, too."

"Did you know them both well?"

Mr. Nesmith rested an elbow against the side of the pump. "Not so much. Neither fella was exactly an open book, at least not around here. I saw them now and again." He grinned. "When you own the only gas station for miles around, you tend to see everybody now and again."

I laughed. "Good point. What about a couple of kids? A young man and a young woman. They would be riding bicycles, a red one and a yellow one."

Mr. Nesmith tilted his head. "Would the girl have colored hair?"

"Yes, blue and green."

Nesmith shook his head. "Kids. If I had come home with my hair painted green and blue, my pop would have shaved me bald!"

"How long ago were they here?"

Nesmith thought a moment. "About two hours or so. They bought some drinks and sandwiches in the store, then headed out." Nesmith's contained a small convenience store inside. Two garage bays sat open to the right. A white pickup sat on a lift in the bay nearest the store-slash-office.

The pump came to a stop and I removed the nozzle. "Did you happen to see which way they were headed when they left?"

Nesmith looked up the road. "West."

"Did they say where they were going?"

"Nope. Sorry. Why do you ask?"

I explained how they had been camping out near the Sherman place and how Chief Kennedy might want to talk to them. I handed Mr. Nesmith my credit card and followed him inside to the register.

He ran my card. "Need a copy of your receipt?"

"No, thanks." I turned toward the garage. "Where's Steve?" I hadn't seen any sign of him or Otelia's minivan, for that matter.

"Steve?" Nesmith removed his eyeglasses, rubbed the bridge of his nose, then replaced them. "Haven't you heard? Steve quit."

"Quit?" I slid my credit card back in my wallet and my wallet back in my purse. "That's news to me."

"It was a surprise to me, too." A black sedan pulled up to the pump. A man in rumpled black sweats got out and went to the pump. "Today was his last day. He came by this morning, packed up his tools, and left." The corners of Nesmith's mouth turned down. "I'm going to miss him. He was a good mechanic."

"Is he going to work at LaChance Motors, or at one of the other garages out near the interstate?" Those were pretty much the only options for an auto mechanic around Ruby Lake—unless he intended to go into business for himself.

Nesmith walked with me outside. "Nope. He said he was retiring."

"Retiring?" I climbed into my van, leaving the door hanging open. He grabbed the squeegee from a bucket between the two pumps and ran it across my windshield.

"Can you believe it?" Nesmith asked with a chuckle. "A man his age? Suddenly, he wants to be Mr. Explorer." He scrubbed at my filthy windshield with sudsy water.

"I suppose it's a midlife crisis," I replied. I fast-forwarded to the future. In it, if Derek and I were together, I hoped I wouldn't have to deal with such things. Hopefully, he'd opt for a red convertible sports car. Odd, though, that Steve hadn't said anything about it earlier. Just the opposite, he'd made plans with Otelia. They were going bird-walking. Was she planning on retiring, too? Otelia and I weren't close, but I would have thought she might have told me if she was.

Mr. Nesmith moved from one side of the van to the other and squeegeed away the water.

Steve might have cancelled on her. If so, she must be broken-hearted. I'd stop by Otelia's Chocolates when I got back to town and see what was going on.

Something nagged at my brain. Mr. Explorer, the gas station owner had said. And what was it that Sally Potter had said? Something about exploring her options?

Suddenly, everything became as clear to me as my freshly cleaned windshield.

I slammed the door shut, turned the key in the ignition and revved the motor. I stuck my head out the window. Nesmith stepped back, the squeegee in his hand dripping over his brown work boots. "Can you tell me where Steve lives?"

"I can't see any harm in it. He lives two streets over on Bland-ing." Nesmith eyed me curiously. "White house with red trim. You can't miss it. It's the only house on the block with a mailbox shaped like a Model T."

"Thanks!" I backed up so I could maneuver around the vehicle parked in front of me.

"Call Chief Kennedy and tell him to come as fast as he can!" I hollered out the passenger-side window as I eased past the other car.

"Wait!" I heard Mr. Nesmith shout as I floored the gas pedal once I hit the pavement. "Where are you going?"

There was no time to answer. If I didn't hurry, a killer might get away.

If he wasn't gone already.

25

Gordon Nesmith was right. It wasn't hard to find Steve Dykstra's house. I drove slowly past, hoping he wouldn't spot me.

A black Model T mailbox sat proudly at the curb. A gravel driveway led up to a single-story white house with red shutters and a red front door. At the end of the drive, ten yards back from the house, sat a white garage. The overhead door to the garage was down, but I could see that the side door hung open.

It was a modest neighborhood, with the houses set on quarter-acre lots. Smoke came from the tan brick chimney of the house on my right.

There was no sign of activity at Steve's house. There was also no sign of Otelia's minivan. The front door was closed and the drapes were pulled.

I drove up to the end of the street and idled for a moment, wondering what I should do next. How long would it take Jerry to arrive with reinforcements?

Worse, what if Steve had already fled? There were a hundred country roads a killer could take. He might never be caught.

I lifted my foot from the brake pedal and eased to within two houses of Steve's home. I turned off the engine, leaving the keys in the ignition. If Steve was there and he came after me, I wasn't going to play hero, I was going to run for my life.

Keeping low, I followed a line of shrubs that divided Steve's house from his neighbor's. There were no windows in the overhead garage door, so I worked my way around to the side door, going the long way around.

A near-empty bird feeder swung lazily in the breeze from the horizontal branch of a pin oak.

In the distance, I heard a radio playing, but I didn't hear a sound from the garage.

Creeping to the side door, I held my breath and slowly stuck my head through. Otelia's brown minivan sat in the musty garage. There was no sign of Steve. I peeked in the back window of the van. There was a suitcase inside, along with several metal tool boxes and two cardboard boxes from which various items of clothing protruded.

Steve's prized De Soto was nowhere to be seen.

And that had been the key to this entire case. The De Soto. I had no idea where it was now, but, if I was right, and I knew I was, then Steve was planning to leave town in Otelia's minivan. And if I was right again, he'd be taking a small fortune in Audubon sketches and books with him when he did.

And I had to stop him.

I backed up slowly and quietly. I'd left my purse and cell phone in the van. I'd get it and call Jerry again.

He should have been here by now.

I felt a bump and froze.

"Going somewhere?"

I twisted around. Steve glared at me with an angry, ugly look on his face. He grabbed my arms and held me in place.

"Let me go!" I tugged but he was too strong. "I'll scream if you don't!" I warned him.

His meaty hand clamped down over my mouth. His other hand gripped viselike around my neck. I felt my vocal cords being crushed. "Try it and you'll take your last breath."

I felt my heart stop.

"Am I making myself clear?"

I nodded as best I could with one hand sticking to my face and the other my throat.

Steve released his hands but remained within striking distance. I rubbed at my throat and resisted the urge to run my hand over my mouth to remove the taste of him from my lips, for fear of making him even angrier.

He was dressed just as I'd seen him that morning. His brown jacket was zipped to the neck.

"You're Mr. Hernando, aren't you?"

Steve sneered. "How did you figure it out?"

"It took me a while, but when Gordon Nesmith mentioned that

you'd retired to go exploring, it all came together in my head. The De Soto, Mr. Hernando." I shook my head. I should have realized sooner. "Hernando de Soto. It's really pretty obvious once you know."

Steve shrugged a shoulder. "I guess it really was kind of dumb of me." He grabbed my arm. "Come on."

"Where are we going?" I demanded. "Where's the Audubon collection? Have you sold it?"

"Not yet," Steve admitted. "But you can bet I will. I've been looking around online. Buyers will pay a fortune for that stuff. And after what happened with the car . . ."

"You mean the El Morocco? Chick Sherman's car?" I demanded as he led me through the back of the house to the kitchen.

Surprise showed on his face. "That's right. Him and me had a deal. We'd sell the car to Lancaster and split forty-sixty." He pushed me down into a chair at the kitchen table. "Sit," he commanded.

I sat. "Why would Chick agree to do that? He loved that car."

"Because he was tired of Parker holding the purse strings. He wanted some money for himself." Steve shook his head in disgust. He fished around in a drawer beside the sink and pulled out a roll of tape.

"Then he chickens out. Decides he doesn't want to sell. But we had a deal!" Steve waved his fist at my nose. "I already took Lancaster's deposit!" He stormed across the linoleum floor toward me. "I've got bills to pay!" he bellowed. "Put your hands down."

I lowered my hands and he started wrapping masking tape around them until I was stuck to the chair. "Is that what happened to the De Soto?" I asked. "It didn't really break down, did it?"

Steve hesitated, then answered. "No. I sold it. I owed some not-so-nice men some money. They took the car in exchange. But it wasn't enough. And they want the rest."

He tightened the bonds around my arms. "They aren't going to get it though. With the Audubon collection, I'll have enough money to start over fresh in a new town."

"With two murders on your conscience."

"No," he said with a wicked grin. He held up his fingers. "Three."

A chill washed over me and I broke out in sweat. The man had no conscience at all. I strained for sounds of a siren and heard nothing. I tested my bonds.

What was keeping Jerry?

"What about Parker?" I had to keep the dangerous blowhard talking. I had a feeling the only thing keeping me alive now was his need to brag.

Steve loomed over me. "When I learned how cheap you'd bought that sketch, I knew that Trudy didn't know what she had. I went back and offered Parker a hundred bucks for the lot of it." His laughter filled the small kitchen. "Later, he learned that I had cheated her, and he demanded I return everything."

"But you weren't going to let that happen, were you? You were the person I'd seen arguing with Parker behind TOTS."

"A deal is a deal," Steve said. "Besides, I'd already lost out on the car. I needed something, and the Audubon collection is that something."

"What about that prototype car Chick was working on? That must have been worth a lot, too."

"Not a chance," he said with scorn. "That hunk of metal was nothing but a one-off deathtrap." He chuckled. "If I hadn't killed him, that car of his would have, one day or another. I guess I should be thanking you."

"Me?"

"If you hadn't researched those books and pictures, I'd have never known what a pile of money they were worth."

"Where is the Audubon collection now?"

"In the minivan." He lifted a box. "And as soon as I get this last box loaded up, we'll be leaving."

I felt another chill wash over me. I had a feeling he was picturing me leaving, permanently. As in dead.

"How did you manage to plant my sketch in Paul's apartment?"

"My dad was in the locksmithing business. I learned a skill or two."

"I'm sure he'd be very proud to see what use you've put those skills to."

Steve glared at me. A line of sweat had formed at his hairline. "You talk too much." He stared at me a moment, the box clutched to his chest. "Don't go anywhere."

He left the kitchen and started down the back steps. I twisted and tugged. I knew that if I got in that van, I was a dead woman.

Risking being heard, I stood quickly and let myself fall back down, lifting my legs so the chair would take the brunt of the fall. My teeth crashed together and a sharp jolt went up my spine. I tested my arms.

Looser.

I stood, glanced out the open door, and seeing no sign that my commotion had caught Steve's ear, I tried once again. And again. On the fourth attempt, the masking tape gave way.

"Should have used duct tape," I muttered as I quickly fought to disentangle myself. I yelped as I ripped the sticky tape from my hairs. This wasn't a process I'd be repeating as a depilatory anytime soon.

I glanced, worried, out the door once again. There was still no sign of Steve's imminent return. I shoved the kitchen table aside and ran to the kitchen in search of a weapon.

"Going somewhere?"

I cried out and spun about. "Steve!"

Steve stood in the doorway separating the kitchen from the living room. He'd come in through the front door.

There was a block of knives in the far end of the kitchen between the stove and the refrigerator, but I knew I'd never reach it before Steve cornered me.

I took one look at the open back door and bolted through it with Steve hot on my heels. I couldn't be certain, but I thought I heard the high-pitched screech of a police siren.

All I had to do was stay out of Steve's reach until help arrived.

I darted past the lawn furniture, tossing a chair in his path as he bellowed with rage. I felt a hand tugging at my jacket as I tried to get behind the pin oak and put some distance between us.

But Steve's fingers held. I reached back and batted at his hand. With his free hand, he reached across my chest, his fingers jumped up to my throat and squeezed.

Half blinded and half winded, I noticed the bird feeder jumping on the branch. I reached out and felt my fingers latch on to the metal wire frame. I yanked the heavy feeder free of the branch. Birdseed went flying as I swung blindly behind me.

Steve screamed as the feeder struck him in the face. He fell and, as he did, his hands grabbed my hips. We fell together, hitting the ground with a thud.

The bird feeder slipped from my grip. I clawed for it, my hand reaching across the long grass.

Steve started to pull himself up, a string of curses escaping his lips. I grabbed the feeder by its hook and swung at his knees. He yelped and went down.

More seed went flying. This time, bits of millet hit me in the eyes. I squinted and grabbed the feeder with both hands. I swung wildly. I could feel Steve grabbing at my feet.

"Freeze!"

I smashed the feeder against Steve's fingers.

"Okay, Simms. Okay," a voice said firmly yet softly.

I opened my eyes. It was Jerry. Officer Sutton had his gun trained on Steve Dykstra, who was balanced on his knees with his hands in the air.

Jerry delicately removed the smashed bird feeder from my grip. "I've got to say, Simms, your swing is improving."

I gulped for air and nodded. I'd take my compliments when and where I could get them.

26

I spent the rest of the day at the local hospital being peppered with questions by Jerry and Derek, who was acting as my unofficial counsel and very official, caring boyfriend. Paul had been released from jail and Steve had taken his place.

By evening, I was exhausted. I was given a clean bill of health and allowed to go home. Which was fine by me. A good night's sleep in the comfort of my own bed was just what I needed.

I woke the next morning feeling refreshed, if a little beaten up. My body felt like one giant bruise and my arms were still red and raw from being wrapped in masking tape. I also bore marks on my arms and legs that were caused from Steve Dykstra's fingers digging into my flesh.

I took the longest shower I could stand, then dressed in my comfiest jeans and an old college sweatshirt. I tied my hair in a carefree ponytail, applied a little lip balm—a necessity this time of year if I wanted to avoid cracked lips—and sat at the kitchen table.

Derek and Mom had kept me company both at the hospital and later in the apartment. I remember dozing off in front of the TV and Derek lifting me in his arms and carrying me off to bed.

I had the apartment to myself now. Mom had let me sleep in. She had told me she was volunteering at the school library this morning. I stood and looked out the kitchen window. The sun streamed in and it looked to be a perfect day.

A robin pecked at the grass near the fence, in search of breakfast. Derek had promised to come by in the afternoon and take me on a picnic once he finished at the office, and I was looking forward to it.

It had been a rough week. Not as rough for me as it had been for Chick Sherman and Parker Sudsbury, but rough enough. Steve was singing like a canary, now that he'd been caged. I'd learned yesterday that Chick's murder had been set in motion by Steve's desperate need for money to cover his gambling debts. Sally Potts was right when she suggested that Steve had an addictive personality, though she'd called them vices. He'd once been addicted to smoking and even chocolate.

But he had a bigger vice that he'd never been able to overcome: gambling.

When he overreached and gambled big on a couple of college football games, he'd found himself unable to pay off his bookie. His prized De Soto had gone toward the debt, weeks ago. That was why he hadn't shown it in the parade and he was driving around in Otelia's minivan.

Steve had tried to convince Chick to sell the El Morocco, with him as the go-between earning a hefty commission. Chick had backed out at the last minute and Steve killed him in the heat of the argument. Paul was, as I had suspected, simply in the wrong place at the wrong time. The night of Chick's murder, Steve had parked on the little-used track near Tam and Dom's campsite.

When the campers told Steve they had seen him, he had paid them to keep quiet. That was how they could afford to feast at Lake House. Chief Kennedy said the state patrol was looking for them now, but I doubted they would ever be found. He didn't even have a last name to go by.

Once Steve learned the police were focusing on Paul as the killer, he did everything he could to frame him—including planting my sketch under Paul's mattress. Planting Parker in the trunk of Paul's Impala had been intended to seal Paul's fate, and it practically had.

Steve had also set fire to the Birds & Brewsmobile as a warning to me and to add to the confusion at the festival. As if there hadn't been enough that day with an escaped peregrine falcon and a dead body in a trunk.

"Enough self-reflection," I said to no one. I didn't feel like being alone. I'd have my coffee downstairs. I slipped my feet into a pair of buttery leather moccasins, tossed my purse over my shoulder, and left the apartment. I went down to the second floor and knocked on Paul's door to see how he was faring, but there was no answer. Was he in avoid-Amy mode again? After all I had done for him?

I grinned. He was probably fast asleep. I'd be, too, after being arrested for murder and spending time in jail.

Deep in thought, I continued down to the first floor, following the sound of murmurs that rose in the stairwell. Jerry was still mad at me, but that was nothing new. I knew he was annoyed that I'd solved his case for him. He was also upset that I'd caused him to miss Cassie's coronation as this year's Miss Fall Festival Queen. My little escapade had come at an inconvenient time relative to the renewal of his nuptials as well. Apparently the last-minute cancellation was costing him plenty.

I did feel bad about that, if not for his sake then for Sharon's.

Jerry had saved my life. If he hadn't arrived when he had, Steve could very well have killed me as surely as he had Parker and Chick. My hand went involuntarily to my neck. It had been close. Too close.

And now I owed Jerry my life. As if his head wasn't swollen enough before—there'd be no living with the man now.

I found myself at the bottom of the steps without quite realizing how I'd gotten there. Kim was seated atop the counter. Esther was perched on a stool.

I walked over slowly, not taking my eyes off Esther. "What's that?" I pointed at her chest.

"What?" Esther blinked at me.

"That." I tapped the painted enamel cloisonné pin in the shape of a parrot that clung to her gardenia print dress. It read: ESTHER PILASTER, ASST. MANAGER.

Esther plucked at the pin. "Barbara got it for me." She pushed out her chest proudly.

"My mom gave you that?"

"Yep. Nice, huh?" She straightened the pin with her fingers. "She had it made for me at the trophy and print shop."

"Hey," Kim complained, "how come Esther gets to be assistant manager?" She stared jealously at the shiny pin. "Shouldn't I be assistant manager? I am your partner, after all."

"Nobody is assistant manager," I said, my voice rising. At the moment, I wasn't even sure I was the manager, with everyone from my mother to my renter running roughshod over me.

"I am," Esther averred.

I pulled a face. "I need to talk to my mother."

"Hey, glad you're okay, Amy," Cousin Riley called, leaving a muddy trail across the floor as he came through the front door, hoe in hand. His eyes fell on Esther, who was polishing her new name tag with a hankie. "If she gets to be assistant manager, shouldn't I be head groundskeeper?"

Kim chimed in. "Amy made Esther assistant manager over me. Does that seem fair to you, Riley?"

"I did not—"

"Really?" Riley pulled off his cap and scratched the top of his unruly head.

A headache sprung out of nowhere and I felt my blood banging against my eardrums. Mom had hired Riley to maintain the grounds. Once a week, he trimmed the hedges, mowed the tiny lawn and weeded the flower beds. He also performed various and sundry handyman duties around the house as problems sprung up. And with a house built in the late eighteen hundreds, something was always springing up. That did not make him head groundskeeper.

"Give me that, Riley. You're leaving a trail of dirt." I snatched the soiled hoe from Cousin Riley's hands. "You can call yourself the King of Marvin Gardens, for all I care. I need some air."

"King of Marvin Gardens?" I heard Riley echo, as I headed out the storeroom door. "What's that supposed to mean?"

"It means get back to work," Esther said sternly. "When the boss is gone, I'm in charge."

It was all I could stand. I tossed the hoe in the shed along the rear of the house. The back door of Brewer's Biergarten popped open and Paul Anderson appeared. He had a hound dog on a leash.

I narrowed my eyes. "Is that Princess?" The dog wagged its tail and pulled Paul along with her as she came running over to greet me. I patted her on the head.

"Yep. I was just showing her to the gang at the biergarten. I took her out for her morning walk." He tenderly slapped the dog's side.

"What's Princess doing here? What are you doing with her?"

"She's mine," Paul said with a touch of pride.

"Yours?"

"Yep." He thumped the hound on her side again and her tail wagged vigorously. "Trudy asked me if I wanted to take care of her. She said she's leaving town to go live with her sister in her condo and couldn't keep her."

Paul knelt and rubbed Princess's snout between his hands. "Princess and I are sympatico. I'm thinking of making her my mascot."

I drew my brows together. "Where are you planning on keeping her?" Paul and Princess followed me back inside the store.

"Here, of course. I've decided to keep renting from you." Paul couldn't stop beaming.

"You what?"

"Yeah, this is more convenient than some house miles from here. The biergarten is next-door. Princess and I can walk to work. You've got to love that commute, right?"

"Paul," I began, folding my arms across my chest, "Princess is great. I love her. But you cannot keep her here. This is my home and my business." I avoided looking Princess in the eye. Dogs can be so manipulative that way. "I have a strict no-pet policy. As for you continuing to rent here, what about your house?"

"What about it?"

"You've been working on getting it fit for occupancy. You've invested a lot of time, energy, and money into it. Are you simply going to let it fall back into disrepair?"

"Nah." Paul waved his hand in the air. "I'm going to sell it. It's already on the market. Kim listed it for me."

That was news to me. "Paul, I'm not sure I want to have a full-time tenant. Nothing personal, but I had plans for that space." I looked around. Kim had conveniently disappeared. "Where is Kim anyway?"

"She went out for coffee and donuts," Cousin Riley answered.

"But I already signed a lease." Paul fished in his back pocket, from which he extracted a crumpled bunch of typed pages. He unfolded them. "See?" He thwacked the pages in my face. "Right here. A twelve-month lease. And it says here"—his fingernail underscored the words—"tenant is allowed one pet."

"Can I have a cat?" interrupted Esther.

"No."

"That's not fair. He has a dog."

"Paul does not have a dog," I sputtered. "I mean, he has a dog." I turned back to Paul. "But he is definitely not keeping her here."

"But it's in my lease."

He threw the papers in my face and I grabbed them. "I didn't sign this." My eyes quickly scanned the pages. When I reached the bottom I understood. I frowned. "Mom signed this?"

"That's right." Paul grabbed the lease papers from me and returned them to his back pocket. "And a deal's a deal."

"I'm getting a cat," insisted Esther.

"You've already got a cat!"

"Not in my lease, I don't." Esther glared at me.

I returned her glare. "So you *do* have a cat?!"

She avoided answering and instead pointed at Paul. "He's got a dog!"

"Right here in the lease." Paul patted his back pocket. He looked down at his side. "Hey, where'd Princess go?"

"Down there." I pointed to the bobbing tail that had just rounded aisle two, a blue and red leash trailing behind.

"Right. I guess she wants to get the lay of the land."

"There is no land to—"

Esther tugged at my sleeve. "What about my cat?"

"Yes," I demanded, drawing myself up, "what about your cat?"

"What's its name?" interjected Paul.

Princess yowled and we could hear her paws scraping against the floor. "Paul, would you mind checking on Princess?"

"Sure thing." He slapped his thighs. "Here, Princess! Here, boy."

"It's a girl," I said, rolling my eyes.

"Oh, right."

Esther snatched a pen from the cup beside the register and held it toward me. "I think you should put an addendum in my lease."

I stared at the shiny black pen. Not an easy thing to do with a ten-megawatt headache pounding between my ears. A sigh escaped my lips as I fought to steady my nerves. "Your lease is almost up, Esther. I thought you were considering taking a condo at Rolling Acres?"

Out of the corner of my eye, I noticed that Princess had picked up a plush toy off the bottom shelf and was gnawing happily away on it at the front door. Eating into the profits—that singing black-capped chickadee Audubon plush toy had cost me over three dollars wholesale.

With each bite, the chickadee sang brightly, impervious to pain and sounding remarkably lifelike. But then it should sound lifelike; the authentic recording within the plush toy had been provided by the Cornell Lab of Ornithology.

"Rolling Acres is fine," replied Esther. "But I've got to live in town—this is where the action is."

I couldn't argue with that. Although, personally, the action was beginning to take its toll on me. I might just check Rolling Acres' minimum age requirements. Even if I was too young to qualify for residency, maybe they'd make an exception in my case. I could probably get Floyd and Karl to put in a good word for me.

"I understand how you feel, Esther." I laid a hand on her shoulder to ease the coming blow. "But, you see, my mother and I have plans for that space on the second floor. I'm afraid you'll have to find other accommodations once your lease is up. I simply can't—"

She pulled away. "But I already got an extension."

"An extension?"

"Twenty-four months, to be exact. Your mom typed it up herself." Esther hobbled over to the counter, retrieved her purse, thrust her hand in, and popped out with her own sheaf of papers. "You wanna see?"

I started for the door.

"Hey!" called Esther, scurrying after me. "Where are you going?"

I didn't want to be rude, I simply didn't have an adequate answer. "I don't know," I replied from the porch.

The patter of feet followed me. "You must be going somewhere," Esther insisted. "And as assistant manager, I have a right to know!"

I watched a pair of chickadees, one male, one female, dance along the wire between the telephone poles across the street. "I have no idea where I'm going."

A flash of red caught my eye. I hesitated for only a moment. Some joker had planted the Lord of Death in the hanging planter next to the front step. He stood there amidst the purple asters, a sick grin on his face.

I pretended I didn't see him and kept walking.

"Hey, aren't you the Wild Turkey Woman?" a man's voice shouted from the sidewalk.

Him, I pretended I didn't hear.

Please turn the page for an exciting sneak peek of
J.R. Ripley's next Bird Lover's mystery
HOW THE FINCH STOLE CHRISTMAS
coming soon!

1

There was a commotion of some sort brewing on the street below, but I chose to ignore it. I was happy.

"Isn't it wonderful this time of year, Derek?" I reached out of the double-hung window and carefully slid the plastic tray from the feeder so I could refill it with sunflower seeds. It felt cold in my bare hand. I had promised Derek that I would give him a bird feeder for his apartment—and further promised to come by weekly to refill it for him.

"Everything is so peaceful, so quiet." I admired the sparkling tinsel lining Lake Shore Drive. "So festive."

"I agree," Derek said lazily.

"For a while there, I was beginning to wonder if I would ever truly settle in here." Since returning to my home in the Town of Ruby Lake, North Carolina, my life had been anything but normal and peaceful. And rarely had things been quiet. Finally, things had settled down.

And with Christmas just around the proverbial corner, my life couldn't be more perfect.

I inhaled the chill morning air. The sweet smell coming from C Is For Cupcakes, located across the street and a couple of shops upwind from Derek's second-floor apartment, was making my mouth water. I looked hungrily at the pink and blue bakery-shop sign and considered stopping in for a midmorning treat. This time of year, I heard Connie added vanilla and peppermint cupcakes to the lineup, and I was dying to try one.

"You moved into a new house, opened your Birds and Bees store. What did you expect? There were going to be some bumps in the road, Amy," Derek said patiently. "I had some bumps of my own when I moved here."

"I know. Thank goodness we're past them." Birds & Bees was the bird-watching and bird-feeding supply store I had started up on returning to Ruby Lake. I operated the business out of the house I owned on Lake Shore Drive, the town's busiest street. I didn't know much about business and I wasn't the world's foremost ornithological authority, but, so far, I was making a go of it.

"I'm looking forward to a bump-free future," I said with a grin.

Derek laughed as his eyes skirted to the muted television screen facing him. Some morning sports-recap show was airing. He had moved to town around the same time as me. He wanted to be nearer his daughter, Maeve, who lived with his ex. He also wanted to be nearer to his father, Ben, whose law office was directly downstairs from the one-bedroom apartment he called home.

"It was hard there for a while," Derek agreed. "But I feel a change in the air, and it isn't only the coming of winter. And it's nice being near Maeve."

A house finch clung to the red brick several feet to my right, one curious eye on me as it attacked the mortar with is stubby beak.

"The sense of home and family. That's a big part of the reason I moved back to Ruby Lake in the first place." Being nearer to my mother and farther from my ex-boyfriend had definitely played a significant role in my decision to move back home.

I turned and looked at Derek as he snorted. "I thought it was so you could meet me," he said with a grin. He sat with his feet up on the green sofa, hands behind his back, eyeing me. He wore a pair of loose-fitting jeans and a rumpled heather sweatshirt, and he still looked gorgeous to me.

As a lawyer, Derek is all suit and tie during business hours, but when he's off duty, he prefers to go casual.

"Very funny." I pushed a wavy lock of brown hair from my eye.

He wiggled his stockinged toes in reply.

The bird feeder was held to the glass via four strong suction cups. The frame of the feeder was made of recycled plastic. It had a sloped roof and a perching tray of clear plastic. The tray slides out, making it easy to bring in, refill with seed, and replace on the window.

I picked up the small tote bag of mixed birdseed, reached my hand inside, and refilled the tray one handful at a time. I carefully slid the tray back into the feeder, dusted off my hands, and closed the bottom sash.

The minute I did, the finch alighted on the tray. Its toes clung to the edge as the bird rooted around in the fresh layer of seed. "It looks like you've got a friend."

Derek squinted at the bird. It was a mere six inches long from the point of its beak to the tip of its tail. "That bird or one just like it is always pecking away at the bricks." He sat up. "In fact, I think he, if it is a he, prefers it to the birdseed."

I smiled. "You don't know much about birds, do you?"

"Nope." He rose and kissed me quickly on the lips. "That's what I've got you for, Amy."

I tapped the end of his nose with my index finger. "I believe you are more interested in my weekly visits than you are the birds that are attracted to your window, Mr. Harlan."

"You won't get any argument out of me, Counselor."

"For your information, that little bird is a house finch. And this one," I explained, pointing through the glass at the bird, "is a male. See all the red?" Our bird sported a red forehead, rump, and chest.

Derek nodded.

"The females are paler, with more of a gray-brown plumage."

"And they like to eat bricks?" Derek whispered, not wanting to spook the bird. I could feel his warm breath on my neck and smothered a sigh.

"There is lime in cement, and lime is a good source of calcium. If you'd rather they didn't eat your mortar, you could try putting out broken egg shells. The birds might eat that instead."

Derek pulled away. "That's okay. There's enough mortar on these old walls to last longer than I'll be living here." He picked up the remote and turned off the television.

"Are you thinking of moving?" Not that I would mind too much, just as long as he remained in Ruby Lake. In fact, if he wanted to move out of the apartment, I would help him pack. His ex had recently partnered in a bridal boutique right next door. I could read the shop's sign from the window: DREAM GOWNS.

It was more of a nightmare, if you asked me.

"No, at least not anytime soon."

I nodded and glanced back out the window. "What *is* going on down there?"

Derek rejoined me at the window, placing one hand on the ledge and the other on the small of my back. "I'm not sure."

Together we watched as what had started as a small crowd on the sidewalk now spread out onto Lake Shore Drive.

As many as twenty people had gathered in a loose crowd. Passersby slowed to watch. Several in the group carried makeshift signs in their hands.

"Can you read what the signs say?" Derek pressed his nose to the window and cupped his hands over his forehead.

"No. Maybe it's a gimmick. Christmas House Village might be running some kind of a midweek sale." Opposite the brick building housing the offices of Harlan and Harlan, Attorneys, sat one of Ruby Lake's oldest and most popular attractions, Kinley's Christmas House Village.

"Say, isn't that Kim?" Derek asked.

"Kim? Where?"

"That blonde on the right in the long red coat."

I followed the imaginary line of Derek's index figure. It led to a pretty, long-haired blonde with a shiny black patent-leather purse over her left shoulder. "I wonder what she's doing there."

"If it is a sale, maybe she's shopping."

"Maybe." But I didn't think so. Several persons in the crowd were carrying cardboard boxes, others toted bags. Some were empty-handed. All appeared agitated.

A man in a black suit soon came down the sidewalk bisecting Kinley's Christmas House Village. A security guard in a holly-green uniform joined him. Kinley's Christmas House Village was a collection of six houses, three on each side of the narrow cobblestone sidewalk connecting them.

The small cluster of multistory Victorian era homes were original to the location. The houses sat on postage stamp–sized lots and had been home to some of Ruby Lake's earlier residents. The charming enclave had been constructed by a small group of immigrants in the late eighteen hundreds.

Families came and went and, after World War II, Owen Kinley moved into the second house back on the left. Sometime in the

1950s, he had turned the first floor of his house into his business, Kinley's Christmas House.

It was to become the beginning of a small-town empire. Kinley's Christmas House grew from first one house, to two, and then three, until finally it became Kinley's Christmas House Village as Owen Kinley and his family purchased the remaining houses in the enclave to expand their holiday-themed business.

"Look! Somebody just took a swing at Kim!" Derek said in astonishment. "That woman hit her in the side of the head with her purse!"

I gasped. "That's Mrs. Fortuny. What's gotten into her?"

"I don't know," replied Derek. "But it appears to be spreading." He clamped his hand on my shoulder and pointed with the other. "Look."

I looked. The street had erupted in mayhem. Kim was now surrounded by an unhappy crowd. I saw Kim pull out her cell phone. She dialed, talked quickly, and then dropped the phone into the front pocket of her coat.

So much for my bump-free future.

"We'd better get down there!" I pulled away and ran for the apartment door.

We grabbed our coats and Derek fumbled into his sneakers. The door to Derek's apartment opens at the rear onto the alley. I led the way down the narrow metal steps with Derek right behind me.

We went around to the main street and had to wait for a line of traffic on Lake Shore Drive to move past before we could cross over. "Kim!" I shouted, signaling with my arms as we approached. "Over here!"

Kim turned and looked at me. She was in the midst of a heated discussion with Mrs. Fortuny, an elderly woman with silver hair tied in a tight knot behind her head and dressed in a baggy black coat that fell to her knees. Kim said something to the woman, then hurried toward us.

Mrs. Fortuny was huddled with a stout older gentleman, who appeared to be consoling her. It wasn't her husband. He'd died years ago.

On the opposite side of the street, I noticed a smaller group that included our mayor, Mac MacDonald, Gertrude Hammer, and a man whose name I didn't know but recognized as the head of our town's planning and zoning commission.

"Amy." Kim gave me a quick hug. "What are you doing here?" She turned to Derek and said hello. My best friend is a long-legged blonde with devilish blue eyes. She is thirty-four, like me, but likes to brag that she's younger. Three months, big deal—I'm taller. We'd known each other practically forever.

Kim had loaned me some startup money for the business. In return, I had made her a partner and part-time employee in Birds & Bees.

Derek nodded in reply.

"Me?" I looked over her shoulder at the mini protest. "Shouldn't I be asking you that question? And let's assume I just have. What's gotten into these people?"

"Them?" Kim waved her hand in frustration. "They're just upset. I called my boss. He's on his way over."

I arched my brow. "I can see that. But why?" There was no sign of the police. I hoped that was a sign that they would not be needed.

"Ms. Christy!" A clear, sharp voice rang out over the murmurs of the crowd. It was the tall man in the black suit. He had a long face, dark brown eyes, and a sallow complexion. The younger man next to him in the green uniform stood at attention, his arms crossed over his chest. "I'd like a word with you, Ms. Christy!" He beckoned her with his hand.

Kim sighed. "Sorry, I've got to go." Her hand brushed my sleeve. "We'll talk later, okay?"

"Okay," I agreed, though I was dying to know what was going on. "Wait." I reached for my best friend's hand and held her back. I nodded my chin in the direction of the man in the black suit, who, at the moment, was checking his gold watch. "Who is that man?"

Kim shot a quick look over her shoulder. "Him? That's Franklin Finch."

"Franklin Finch?" I asked.

Kim's phone chimed before she could respond. She retrieved it from her coat. "Hello, Mr. Belzer," she said quickly. "Yes, that's right." She twisted her neck and looked at the crowd gathered on the sidewalk outside Christmas House Village. "Yes, I know. Okay."

Kim turned her attention back to me and Derek as she once again dropped her phone in her pocket. "I'd better get back."

Kim turned to go and I grabbed the bottom of her coat to prevent her slipping away without further explanation. "Franklin Finch?" I repeated. "Just who is Franklin Finch?"

"You'd better tell her, Kim," Derek chided. "Or she might never let go. You know how stubborn Amy can be."

Kim rolled her eyes in a *don't I know it* fashion. "Franklin Finch," she said hastily. "He's the new owner of Christmas House Village."

Kim swatted my hand and I lost my grip on her coat. She disappeared into the crowd, moving toward Mr. Finch and his security guard.

"New owner of Christmas House Village?" I looked at Derek in wonder and surprise.

I tilted my head up in the direction of Derek's apartment window. A trio of nuthatches danced around the window feeder, taking turns. "If only the folks on the street were behaving that orderly."

"What?"

I pointed to the birds. The small but large-headed birds skittered happily upside down along the brick, hopping in and out of the feeder for seeds. "No pushing, no shoving. Peaceful coexistence."

"What kind of birds are they?" asked Derek, squinting to see.

"Those are nuthatches," I replied. "And those"—I pointed to the agitated cluster of folks on the sidewalk—"are nut cases."

Derek chuckled. "What do you say we get out of here?"

"What about Kim?"

The corners of Derek's mouth turned up. "I'd say Kim has her hands full."

Kim stood in front of Franklin Finch. His hands were gesticulating toward the men and women swarming around the perimeter. A three-foot-tall white picket fence separated the sidewalk from Kinley's Christmas House Village. Finch, Kim, and the security guard stood on one side. The guard appeared to be unarmed except for a walkie-talkie.

The rest of the protesters stood on the street side of the fence. However, there were more people watching from the front porches of the houses that comprised Christmas House Village—shoppers, employees, or both.

Kim stood stiff-backed, taking it in. Even in profile, I could see the frustration on her face.

I felt Derek's hand on my elbow. "Can I buy you a cup of coffee?"

I took one last look at the crowd. Mayor MacDonald and the man from the planning and zoning commission had disappeared. Only Gertie Hammer remained—a distant observer. Her hands gripped the handle of a Lakeside Market shopping cart laden with stuffed plastic grocery bags. Had she had something to do with all this commotion, or was she simply a curious bystander?

The crotchety old woman had sold me my house, then tried to buy it back again. When she couldn't buy it from me, she tried to snatch it by other means and had failed.

I'd had little to do with her since then, and preferred to keep it that way. "Only if it comes with a cupcake," I said in response to Derek's offer of coffee.

"Deal." Derek and I started down the block. "Don't worry about Kim," Derek said. I swiveled my neck for the second time to look back at the scene as we strolled hand in hand, ever closer to the smell of freshly baked cupcakes. "I'm sure she can take care of herself."

I nodded. "Kim's tough, all right." But little did I know how tough her situation would prove to be.

2

Derek stepped to the side and pulled open the glass door of C Is For Cupcakes.

I moved inside, enjoying the scent of sugar and cake as much as I enjoyed getting out of the cold. I unbuttoned my coat and draped it over a hook on the coatrack near the entrance. Derek did the same.

"Welcome to C Is For Cupcakes!" An exuberant young man behind the counter, wearing a blue hat and apron, waved to us. A woman wearing a pink hat and apron stood behind him, filling a plastic to-go tray with cupcakes.

We approached the pine-topped sales counter, which was flanked by two long glass cases filled with every flavor of cupcake imaginable and then some. The bakery's walls were painted in stripes of pastel pink and blue. The floor was wide-board yellow pine.

"Do you know what you want, Amy?" Derek asked.

"Vanilla peppermint," I replied without hesitation. I pointed my finger at a particularly thick-frosted one near the front of the glass case.

Derek ordered a pumpkin spice cupcake with maple cream cheese frosting and two large coffees. The ever-smiling youth filled our order and placed it on a plastic tray. Derek carried the tray to a small round table on the far wall and we sat.

"I'll get us some napkins." I rose and crossed to the serving station that held napkins, utensils, and coffee additives. I added some sugar and cream to my coffee and picked up a wooden stir stick. I knew Derek would drink his coffee black.

I returned to my chair and peeled back the wrapper on my vanilla peppermint cupcake. I carefully removed the lower half of the cupcake, broke it into two pieces, and popped one in my mouth.

"What are you doing?" Derek watched in wonder.

"What?" I licked my fingers.

He pointed to my decapitated cupcake.

"I always eat my cupcake like this. I like to save the part with the frosting for last." I eyed his own half-eaten cupcake. He'd taken a man-sized bite out of the side. "Primitive," I quipped.

Derek chuckled. "It seems there is a lot I don't know about you yet, Amy Simms."

I plucked the second chunk of cupcake and popped it in my mouth. "Consider that a good thing."

"Believe me, I do and I . . . uh-oh." Derek stopped as his eyes shifted to the door.

"Uh-oh what?" I turned, catching a frigid blast of air in the face. Mrs. Fortuny and the elderly gentleman who'd been consoling her outside Kinley's Christmas House Village had stepped inside the bakery.

Though why she had needed consoling after knocking my best friend upside the head with her big purse was beyond me.

Irma Fortuny was a small, thin woman with a bowl of silver hair on her head. I knew her to be in her upper seventies, but she was still sharp as a tack—and apparently still packed a mean punch, albeit with her purse. Her blue eyes were equally sharp.

She spotted me, patted the arm of her companion, and walked slowly to our table like the world's most sluggish bird of prey.

Up close, I noted her owlish features—the rounded skull, big eyes and flattish face. "Good morning, Mrs. Fortuny." I extended my hand across the table. "Do you know Derek?"

The corners of her thin lips turned down. "I've not had the pleasure." Finger by finger, she pulled off her brown suede gloves and draped them carefully over her pocketbook.

Derek stood. "Pleased to meet you, ma'am."

Mrs. Fortuny nodded. "You're Ben Harlan's boy, aren't you?"

"The one and only. You know him?"

"Sit," Mrs. Fortuny said with a wave of the hand. "Are you a lawyer, too?"

Derek sank back into his chair. "Yes, ma'am." He winked at me. I gave a small shrug in reply, hoping Mrs. Fortuny wouldn't notice.

If I remembered correctly, Mrs. Fortuny had been widowed some years ago. "I hear that Christmas House Village has a new owner," I said, putting some cheer in my voice. My fingers toyed with the upper half of my cupcake, the thick frosting beckoning. "That must be quite exciting."

"Huh!" snorted Mrs. Fortuny in reply. "Is that what you think?" She shook her head side to side. "But then again—" She paused to snatch her gloves, which had been in danger of slipping to the ground. "But then again, you would, considering you and Ms. Christy are friends."

"Kim?" I frowned. "What's Kim got to do with this?"

"Why don't you ask your friend, Kimberly Christy? She and her boss are the ones who are destroying this town!"

Mrs. Fortuny's companion sidled up to her, tray in hand. On it were two coffees, one carrot-cake cupcake and one dark chocolate. "Hi, folks." He nodded to us. "Ready, Irma?"

"One moment, William," Mrs. Fortuny answered. "This is William," she said for our benefit. "He works in the Christmas House Village stockroom. At least he did."

Her companion, William, was a broad-shouldered man of about seventy years. Big brown spectacles rested on a nose that would have looked at home on a former prizefighter. He carried a burled walnut cane in his craggy left hand. William managed a small smile as he settled the tray against his stomach.

"Isn't that right, William?"

"Yes, Irma," he said, his voice low. "But do try to stay calm. You remember what the doctor said about your blood pressure."

She nodded curtly and the elderly gentleman moved to an empty table near the door and sat with his back to us.

"Oh my gosh," I gasped, thinking I had finally figured out what Mrs. Fortuny was saying between the lines. "You haven't been fired, have you, Mrs. Fortuny?"

"Fired?" Derek said.

I nodded. "Mrs. Fortuny works at Kinley's Christmas House Village." I turned to the woman. "How many years has it been now, Mrs. Fortuny? Thirty?"

"Twenty-seven," she answered, clutching her gloves in both hands. "It would have been my twenty-eighth Christmas season, too." The poor dear looked angry and upset.

"I was fired once myself," I said, reaching out and patting her arm. "I know exactly what that feels like."

Mrs. Fortuny drew herself up. "Young lady, I was not fired. I quit!"

My eyes grew wide. "You quit? Why?"

"Because I have always worked for the Kinleys. I will not work for some New York incomer."

"I'm sure the new owner will be fine," Derek bravely interjected. "If you'll just give him the chance. I'm something of a newcomer myself."

"That may be, Mr. Harlan, but you are not intending to rename the town after yourself now, are you?"

"I don't understand . . ." Derek turned to me for help, but I had none to give and could only throw up my hands.

"What are you trying to say, Mrs. Fortuny?" I inquired.

"Mr. Franklin Finch—"

"The new owner," I interjected.

"Yes," Mrs. Fortuny said with clear disdain. "Mr. Finch intends to replace most of us with younger, cheaper help."

"I am so sorry," I said. Derek echoed my sentiment.

The corners of her lips turned down. "He had the gall to offer us thirty days to stay on, with pay, if we help train the new staff. After that, he's letting us go."

"Well, I, for one, will not give him the satisfaction. I quit today." She slapped her gloves against her leg. "And good riddance to him, I say!"

"That's terrible!" I squawked. "I wish there was something I could do. Derek?"

Derek threw up his hands. "It's not illegal to hire new staff. In fact, it's not uncommon for a new owner to want to bring his own people in."

I frowned. "I never dreamed Kinley's Christmas House Village would not belong to a Kinley."

"Oh, it won't be Kinley's Christmas House Village any longer," Mrs. Fortuny said with a touch of bitterness.

"What do you mean?" I asked.

"It is going to be Finch's Christmas House Village." The elderly woman arched her brow at me. "And this is all your friend's fault."

"I don't see how Kim—"

"I don't know how the woman can live with herself." Mrs. Fortuny turned without further ado and took a seat beside her companion, William.

I picked up my mug. My coffee had gone cold and I'd lost my appetite.

Derek reached across the table and patted my hand. "Are you okay, Amy?"

"Finch's Christmas House Village?" I said with a pinched voice. "It just doesn't sound right."

In fact, something was very wrong.

3

That evening, after closing up Birds & Bees for the day, I locked up, climbed into my minivan, and drove to Kim's house. I had not heard a single peep from her the rest of the day, despite having left her two phone messages.

It was time for the personal touch.

The sun sets early in western Carolina this time of year. It was long past dark as I pulled into the steep drive behind Kim's sapphire-blue Honda.

The front porch light was off. The curtains were pulled and there was no light visible inside the house from the street. Kim lives on the opposite side of town from me in a Craftsman-style bungalow in her parents' old neighborhood. An expansive front porch with white square posts atop chestnut redbrick piers rising to slightly above the white porch railing was a great place to while away a warm summer afternoon.

An ever-empty red flower box attached beneath the triple attic window held the occasional bird's nest but never a flower. The bungalow, with its stone-colored weatherboard, white trim, and deep red front door, reminded me of the house I'd grown up in.

Though Kim's car sat in the drive, she could have been out on a date. My gut told me she was home.

I turned off the motor, dropped my keys in my purse, and pulled my collar tight as I marched determinedly around back to the kitchen door. I didn't bother knocking. When Kim was in a mood, she wouldn't answer anyway, not even for me.

I bent and reached for the spare key she keeps hidden beneath a flowerpot on the back stoop. I didn't get a chance to use it.

The door shot open. Kim stood at the entrance in a pair of brown corduroy jeans and a billowy cream-colored sweater. "Come on in," she said rather wearily.

"That was my plan," I quipped as I replaced the key under the pot.

Kim turned and walked to the kitchen table against the far wall. Furry yellow slippers covered her feet. When she moved, it looked like two baby chicks were following her around.

"Can I get you anything, Amy?" A crumpled package of pecan sandies and an open bottle of rum sat within hand's reach of her.

"Are you okay?" I removed my coat and hung it over the back of an empty chair.

"Everybody hates me," Kim said, wrapping her fingers around a crystal tumbler with a splash of dark liquid at the bottom.

"Don't be so gloomy," I replied. "Things can't be that bad." I pulled a cookie from the protruding sleeve and took a nibble.

"Are you kidding? The entire town hates me." Kim brought the glass to her lips and polished off her drink. She reached for the open bottle of rum.

I grabbed the bottle and set it out of reach atop the fridge. "How about if I make us some coffee?"

Kim pulled a face but did not protest. She reached for a cookie, put the whole thing in her mouth, and clamped her jaws down on it like a vise.

"How's your head?" I called as I grabbed the glass carafe from the coffee maker and filled it from the tap.

"What?"

"Your head. I saw Mrs. Fortuny clobber you with her purse."

Kim made a face as her hand went to her ear. "You saw that?"

I nodded. "Half the town saw it. It was kind of hard to miss."

Kim rubbed her ear once more, then dropped her long locks over it. "Mrs. Fortuny didn't miss, that's for sure," she muttered.

I couldn't help but laugh.

"It isn't funny, Amy Simms."

"Amy Simms?" I poured the water into the coffee maker and popped in a fresh paper filter. "Now you sound like my mother." I scooped a half-dozen spoonfuls of ground coffee into the filter, closed the lid, and hit the brew button.

I pulled out a chair and sat across from Kim. "I ran into Irma Fortuny at C Is For Cupcakes. She told me that the new owner of Christmas House Village is getting rid of all the employees and replacing them with younger, cheaper help."

Kim groaned and held her head in her hands. "He promised he would keep everything the same." Kim looked up at me. Her eyes were red and bloodshot.

"So it's true?"

Kim shrugged. "Pretty much."

"Is it true that he also intends to change the name of Kinley's Christmas House Village to Finch's Christmas House Village?" The coffeepot hissed and burbled in the background. I rose, pulled two mugs from the mug tree, and filled them. I set one in front of Kim. I added cream and sugar to mine.

Kim dunked a pecan sandie in hers and let it sink to the bottom. I tilted my head as she did so, thinking that it might actually be quite flavorful. I plucked a cookie from the sleeve and followed suit. "Franklin showed me the rendering for the new sign." Kim tugged at a strand of her hair. "It's true."

I brought my cup to my lips and drank. "Why didn't you tell me that Kinley's Christmas House Village had been sold?" I set my mug on the teak table. "I didn't even know it was for sale."

Kim picked up her spoon and stirred it slowly around the lip of her mug. She fished out the sodden cookie and popped it in her mouth. She chewed and swallowed before answering. "It was a secret. Mr. Belzer said the Kinley family insisted that everything had to be kept confidential."

Ellery Belzer, Kim's boss, was the owner of Belzer Realty. Ellery was a widower and worked seven days a week at his business. Kim worked for him on a part-time basis. After graduating junior college, she had started selling real estate in the office of Mac MacDonald. But he had closed his office after becoming our town's mayor.

"Why the secrecy?"

Kim leaned back in her chair. "It was meant to ensure that the sale went through without a hitch and without creating any disruption to the business."

"I'd say that plan backfired."

"Big-time," agreed Kim. She rose, fetched the rum from atop the fridge, and poured a splash into her coffee, giving me a look daring me to admonish her as she did so. She tilted the bottle my way.

"No, thanks." Coffee, rum, and pecan sandies did not sound like a winning blend.

Kim replaced the bottle and sat. "I still don't get it. The entire time the sale was being negotiated, Franklin repeatedly assured Mr. Belzer and me that he was going to keep Christmas House Village just the way it was.

"Then, the day he takes over . . ." Kim threw her hand in the air. "Whoosh! Everything goes out the window!"

"I'm surprised that the Kinley family agreed to sell. It has been in the family forever."

Kim nodded. "Yes, but when Tyrone died last year—"

"Tyrone?"

"Tyrone Kinley." I nodded and Kim continued. "Anyway, when he died a widower, that left only his grown kids, two boys and girl. They all live out of the area and had little interest in running the business. I guess they have careers of their own."

As Kim talked, I borrowed her spoon and used it to fish out my own submerged cookie. I lifted it carefully and popped it on my tongue. It was delicious.

"The kids decided to sell?"

Kim managed a small grin. "They wanted to. They contacted Mr. Belzer and asked him to try to work it out with Virginia, but she absolutely refused to sell."

"Virginia?"

"Virginia Kinley Johnson. She was Tyrone's sister. She was married to Chris Johnson. He passed some time ago, leaving her a widow."

"With no children of her own?"

"That's right. Virginia owns, or owned, ten percent of Christmas House Village. Tyrone's children owned thirty percent apiece."

"And she wouldn't sell her share?"

Kim shook her head. "The nephews and niece reached out to her several times. Each time, she steadfastly resisted the idea of letting Christmas House Village out of the family.

"Finally, Tyrone Kinley's children contacted us. Belzer Realty, that is." She pouted and took a drink. "The rest is history."

I fingered the handle of my mug. "Virginia . . . I seem to remember her. Gosh, she was old even when I was a kid."

Kim nodded. "Ninety-two years old when she died."

"She died? I didn't know."

"Yes. It was a couple of months before you returned to Ruby Lake." Kim's face took on a funny expression.

"What?"

Kim pulled a face. "Well, it's kind of sad really."

"This whole day has been sad." I wiggled my fingers at her. "Spill it."

"Virginia committed suicide."

"Suicide!" My arm shook and I spilled coffee all over the table. I jumped up and grabbed the dishcloth hanging over the edge of the sink. I wiped up the spill and rinsed out the dishcloth. I gave it a squeeze and hung it over the faucet to dry.

"Why would a ninety-two-year-old woman commit suicide?" I asked, following Kim out to the living room, where she threw herself down on the sofa and stuffed a pillow behind her neck.

"I don't know." Kim's fluffy yellow slippers dangled over the side of the couch. "But the police found her hanging in her garage."

"Hanging?" My hands went involuntarily to my neck.

Kim nodded. "From the rafters."

I settled myself on a big chair near the cold fireplace. "Did she leave a note?"

"I have no idea." Kim's mouth stretched open in a yawn. The stressful day was starting to catch up with her. "Anyway, when Virginia died, a widow with no children—"

I leaned forward and pulled off my shoes. "What about a will?"

"I was just getting to that. With no immediate family of her own, she left everything to Tyrone's kids."

I let out a breath. "And the three of them were free to sell Kinley's Christmas House Village."

"Finch's Christmas House Village," Kim said with dismay. "And now I can never show my face in town again."

"You? I can only imagine how Mr. Belzer must be feeling. Christmas House Village was his listing, after all, right?"

"Yes. I spoke with him several times on the phone today. He says he was as completely blindsided by Finch's actions as I and everybody else was. He said several townspeople have already come to his office and his house to strongly express their opinions."

"I'll bet. I can picture the barbed comments he must have endured from the likes of Mrs. Fortuny and all the other disgruntled employees, soon to be former employees, of Christmas House Village."

Kim nodded her agreement. "And don't forget everybody else in town who sees Christmas House Village as a Ruby Lake institution. Once everybody hears it has been sold—"

"News does spread like wildfire around here."

"Yes, and when they also learn that the new owner is renaming Christmas House Village for himself"—Kim dragged her teeth over her lower lip—"things are bound to get worse."

I forced a smile I wasn't feeling. "I wouldn't worry about it. In a day or two the whole thing will have blown over."

"Do you really think so?"

"Of course." I slipped back into my shoes. "Get some rest. I have to go. We'll talk more tomorrow."

"Fine." Kim picked up the TV remote from the coffee table and hit the power button. The TV came to life.

"You are coming in tomorrow, right?" I asked. Kim was scheduled to work half the day at Birds & Bees.

Kim nodded.

I said goodbye and left through the kitchen, grabbing my coat and bundling up before exiting. I had not wanted to say it to Kim because she was distressed enough already, but she was probably right.

If the scene outside Christmas House Village and the sentiments of others like Mrs. Fortuny were any indication, the situation was bound to get worse.

ABOUT THE AUTHOR

In addition to writing the Bird Lover's mystery series, J.R. Ripley is the critically acclaimed author of the Maggie Miller mysteries and the Kitty Karlyle mysteries (written as Marie Celine) among other works. J.R. is a member of the American Birding Association, the American Bird Conservancy, and is an Audubon Ambassador with the National Audubon Society. Before becoming a full-time author, J.R. worked at a multitude of jobs including: archaeologist, cook, factory worker, copywriter, technical writer, editor, musician, entrepreneur, and window washer. You may visit jrripley.net for more information or visit J.R. on Facebook at facebook.com/jrripley.

J.R. RIPLEY

A Bird Lover's
Mystery

First in a
new series!

DIE, DIE
BIRDIE

J.R. RIPLEY

A Bird Lover's Mystery

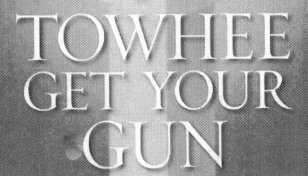

TOWHEE GET YOUR GUN

THE
WOODPECKER
ALWAYS PECKS
TWICE

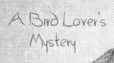

A Bird Lover's
Mystery

J.R. RIPLEY

Printed in the United States
by Baker & Taylor Publisher Services